The Death of Jacob Track

Book One of the 33X Series

by

Natasha Gilbert

Dedication

I would like to dedicate this book to all of those who are suffering in their grief, and to those that have trouble finding light in their lives. There is always hope.And also to you for deciding to buy this book and support this first-time author. It means the world to me. It's been an extremely long journey and I hope you love it as much as I do! I did all I could to make sure it was as close to perfect as possible. I'm sorry if it's not!

I'll try to write the second part as fast as I can!

Xoxo.

Contents

PART ONE: MURDER

Chapter 1

Murder. It covers the course of humanity, littering the pages of history books with its bloody path. There are numerous reasons why people kill: jealousy, power, rage, passion, obsession, psychosis, money, etc. Society has tried to understand and categorize it, but still we don't understand it. We're left with more questions than answers and nothing but grief eating away at our souls. The answers about murder or death won't be found in this story. This is a story about Jacob Track, a seventeen-year-old boy, struck down in the prime of his life. Jacob's murder looks as cut-and-dry as any murder could be, however, it is not. Jacob was a well-loved boy, more loved than most, but still someone felt he had to die. There is more to his death than meets the eye. The only way to understand his death is to look at the lives of all those around him. The death of Jacob Track came quick and swift in the night, and the eyes in the shadows saw all.

* * * *

October 28, 2013

"Hey!" Bobby Woods waved down the almost deserted school hallway, trying to catch the attention of his best friend, Jacob Track. There were still a few kids shoving books in their lockers, some moving dreadfully slow to their next class.

"Oh, hey, Bobby what's up?" Jacob smiled as he made it to Bobby's locker. He gave Bobby a quick high five.

"I was just wondering if you wanted to stop by after school and play some video games. Trevor's coming over too. Dad just bought me the new Xbox One, can't wait to try it out!" Bobby exclaimed as he shoved a book into his locker.

"Ooh, sounds awesome! It looks so cool from the commercials! But I can't. The coach is giving us an extra football practice tonight for the game on Friday, which kind of sucks. It's supposed to rain tonight too. Hope it doesn't rain on us at practice; I'll be drenched! And Mom will want me home right after that. You know how she worries when I'm out after dark." Jacob chuckled and rolled his blue eyes. "Like I'm going to be snatched right off the street and murdered in the woods!"

Bobby laughed with him. "Most parents seem to think that we're so dumb we can't fend for ourselves

I guess. I clearly walk around aimlessly bumping into walls!"

Jacob laughed his loud, cheerful laugh. He was well known for it. "You almost do run into walls, Bobby!"

"Hey! I'm not that clumsy. I'm not Tim!" Bobby laughed.

"Very true, our sweet, clumsy Tim! Well the bell's about to ring. Hopefully we can meet up tomorrow then."

"Holler at me at lunch. We can talk about it some more. You have to play it! You just have to! It's amazing. The graphics are killer."

"I definitely, will do, my good man." Jacob smiled. "Well I'm off to Biology. I just cannot wait to find out what's inside of this frog..." Jacob chuckled and hurried down the hallway to his class.

He had laughed about it, but sometimes his parents really were overprotective. Larned, Kansas, was a small town—about five thousand people. The only dangerous people in it were in the prison about three miles outside of town. The prison was well guarded and almost never had escapees. The crime rate was pretty low as well. Mostly, the transgressions were minor drug offenses. Jacob knew a few of his classmates did some recreational drugs on the weekend, but he had stayed away from them. He preferred to hang out with his group of friends, who were, as far as he knew, drug-free.

When Biology had finished, Jacob and his classmates headed to lunch. It was Jacob's favorite part of the day. He got to enjoy some good food (even though most of his classmates complained of the cafeteria food, he actually quite enjoyed it) and catch up with all of his friends.

He found a seat near Bobby and they continued their earlier chat about how amazing the Xbox One was and all the games that Bobby already had. Also at the table were Trina Johnson and Tim Meadows. Soon Zacchya and Trevor Packers, a sister and brother set of twins, sat beside them. Zacchya was the most beautiful and kind person Jacob knew. She had long, blond, wavy hair and bright blue eyes. All of the guys in school thought she was a knock-out. He had dated her over the summer, but their relationship had ended about a month before. He still had feelings for her, but tried to hide them as much as he could. Jacob didn't want to put a rift in between the group.

"Seriously if I have to sit through Mr. Henson's lectures one more time, I might have to like hang myself!" Trina exasperated, rolling her blue eyes. "He has the most boring voice on the earth! I swear to it! You could travel the world and never find anyone more boring!"

"Oh, Trina, I don't know about that... Tim's voice is pretty boring to me!" Jacob grinned.

"Oh thanks a lot, Jacob! At least I don't have to walk around with that ugly mug you got!" Tim pointed and laughed. Jacob smirked at him. It was well known that Jacob was the most attractive and popular boy in school. He had shaggy blond hair, blue eyes, and a sweet bright smile which all of the girls found attractive. Tim liked to hassle him about it quite often.

"I don't know, Tim, Jacob's very pretty to me." Bobby winked.

"Oh goodness... shall we get you a room, boys?" Trevor joked. The group laughed along. They were the best of friends, had been since elementary school. Tim had moved to Larned a few years ago, but he fit along with the rest just fine. They did everything together: sleepovers, camping, games, trips, whatever they did, they did it together.

"Hell yeah, we want a room! Jacob, come give me a big kiss!" Bobby puckered his lips toward Jacob. He was the jokester of the group and would do anything for a laugh.

"Hey now! If anyone is kissing Jacob, it's going to be ME!" Trevor winked, his green eyes twinkling mischievously.

"You boys are so weird!" Zacchya laughed, her bright blue eyes sparkling.

"And we're your best friends… so what does that make you?" Tim grinned.

"I think it means we're really stupid…" Trina shook her head, her blond hair falling around her face, smiling.

Just then, April Walker walked by and found a seat at the table. She was being particularly quiet, but she usually was soft spoken anyway. Alicia Green joined the table as well, but unlike April, she was full of things to say. Alicia was very social and head cheerleader. After lunch, the group parted ways. Jacob headed to his locker, opened it and found a note inside:

Meet me at the railroad tracks tonight. You know the spot. Our first kiss.

It was signed with a little drawing of lips inside of a red heart. He knew what it meant, of course. But he was surprised that she was passing him notes like this. It wasn't like her. As odd as it seemed, he would meet her to see what she wanted. It would have to wait until after football practice though. He would just send her a text when the practice was over.

Football practice ended a few minutes early, as the skies threatened to pour down rain and lightning. Jacob changed into his regular clothes and headed toward the railroad tracks. He hopped in his '99 Chevy S-10 Pickup and drove toward the south end of Larned. He hoped she wouldn't take long. His mom would be furious if he were out late, especially in a storm. She had texted him already, telling him to get home as soon as practice was over. He figured she was worried that he would get struck by lightning or something. As much as she worried, he adored his mom.

He reached the south edge of town, where the tracks started. Parking the truck, he headed out on foot toward the west, heading into the small forest area that the railroad tracks traveled through. About a half a mile in, he saw her standing on the bridge. She waved to him and he approached her. It had been one of their favorite spots to relax when they had dated. The sky was extremely dark and the only light that came was in distant flashes of lightning. There were no streetlights in this area; it was too far away from the roads. The air was chilled from the briskness of fall. The lightning was still a ways off, but it didn't calm his worries about getting struck standing on a metal railroad track. He loved storms, always had, but didn't want to die in one.

"I'm really glad you came," she whispered.

"Yeah, I really can't stay long. Mom's going to be worried. What's up?" Jacob replied.

"Oh... I just had to see you. Today at lunch, I knew you felt the same way. I thought..." She smiled, but he could barely see it. The sun had set about an hour before and the sky was quite dark. The railroad bridge was more open, trees at both ends of the bridge, but it was still quite dark because of the incoming storm. He could hear the Arkansas River running below the bridge ready to be filled with rain.

"I don't think I know what you mean..." Jacob replied, trying not to hurt her feelings.

"Oh, I know you do. Jacob it's time for us to be together again. For good this time." The lightning flashed as she spoke, almost distorting the angles of her face.

"Listen, I have to go. I'm sorry. We can do this another time, really! I don't have time for this..."

"Oh Jacob, just call me what you did when we were dating. Please! I need to hear it. I know you still love me! I NEED to hear it!" She edged closer to him, only a mere foot away from him. The lightning filled the sky again. Her eyes were filled with passion that he couldn't miss, even in the dark.

Jacob slowly backed away from her. His gut was telling him something was wrong and he couldn't trust her. He shook his head, just wishing to leave. He didn't love her.

"Jacob! I NEED to hear it! Please. And then you can go!" she demanded.

"Fine, Lips! Are you happy now? I really need to go. My mom..."

"Why did you call me that, Jacob?" She leaned closer to him, seductively.

"Because you were a good kisser, you know that! Seriously I got to go..." He turned to leave.

"No, Jacob... I don't think so," she said quietly as she lightly grabbed the corner of his jacket, the thunder pealed above her. "You are going to stay with me."

"I'm not staying anywhere! Let go of my jacket, please. My mom's going to kill me!" Jacob asked as the thunder boomed above him once more, trying to edge out of her grip.

"No, Jacob. She won't," she sneered at him.

Jacob stared into her eyes. There was something in her eyes that he didn't recognize. Jacob frowned at her and turned to leave. He didn't know what was wrong with her, but he didn't have time for her games. However, she grabbed his arm more forcefully.

"Seriously?"

"You're NOT leaving, Jacob. We are going to be together. Or nothing at all! We belong together!" She screamed over the sound of the thunder.

"You've gone mental... We can't be together. Especially when you're acting like this! Maybe I was wrong and we can't be friends. I tried to trust you again, but look what it's getting me!" Jacob snapped at her.

"What's wrong with me, Jacob?" She laughed loudly. "Nothing's wrong with me! Jacob, I'm thinking perfectly clear! I want you. I've always wanted you! Kiss me."

"You've gone completely mental. Let me go!" His heart raced. He wasn't sure what had come over her, and wasn't sure he wanted to know. All he wanted was to get the hell out of there as fast as he could.

"No, Jacob... You're not leaving." She put her face right next to his. Her hot breath wafted over his face. He wanted to run, but her grip was so tight on his arm. She was actually hurting him, scaring him. He wondered when she became so strong. "You either kiss me, you love me, or ... I'm going to have to kill you."

Jacob looked into her eyes, wanting to laugh off such a ridiculous comment. The lightning crashed and her face lit up, leaving him able to see the madness in her eyes. He felt like he was in some awful B-list horror movie. She was a good person with a good heart. This didn't make sense.

"You're going to kill me?" Jacob forced a chuckle, hoping to lighten her mood a bit. However, she stared intently at him, her face unchanged. "Listen, Lips... I think you need to go home and rest. We can talk about this another day. Really, I have to go. Let's just both go home! I feel like we're in some cheesy horror movie right now! This is just ridiculous. I don't want to kiss you. I want you to act like a normal person, the girl I've known forever." He pleaded with her, keeping his voice calm and quiet to not agitate her further. But her eyes showed nothing new. She was frenzied.

"We're not going home, Jacob. There's no more waiting, either." Lips chuckled. "You don't want me! Fine! Then I'm going to kill you. If I can't have you, no one can! NO ONE, JACOB! NO ONE! I tried to move on, but I can't. So neither can you!" she screamed. She grabbed his face with all the force she had, planting a painful kiss on his face. He tried to get away from her, but she was so strong. He had heard about people exerting strength in moments of madness before, but this seemed extreme even for her momentary madness. Finally she let go of the kiss, Jacob felt his lip bleeding from the force of her teeth smashing against him. He reached a hand to wipe away the blood trickling down his chin.

She sneered at him. "I've always loved you, Jacob. Always. We'll always have that kiss." She licked Jacob's blood off of her lips and smiled. She loosened her grasp on his face and arm, throwing him to the ground. Jacob smashed into the rail of the tracks. The nerves in his spine tingled oddly. Pain shot throughout his body. The air was forced out of his lungs. He wanted desperately to scramble away from her and off those tracks, but his body was temporarily paralyzed with pain.

She stood above him, watching him try to move away, but not being able to. She laughed. The lightning crashed above them. She stepped closer to him, smiled then kicked him in the rib cage. Hard. Jacob yowled in pain. "Oh, parting is such sweet sorrow, Jacob!" She ran from the bridge and headed into the woods, away from the exit.

Jacob, thinking he was free of her, managed to get on his hands and knees and tried to crawl away. Oh, if she would stay in the woods, if she was gone, he could get away. She was crazed; she wanted to kill him. He couldn't understand it. They were once so close. What happened to her? He didn't know, and wasn't sure he wanted to find out. He managed to crawl a few feet to the edge of the railroad bridge. He looked toward the tree line and didn't see her. Maybe she really was gone for good. Maybe she ran home. He tried to stand, but his legs felt rubbery. He was sure his rib was cracked. His breath was wheezy and strained. He had to get out of there. All he wanted was to get to safety, to his mom and dad. He stumbled to get on his feet a few more times, and finally got in an upright position. He slowly stumbled along, his hand on his ribcage. Oh, freedom was close, only half a mile before the road. Once he got to the road, he could get in his truck and drive home to safety. But there in the woods, on the railroad tracks, he was alone. He was far enough in that no one could see him or come to his aid. If he screamed for help, no one would hear it. He continued to stumble along for another fifty feet or so when the thunder rolled so loudly, he jumped with surprise. And then he saw her, standing about fifteen feet behind him. The lightning flashed again, lighting up her wide grin. He could hear her giggling. She walked towards him slowly.

"Oh, Jacob. I told you, you were not going home. What are you doing? This is the end, Jacob." Lips grinned widely, suppressing a laugh. She enjoyed watching him limp sadly along.

"Why? I... I..." he wheezed out a few words. The pain in his ribs was becoming too much, making it hard for him to talk.

"Why? I explained that already. Are you that stupid?! I must kill you, Jacob. I must! No one else can have your love! Your lips, your kiss! Your desires, your passion! I am the only one! Forever! No one else will love you the way I do! I can't watch you love another woman. I won't do it. Absolutely refuse!" She grabbed his face again, looking deeply into his eyes. She pressed another forceful kiss upon his lips, this one more forceful than the first. Her hands were on his face and she began to claw at him deeply. He tried to get away from her, but yet again, her strength was too much. He was weak and hurt now, he couldn't fight her. He realized it probably was the end for him. He was going to die. She had lost her mind with this obsession over him, and she had made her choice. She wasn't going to see him with another woman. A tear began to roll from his blue eyes. He had always been strong and athletic, but he was failing now. He had done so much to stay healthy and fit, but none of it had mattered at all. He was defeated by her, a girl he had once cared about. With what felt like a cracked rib and a tingling spine, it was over. She knew it.

She pulled away from the kiss, staring at the blood trickles from his face and mouth. She smiled. "You are so beautiful, Jacob. Even now, when you're so disgustingly imperfect, I love you. I always have. I always will. Forever, my Jacob." And she released her grasp from his face. She grabbed something out of her back pocket, a sturdy, sharp stick she had plucked from somewhere in the trees.

"Please...don't..." he whimpered out.

"Forever, Jacob!" She touched his bloody lips once more, took a moment to lick the blood off her fingers, savoring it. "I'll miss this, Jacob. Mmm, you're so good."

She plunged the stick into his chest. Jacob let out a yowl of pain. His face contorted from pain, shock, and sadness. He pictured his mother and father's smiles one last time. Oh, how he loved them so. He felt the life draining out of his body. There was nothing he could do now. He was too far away from a hospital. He screamed in pain.

"Why?" he winced in pain and sadness. He expected to see his life flash before his eyes, see the good and bad times, but none of that came. The pain became overwhelming. Jacob's blue eyes rolled back into his head.

Lips pushed him to the ground, watching the little bit of life he had left inside of him wither away. She grabbed his shirt collar and dragged him back onto the bridge, his body bouncing off of the railroad ties. She gave him one last look as she reached the bridge again. The light that she had once loved so much in Jacob's eyes was gone. He was motionless. He was dead. Her mission was complete. She kicked him over the side of the bridge and watched him fall into the cold water below. Lips watched his body as it was carried on by the current and then turned to leave. Jacob Track was dead. She did what she came to complete. Now no one else could ever love him again. As if they could love him the way she did, anyway. They couldn't and she knew that.

No one would ever know of this peace she gave him. As she had written out a suicide note and left it in his bedroom hours ago. His poor parents would think they had failed at their job and their precious Jacob killed himself. She had written:

Dear Mom and Dad,

I'm sorry it has to come to this. You see life and its pressures have been weighing on me for so long. I tried to hide it from you and my friends, but I cannot hide it from myself. It has been a daily struggle to keep my head above water. I've been depressed for quite some time. I have been so overwhelmed with school and football and then my girlfriends as well. As you know I've dated a few girls over the past two years, but only one has ever meant to me as much as her. When we broke up, I felt like something was wrong inside of me. I tried to hide it and pretend it wasn't there. But it's always there, gnawing at me. So with my heartbreak and the pressure to be perfect, it became too much. I did everything I could to cope with the pain, but nothing worked. I'm sorry to tell you like this, but I have ended my life.

Forever, Jacob.

Her plan had gone perfectly. Well, as close to perfect as it would ever get. The thunderstorm was a bit cheesier than she hoped for, made it seem like a bad horror movie. She really could never stand cheesy horror movies; they were so ridiculous and nowhere near scary. As she turned to leave the bridge and head back into a town, he stepped out behind a large oak tree.

"Is it done?" he asked curiously.

"Of course, it is. Just as you wanted," she replied, a smile on her lips.

Chapter 2

October 29, 2013

"I don't want the funeral on Halloween. Oh God, that would be awful. Any day but that, Edward, please!" Elizabeth Track sobbed into her husband's shoulder. His black T-shirt was already soaked from her tears, but he didn't mind. They had both lost a child. A tear-soaked T-shirt was nothing to be concerned about. There were no words to express that could ever come close to explaining their loss.

"It doesn't have to be on Halloween, Liz. It could be after it. We just tell the funeral director our stand," Edward said as he ran his fingers through her auburn hair, tears slowly dripping from his blue eyes. "It's not like we…" his voice trailed off. He hadn't been able to say it yet. Saying it made it too real, too painful.

Elizabeth sat up, looked into Edward's blue eyes. She knew what he couldn't say. She hadn't been able to say it yet, either. But the fact was in the room with them, weighing so heavy on their shoulders. Jacob was dead, suicide. And the rain had washed away his body. The

police had only found a T-shirt snagged on an overhang-
ing tree limb. They had no body to bury, no closure. The
thought of having a funeral with no body, made it seem
harder, as if Jacob wasn't really dead. In her overwhelming grief, she needed that closure to know he was gone
and never coming back.

She wrapped her arms around Edward's waist and
fell onto his shoulders again. They continued to cry and
hold each other for a long time. She tried to enjoy the
things about Ed that had always been her favorite: his
smell, his warmth, the way his arms fit around her so
perfectly, the gentle way his fingers touched her face and
hair. But it all felt so selfish. She wanted the comfort,
needed it really. The pain should be gone. It should have
never come. Why would God take her son? Her precious
Jacob had so much life yet to live, so many hopes and
dreams. He could have accomplished anything, but he
gave it all up. All of his dreams and hopes were gone,
over a girl and being overwhelmed by stress. She wondered who the girl was; she had her suspicions, but there
was no way to be sure.

Liz didn't believe it, couldn't believe it. It just felt so
false. Jacob was a great boy. He was honest with Liz and
Ed all of the time, more honest than most teenage boys
were with their parents. He barely ever kept secrets from
them. They knew he had some close girlfriends, even

gave Zacchya Packers a promise ring, but that relationship had ended. He had been very sad about his break up with Zacchya, but he had seemed to cope all right. He had even stayed friends with her. So why would he hide this deep love and emotional struggle from them? It just made no sense. Liz wasn't sure if it was her heart or her gut gnawing at her, but it just felt off. She wanted to know the truth. Why couldn't God just give her the truth?

The few words Liz and Edward had spoken since they found Jacob's suicide note told her Edward agreed. Sometimes Edward wasn't the best at expressing his thoughts, however. But Edward felt like a part of him had died. It wasn't fair. They had already lost a kid, a miscarriage, a few years before Jacob had been born. All the excitement and love blossoming between them was gone two months later. No idea if the baby was a boy or a girl. No name. It was just science being science. The doctors told them, "It just happens sometimes." What the hell did the doctors know, anyhow? A life was there and then it was gone. Only a dandelion puff in a field full of dandelions. Nothing about that could ever feel right. And now their Jacob was gone too. Edward didn't know how to cope. He caressed Liz's hair like he always had, partly for her, partly for his own comfort. He missed the days, some of them only the week before, where he could hold her and kiss her, get lost in her hazel eyes and forget the world existed, nothing but their love and their souls intertwining. Liz was his soul mate, he was sure of that. But even through the worst times, which he thought had already passed but clearly hadn't, she had kept him strong. He just didn't know if this time, he could stay strong. The road ahead looked harder and longer than any he had ever seen before. He prayed for strength to God, even though God felt like their number one enemy.

* * * *

November 2, 2013

The cars lined around the church for blocks. Inside the church were about three hundred people, most standing, as the chairs were full. But people didn't mind standing. They came to pay their respects. There was a white casket in the center of the altar. Assorted bouquets of roses, carnations, and other flowers covered the rest of the altar. The preacher spoke of loss and finding forgiveness. He told of finding peace and hope in the midst of a tragedy.

"Never forget the one who will carry you through the hardships, Jesus. The road will be long and tiring and most days you're not going to feel like you can make it. But through Jesus' strength, he will carry you through."

The tears flowed heavily over this teenage boy who had touched so many lives in his short seventeen years. Jacob had been a member of the church did a lot of volunteer work, was a star football player, handsome, and extremely kind. He had been a friend to everyone he knew. No one could make sense of it. After the funeral, hugs and tears continued to flow through the church. The crowd gathered to their cars and drove the three miles out of town to the cemetery. The procession line was over a mile long. So many people had come to lay Jacob Track to rest.

Finally, most everyone had made it to the gravesite. A few found seats, family and a few close friends, and the rest stood. Within the crowd of tears stood a girl, wearing black like everyone else, staring nervously at the ground. She had gone to school with Jacob, dated him once in the seventh grade, but found they were better friends. She adored Jacob, like everyone else did. He had been so kind to her when others weren't. Jacob even let her into his close group of friends, The Misfits. They were all still friends now. But April Walker was feeling uneasy. And oddly enough, it wasn't because her good friend was ready to be buried. No, it was because she knew the truth. Jacob never committed suicide. Jacob was murdered and she had seen the whole thing. She shifted uncomfortably, kicking the dirt with her feet, looking nervously for the culprit. Her heart raced while her stomach swirled nervously.

Don't think of it, April. Focus on saying goodbye. You'll never get another chance, she thought to herself. She prayed it was all a bad dream and she'd wake up to find out she hadn't seen Jacob get murdered. She forced her deep-set brown eyes to stare at a nearby patch of grass, purposely not looking up or around at anyone until it was over.

Well that was her plan anyway. However, once the preacher finished his prayer and the gravesite service was set to be over, things suddenly changed for the worst.

It was like a nightmare coming true, especially for Elizabeth and Edward. They were sitting there, sobbing, Edward's arm around Liz's waist. Both were staring helplessly at the white casket, wishing for a way to change it all. The casket that held nothing but a T-shirt. That's when it happened. Zacchya Packers ran from the back of the crowd, screaming. She pushed people down on her way to the front. Zacchya ran to the casket and threw her arms on top. She screamed and screamed. People stared, not knowing how to react to her immense grief and loud screams. The preacher walked over to her, to calm her, but it was too late. The moment he touched her shoulder, Zacchya came unglued.

"NO!" she screeched. Her arms left the casket and reached inside of her small black handbag. It happened so fast, almost no one saw the gun at first. But then she was waving it at the preacher, and at her own head.

"I can't! I won't live without him! I WON'T!" she screamed as the gun shook in her small hands. She pointed it at her skull. The crowd gasped.

"Zacchya! No, please stop!" Trevor Packers, Zacchya's twin brother, came bolting through the crowd. He had the slightest resemblance to Jacob, with his shaggy blond hair, that stopped Liz's heart for a moment. It was the only resemblance the boys had, but it had given Liz hope for only a second. His green eyes were full of fear. "Sis, please stop!"

"Trevor!" she cried harder, but her grip on the gun stayed as tight as she could hold it. Her knuckles were white from the grip, but she wouldn't let go.

"I know sweetie, I know. I loved him too. I loved him too!" Trevor cried. Jacob had been his best friend since third grade.

"You don't know! You don't! He didn't... He didn't..." she trailed off, lost in tears.

"It's not your fault, sweetie. Just put down the gun. Please talk to me. Please!"

"It is my fault! The note... I was the last girlfriend he had. It had to be me! He was my soul mate!" Zacchya's legs quivered. She didn't know how much more she could take. The gun was so heavy in her hand. She leaned on the casket for support. Her blue eyes were bloodshot and burning. Her long blond hair flew wildly around her face. She just wanted it to be all over. No more pain. No more pain.

"No, it's not your fault! It's nobody's fault. Zacchya! It's nobody's fault!" Trevor pleaded as he slowly inched closer to her. He didn't want to rush next to her, in fear that she would just pull the trigger.

By then the police who had escorted the procession were standing close by. Officer Nick Walker and Zac Reynolds were only feet five away, in case they had to pull Zacchya or the gun away.

"Zacchya, can you please put down the gun? We don't want anyone to get hurt, please," Officer Reynolds asked quietly, not raising his voice to keep her calm.

"Hurt? We're all hurt! I just want to make it stop! The hole inside… just make it stop! I only want to be with him again." She cried even harder. It was time. No more pain. She threw her arms around the casket again and lifted the lid up.

"NO!" Zacchya scream pierced the air. "Where is he? WHERE IS HE?"

Liz and Edward, who had been sitting dumbfound-ed and hurt by this turn of events, stared up at Zacchya, who was screaming at an empty coffin. Zacchya, gun in hand, began running towards them.

"Where is he?" she screamed in their face.

Elizabeth looked up at her, too scared and upset to answer. Edward, however, stood up. He didn't deserve this. No parent did.

"There was no… body. He was our son, Zacchya. We're all upset. This is unnecessary! Stop this please…"

"I need him! I need him!" Zacchya screamed through her madness. She had stopped pointing the gun at anyone leaving it to hang to her side. The tears flowed heavily down her reddened cheeks.

"I need him too," Edward replied and reached out for her hand. She stared at it for a moment. He looked into her wild eyes, unsure of how to comfort someone when he needed comfort himself. He knew grief did horrible things to people, but he couldn't understand how this girl he had known for years would act like this.

Zacchya shook her head and stepped away from Edward's hand, then walked back to the coffin. The empty coffin… No Jacob. So it was time. No her. She fell hard to her knees, shaking uncontrollably through her tears. The ground was hard and cold from the November chill. It hurt her knees but she didn't care. She looked up at Trevor, helplessly. She could see her mom, Hollie, about ten feet away, looking scared and sad, tears pouring down her cheeks.

She whispered softly, "I'm sorry." She closed her eyes, her finger on the trigger and said a prayer of forgiveness.

Chapter 3

November 2, 2013

It was over. Officer Reynolds was close enough to grab the gun before Zacchya pulled the trigger. He got her handcuffed so everyone was safe again. Zacchya sat in the backseat of the police car, sobbing. She was so angry that she didn't die. She was supposed to die! How could they do that to her? It was the only way. *"It should be over,"* she whispered through her tears. Nothing could soothe her now. She pulled her knees up to her chest. She cried harder, wishing that she could disappear forever.

The crowd watched as the police car took Zacchya away. Trevor and Hollie were holding each other tightly, sobbing. Neither understood what had caused her to do this. Zacchya had never had depression issues. She was never suicidal before. Something was definitely wrong. They knew Zacchya had loved Jacob, but she had been the one to break off the relationship.

"I don't understand, Mom. I just don't understand it at all," Trevor cried, his arm wrapped around his mom's shoulder.

"Neither do I… she's going to need us more than ever, Trev. Whatever she's feeling now, it might get worse before it gets better. She needs us as a family. It's going to be a hard route for all of us," Hollie spoke as a few tears rolled down her reddened cheeks.

"I'm not ready for any of this. Not ready for Jacob… not ready for Zacchya… I can't do it," Trevor cried.

"Yes you can, baby. She's your twin sister, Trevor. You're going to have to be strong for her, even when you don't want it. We both are. There are going to be days we will both want to disappear, but we can't. If she needs us, we have to be there. Depression is a hard, long road. She's going to need support from both of us," Hollie said soberly.

"I'll try, Mom." Trevor frowned as they headed toward their car. It felt wrong leaving without Zacchya. They'd have to go to the police station to see her. He didn't feel strong enough to deal with any of it. How could he watch his twin sister almost shoot herself in the head and ever be okay with it? As the people made it back to their cars, some running, some walking, one man smiled. It was a wide grin in a sea of sad scared faces. Now, what that smile meant… it was more than anyone could say. But that man was happy, extremely giddy inside. And it was eating away at him to hide it. A small part of him was afraid someone would notice the smile spread across his face, but knew that Zacchya's near suicide was a good enough distraction.

If they only knew, he thought to himself. He had hoped Zacchya's suicide wouldn't be stopped, but it was okay for now. There was always ways to fix the mistakes of others. He suppressed a chuckle. He had so much work to do this week, but the funeral couldn't be missed. The crowd didn't know, but he had his hand in the pot. How? He would never say. The truth would come out at the right time, and this was nowhere near the right time. He smiled as he slid into his car. As he made his way out toward the highway, he laughed. He didn't hold in his laughter. How could he? Nothing had excited him more. *Today was beautiful,* he said to himself, smiling.

So beautiful in fact, that instead of going home right away, he found a dirt road, drove into the country to be alone for a bit. He stopped the car and pleasured himself. His life's goal was coming true. He had planned it all for years. No one knew the plan, and no one would stop it. It had taken a lot to get where there. He had planned everything down to the last detail; made sure that even if the plan changed, he had a Plan B, C, and even a Plan D. Everything was perfect. Oh, so deliciously perfect.

Chapter 4

September 27, 2012

Jacob Track sat at the lunch table waiting for his friends, The Misfits, to join him. As he waited, his mind wandered with thoughts of Zacchya Packers. She was in The Misfits, and one of the most beautiful girls he'd ever seen. She had long wavy blond hair, big blue eyes, and a wide sincere smile. Jacob always felt butterflies in his stomach when she smiled at him. He had always found her beautiful, since they'd met as kids, but over the summer she had particularly blossomed. Her body began to fill out, giving her more womanly curves and her face lost some of its childish features. Now she was simply stunning and his thoughts continued to drift towards her. She was more than just a pretty face to him, however. Zacchya was one of his favorite people to talk to. She was always cheerful and so easy to like.

He had dated Trina Johnson over the summer, but it had ended after school started. He had an amazing summer with Trina, but even though he cared deeply for her, she wasn't the right girl for him. She cared more for him than he did for her, unfortunately. Relationships were hard enough, why make it worse with uneven attraction? He was sad to dump her, but knew it was the right decision. They were just better as friends. She had seemed to be coping with that fact so far.

The group slowly made their way to Jacob's table. Bobby, Tim, Trevor, Alicia, Trina, April, and Zacchya all found a seat.

"How do you always beat us here?" Trevor asked as he stuffed a bite of roast beef sandwich in his mouth.

"History is so boring, even the teacher gets tired of it! He lets us out a minute or two before the bell. Everyone knows Colonel Mustard started all the wars with the wrench in the study!" Jacob laughed.

"You're an idiot... Colonel Mustard..." Tim chuckled as he rolled his eyes.

"And you know that cafeteria lady likes my big blue eyes. She gives me whatever I want." Jacob winked.

"She's about 150 years old, too!" Bobby snorted.

"Jealous, I see. No old broads giving you extra potato chips, hmm?" Jacob grinned widely.

"Well son of a bitch!" Bobby laughed when he noticed Jacob really did have an extra helping of potato chips.

"Silly boys! So, Jake, your birthday is coming up in a few weeks. Did you decide what you want?" Zacchya asked with a smile.

"Um…" Jacob shifted nervously in his chair. He knew what he wanted: to be Zacchya's boyfriend, but he couldn't tell her that, obviously. "What about a yacht?"

"I'll get right on that!" She giggled.

"Ok… fine, fine. I'll just hang out with my best friends… even though money is *quite* acceptable."

"Well I'm your best friend. My company is enough!" Trevor laughed.

"No, no, Trev, I'm his best friend!" Bobby said firmly.

"And we're all chopped liver, I suppose?" Alicia rolled her eyes.

"Yes, you are!" Bobby smiled, sticking out his tongue.

"So mature there, Bobby." Alicia rolled her eyes.

"I'd rather be a hamburger at least." April chimed in.

"Tacos would be better if we have to be a food item." Trina smiled.

"Is it weird I want to be a block of sharp cheddar cheese?" Zacchya giggled.

"Nah, you're cheesy already! It makes sense!" Trevor laughed.

"You guys are really freaking weird…" Tim rolled his eyes.

"But you like us!" Jake smiled widely.

"Only on Tuesdays!" Tim winked.

"Well damn, it's Thursday! We're just shit out of luck, I guess." Jake smirked.

The bell to end lunch soon rang, and they headed to dump their trash. As they walked toward their next classroom, Jake stayed purposely beside Zacchya.

"Hey, so I was thinking me and you… we should… um… hangout this weekend or something," Jake mumbled. Why did she have to make him so nervous?

"Oh that'd be cool. I'd like that." She smiled sweetly at him.

He tried not to stare too long into her bright eyes. They seemed to mesmerize him. "Sweet, I'll text you after school."

"Cool. Is it just going to be me and you?"

"Yeah… but not like … a date, I mean, not that you're not dateable… or whatever. Oh, God, you know what I mean?" Jake couldn't look at her; he was too nervous, fumbling with his hands.

"Ooh… right… of course." She slipped into her seat, trying to conceal the joy in her blue eyes. "It wouldn't be like awful though if it were a date, right?" she whispered, her eyes still on him.

"No! I'd… I'd like that actually…yeah." He smiled, gazing into her eyes one last time before he took his seat. He felt like the happiest guy in the world. Zacchya wanted to go on a date with him. He was a little bit worried her twin brother, Trevor, would want to kick his ass though. But Trevor was a great guy, one of the best he knew. Jake knew he'd eventually understand and be cool with it.

* * * *

October 17, 2012

All of the Misfits were gathered at the bowling alley for Jacob's sixteenth birthday party. Jake, Bobby, Trevor, and Zacchya were in the lanes bowling against each other. Zacchya and Jake were on a team against Bobby and Trevor.

Alicia, Trina, April, and Tim were in the back gaming area playing pool and picking songs for the jukebox. Alicia wasn't too interested in pool and focused on texting her new boyfriend, Alex. Alicia loved all the attention she got from the boys at school, and Alex fed right into her ego. Alicia was very beautiful, slender, athletic, and she knew it.

Tim was watching April and Trina playing pool, while reading a book. He loved hanging out with The Misfits, but he wasn't feeling particularly social. He preferred the company of books, usually, but came because he cared about Jacob. Jacob had been a friend to him and accepted him into The Misfits clan without a second thought. He knew Jacob was a good friend, so he'd be there for him even when he didn't want to.

"Can I ask you something?" April asked quietly.

"Sure, go ahead," Trina said as she hit the ball.

"Does it bother you? Jake and Zacchya, I mean…"

"Oh…" Trina swallowed hard. "I'm happy for him."

"That's not what I mean."

"I know what you meant…yeah, it does a bit. I'm trying to be okay with it. I am! But she could have at least asked me first about it. You know? We are friends," Trina grumbled.

"She should have, I agree. I know he likes her a lot, and I'm glad. But I worry about you, Trina. I know you really cared for him," April said sympathetically.

"I did…" Trina forced herself to concentrate on the pool table. She wouldn't let herself get carried away with emotions. Emotions were for weak people, and she didn't want to be weak. "I've moved on."

"I'm sorry. I don't want to upset you. I just worry about you, like I said."

"Don't. I'm fine, really, totally fine. Don't worry about me at all." Trina made her shot; sinking the ball she was aiming for.

"Okay, if you say so. Just know that if you need to vent, I'm here for you. Don't let my friendship with

Zacchya make you think you can't talk to me. That's all I'm saying." April smiled.

"Thanks, but I'm cool." Trina shrugged. "It's your shot."

April took her shot, wishing that Trina would trust her more. She was closer to Zacchya than Trina, but she longed to help the girl. She could see Trina's struggle with the budding romance every day. But she also understood not wanting to talk about it.

April had a little crush on Tim, but never told anyone. Tim was smart and quiet, yes, but he was always polite. She had a soft spot for kind-hearted guys. It was probably because of her dad, Nick, who was a cop and the definition of a good guy. They always said that girls seemed to like guys like their fathers, which was a little weird in a way, but it made sense to her. Dads, for better or worse, are the first male role models girls have. If he treats the women in his life with respect and love, then she will try to find a man that does the same. Unfortunately there were a lot of girls who had bad male role models and get stuck in bad relationships full of abuse: physical, mental, and/or sexual. She was glad she had a good male role model in her life to look up to. But her crush on Tim would stay a secret, though. She was just too shy to ever tell anyone about it.

She'd only ever had one boyfriend, Jacob, actually, when she was in eighth grade. They dated for a week. Jacob had been the first boy to give her any attention at all. She was a bit of a wallflower, and most boys found her to be too plain and quiet to give her a chance. She was too shy to deal with the attention he gave her, however. Jacob was a bit too cute for her, out of her league. She felt average, just a plain Jane, not that pretty. People would tell her that she was a "girl next door" all the time. It was ingrained in her mind. And Jacob was a pretty boy— charming, popular, liked by everyone. It made no sense to her that he would ever like her, let alone that they'd end up together. She let her insecurities end the relationship, but stayed friends with Jake.

She was happy that he and Zacchya were together, though. She glanced down at their lane; they were laughing and smiling together. She noticed that Jake seemed to always find a reason to touch Zacchya, on the shoulder or arm. He was very smitten with her already. April was sure he was already in love. She hoped that Trina would find a way to cope with the hurt and mistrust she felt. Clearly Jake and Zacchya weren't breaking up anytime soon; they seemed perfect for each other.

After the bowling game was over, Bobby gloated happily over his and Trevor's victory. He bought everyone a root beer, cheering. "To the most awesome bowlers of ALL TIME! The champs, Bobby and Trevor! Sorry birthday boy!" Bobby gleamed.

"Ha. Ha. We're going to step outside for a minute. Gloat away, Bobby." Jake smiled with his hand on Zacchya's back.

"Ooh yeah, baby!" Bobby winked. Jake rolled his eyes and walked outside.

"At least it's not too cold out yet. I really can't stand the cold weather. I belong in the tropics, I think!" Zacchya said, looking up at the stars.

"Yeah, same here. I was looking for a reason to hold you, though."

"Well, I'm okay with no-reason holding." She smirked at him.

He wrapped his arms around her waist, kissed her softly. "Mmm… you really have the most amazing lips." Jacob smirked.

"Why thank you, sir." She blushed.

"I know we haven't been dating long…" Jacob paused, nerves swelling in his stomach.

"What is it?"

"I think… I mean, I know…" Jacob stammered, too scared to look into her mesmerizing eyes. "I love you, Zacchya."

"You love me?"

"Yes, I do." Jacob tried not to blush, but felt his cheeks already reddening.

"Me too! I've known for weeks really!" She smiled widely, her eyes bright.

"Really? Oh good!" Jacob smiled and kissed her again. He couldn't believe she loved him too. He felt like the luckiest sixteen-year-old in the world. He wanted to run around the town, high-fiving everyone. Nothing was better than knowing the girl he loved loved him too. "Best birthday ever, dude!"

* * * *

May 21, 2013

The rest of the sophomore year went fast for The Misfits. Alicia had moved on from her boyfriend, Alex, then onto Clark, and then James. The kids worked through their schoolwork mostly with ease. Tim finished with a 4.0 and was very happy about it. The rest finished with As, Bs, and an occasional C. None of them were upset with their grades.

School was over and the official first day of summer was upon them. Jake and Zacchya were still going strong. They were barely out of each other's sights at school or after school. Hollie, Zacchya's mom, was happy to have Jake around the house. She also loved how happy he made her daughter. Liz, Jake's mom, felt the same way. Liz had even joked about planning a future wedding.

Jake had a special date planned for the night. He had gotten his first vehicle with money he saved from his part-time job at Sonic. He bought a '99 Chevy S-10 pickup, with a little help from his parents. He loved having a vehicle and the freedom it gave him. He lived close enough to school to walk most days, but used it on the weekends when he wasn't working. He had planned on taking Zacchya out to the country to look at the stars. They both had a deep appreciation for space and its infinite magnificent beauty.

Jake loved that Zacchya was a wonderful, but mostly easy-to-please girl. They barely fought, and even when they did, it was over small stuff. He longed to make her happy, and she felt the same way. It was two days before her and Trevor's seventeenth birthday, but Jake wanted to have a special night away with just the two of them. He would have to share his time at their birthday party, as Trevor was one of his best friends. He wanted something special with Zacchya alone.

He picked her up at eight. They went to Pizza Hut, splitting a pepperoni pizza. After pizza, they drove around on the country roads with the windows down, enjoying the fresh summer air. The wind whirled Zacchya's blond hair around, which made her look even more beautiful. He had a hard time concentrating on the gravel roads, when all he wanted to do was gaze into her eyes. He found a remote spot, a few miles out of town and parked on the grassy shoulder.

"Why did we stop?" she asked.

"Get out, babe. I'll show you." He smiled, touching her cheek softly. She stepped out of the truck. Jake grabbed some blankets he shoved behind the driver's seat. He walked to the back of the truck, putting the tailgate down.

"I thought we could spend some time alone. Gaze at the stars… make out… gaze at the stars some more. Romantic stuff, you know, an early birthday present." He smirked.

"Ooh! That sounds awesome!" She hugged him tight. They spread out the blankets in the back of the truck bed, and then climbed in. She welcomed his embrace, lying on his chest, her arms wrapped around him, his arms around her.

Jake did all he could to focus on the thousands of brilliant visible stars, but he was so distracted by the smell of her shampoo and her arms around him. He reached for her chin, lifted it so he could look into her eyes.

"You're more beautiful than every star."

"Oh, Jake." She kissed him, taking in all of his warmth. She couldn't imagine a man more perfect for her than Jake. He was always sweet, loving, caring, funny, charming, and easy to talk to. He loved everything about her, even her flaws. The things that she found terrible, he thought were adorable on her. She loved him just as much too. He was perfect to her, every single part of him. She hoped that their love would never fade away or get dull like some people's relationships do. She wanted to forever look at him with the same spark in her heart. She never wanted his flaws to cloud her vision. If they were in love and together, it would be right. That was all that mattered. Even when times would get hard, she wanted to choose to love him over fighting with him. The world would never be right without her Jake. She never wanted to be anywhere where he wasn't.

Jake let his hands run over her face, then her waist and hips. He leaned closer to her, their bodies as close as they could be. He longed to stay touching, kissing, and loving her always.

He pulled away from the kiss, cupping her face in his hands. She was breathing hard, but smiling.

"I don't want to go any further in this life without you. Promise me we'll be together forever. Just you and me," Jake said, tears forming in his blue eyes. He loved her so much.

"Of course we will! If you don't marry me, Jacob Track, I swear I'll kill you!" She chuckled, lightly wiping a lone tear off his cheek.

"That's a deal to me! I bought you something…" He kissed her forehead, and then grabbed something from his jeans pocket. It was a ring box.

"Jake!"

"It's just a promise ring. After high school, you promise to marry me. Then nothing will keep us from being together. And we can stay just like this forever."

"Of course I promise! I could never love anyone but you!" She kissed him sweetly on the lips. The ring was silver with a small heart shaped group of stones. "This is beautiful!"

"Real diamonds too. Only the best for you, babe."

"Oh! How did you…?"

"Don't worry about that. It doesn't matter. What matters is there's proof now for everyone to see. That we will be together, no matter what! And that's enough for me." He kissed her again, more passionately. His hands and hormones were running wild. She had said she would be his wife. He had never been happier in his entire life. They kissed and touched, just happy to be together.

"Jake…" Zacchya paused hesitantly as she felt his erection against her.

"What?"

"Um… Jake, I'm not… ready for… that," she stumbled her words. It had been such a beautiful night. She didn't want to ruin it. She wished that she was more comfortable with the idea of sex, but she wasn't.

"Oh! Sorry. I'm just happy to be with you. I wouldn't try… if you're not ready," Jake stammered, embarrassed by his hormonal reaction.

"Good. Is it weird that it still scares me?" She frowned.

"Sex? No! No, it still scares me sometimes too."

"Really? I felt like the only teenager left not ready for it."

"Well there's always Tim and April." He chuckled. "But nah, we're all scared, we just don't show it. I want our first time together to be special and amazing. I'll wait as long as you want. I promise." Jake kissed her forehead.

"Thank you. I love you so much. No girl in the world is as lucky as I am. No one!" She hugged him close. And she meant it. Jake was an amazing boyfriend who respected her all the time. She couldn't be happier.

"Let's just watch the stars, okay? Maybe we'll see some shooting stars and make some wishes," he said, caressing her hair.

"Sounds good to me, but I have nothing left to wish for, though. You're all I ever want, Jake."

Chapter 5

December 5, 2013

"Now, we all have struggles, Zacchya, but you have been doing very well since last month. You have made plenty of progress but I still want to give it a few more weeks before we release you back home. Make 100 percent sure the medication is working at its prime for you. How are you feeling?" Dr. Loden asked.

Zacchya smiled at her. She liked Dr. Loden… well, most of the time. "Yes, I understand. I really do feel so much better," Zacchya said.

"Good, glad we are on the same page. The RN tells me you have been taking your medications every day, so that's good as well. Plus, you haven't had any self-harm attempts in over two weeks. Progress is definitely being made here. If you continue to work on your coping skills and taking your medications, I would think you'll continue to get better."

"I don't feel like hurting myself anymore. The classes and the pills have really been helping."

"Good. Well I think if you can make it two more weeks without self harm or threatening of self-harm, I think we'll be able to send you home." Dr. Loden wrote some notes on a paper, but still kept eye contact with Zacchya.

"That would be awesome. It'd be just in time for Christmas too. Trevor and Mama would love that. I would too." Zacchya smiled sweetly at the thought.

"Well I think that's good for today. I'll walk you back to your unit if you want." Dr. Loden smiled at her.

Zacchya really felt like out of the entire group of psychiatrists at Sunnyvale, Dr. Loden seemed to really care about the patients.

"It's okay. I wanted to hang with Marissa for a bit."

"Excellent, well have a good afternoon. I'll see you next week."

Zacchya exited Dr. Loden's office. She walked the long, gray corridor toward the unit where she stayed with thirty-two other female patients. It was a large concrete building with two separate units. She was on the female unit; the male unit was on the opposite side of the building. The rest was offices for doctors and psychiatrists. She reached the glass door to her unit and rang a bell so someone would let her in. An aide soon approached and let her in the unit.

"Good meeting?" the female aide asked.

"Sure was, is Marissa in her room?"

"Nope, she's sitting in the reading room," the aide answered. Zacchya nodded and headed down another gray hallway, this one much shorter and where the patients stayed. There were numerous bedrooms, some with single beds, and some with two to four beds. She thankfully had her own room because of her suicidal tendencies. She had been luckier than expected and received a mental health screen and sent there, instead of jail. She hadn't hurt anyone at the funeral, but she knew that didn't mean they wouldn't find a way to arrest her. Her depression and self-harm issues were more of a concern than of her being a danger to society. She was admitted to Sunnyvale Hospital, a hospital for people with all different types of mental health issues: depression, schizophrenia, drug addiction, paranoia, etc.

Everyone in Larned knew of the incident at Jacob's funeral, of course. But since her admittance, she had attempted suicide two more times. For about two weeks, she was constantly in the company of one of the staff members. It was called "one on one." This meant she had no privacy at all. They watched her sleep, shower, use the toilet, all of it. It was very annoying and discomforting to have someone watch you pee and shower. But it was all to keep her safe, they told her. She kept planning of ways to hurt herself, though. For some reason, her mind thought about it constantly. Some days it felt like she had nothing to live for. Something inside of her cracked the day she found out Jacob was dead, a rip in her heart so deep that she didn't know how to cope with it. Some days, it was even hard to breathe. Romantic love was one of the best and worst things in the entire world. It was completely encompassing, not letting in any other thoughts, except for the beloved. And losing the man she loved, the only man she ever loved in her seventeen short years, was just too much to bear. So much emotion and passionate feelings for him, and then he was gone. It was something she didn't always know how to deal with. She wasn't sure anyone did know how to deal with it, especially when it was all of her fault. No matter what they told her, she knew it was her fault.

She was finally starting to feel like her old self again though. There was a small light in her dark world. Maybe it was the drugs, or the classes, but something had finally started to work. She could only pray that her family and friends would forgive and accept her back. Trevor and Hollie visited her once a week and swore they forgave her. But she knew they were still mad, still hurt by what she did. She definitely never forgave herself and wasn't sure if she ever could.

She made it to the reading room and sat by Marissa. It was an open room at the end of the hallway, with chairs and windows, where people like to read books and enjoy alone time. Marissa had become one of her best friends. Marissa had a horrible past of sexual and physical abuse. She was in a foster home after the SRS removed her from her abusive family at the age of six. She had been in and out of Sunnyvale since she was ten. Marissa had tried over thirty times within six years to end her life or cause harm to herself. She was a very troubled girl, but had a big heart.

"How did the meeting go with Dr. Low Down?" Marissa giggled.

"It was good actually. Be good for two more weeks and I can go home. FREEDOM!" Zacchya said. Dr. Low Down was their nickname for Dr. Loden. She had no idea how it started but it made them both giggle.

"Sweet! Sneak me out in your back pocket please!"

"Sure, hop on in!" Zacchya laughed and pointed to her jeans pocket. The girls laughed and talked for a while. Zacchya was glad to have found a friend, especially one who understood her desire to want to die. Most people would label them "crazy" and act like it was a horrible catching disease. The girls would laugh about "catching the crazy" but really, they were both secretly offended by it. It was newer to Zacchya than Marissa, but the sting of the words never really stopped. Everyone was flawed in his or her own way, but being admitted to a mental health hospital didn't help with self-esteem issues, for sure. Depression was a real issue, but so many acted as if it was just a passing phase.

It also didn't help that the only visitors allowed were family members. Marissa didn't have any family, well she did, but they were either in jail or dead, or who knows where. Zacchya was her only friend. Most people couldn't handle her when she was doing badly. Marissa had come to the realization she was unlovable, but Zacchya tried to help her see otherwise. The sexual abuse of her past really had messed with her self-confidence issues. She was a pretty girl, tall, long dark hair, brown eyes, but carried about 50-60 extra pounds. Her weight was an issue she had trouble getting past. But her emotional trauma of the past had made her an overeater.

The next afternoon, Zacchya was awoken from a nap by loud screams. She had been surprised that she could sleep at all. The unit was very loud all day, one of the patients, "Terrible Teresa" as the patients called her, was screaming up and down the halls, and trying to flush clothing down the toilets. Terrible Teresa could really make the unit a nightmare sometimes. She'd go in phases where she would terrorize the entire place, smearing feces on the walls, and trying to throw urine on people. It was awful. The rest of the time she was perfectly friendly. Zacchya was sure Terrible Teresa was just evil. That woman always knew exactly what she was doing. *Mental illness, my ass!* Zacchya thought.

"Zacchya, your uncle is here in the visiting room," The aide came to her bedroom to tell her. She headed to the visitation room, found Larry inside and hugged him. Larry hadn't come to visit her since she was hospitalized. He was her only uncle, Hollie's older brother, and a really great guy. Larry was a medical doctor at the Larned Community Hospital. He also had a degree in Chemistry, along with numerous awards for his recent discoveries in the Alzheimer's field.

"It's great to see you, kiddo." Larry smiled and sat down in a brown plastic chair across from her. "So how has my favorite niece been?" Larry's green eyes sparkled. He was a very handsome man with salt and pepper hair. A lot of Zacchya's friends found him to be an attractive older man. He was what some called classically handsome.

"I'm you're only niece, for one. And for two I'm feeling much better. My head is finally starting to clear up a bit. Feeling like a human being again, which is awesome." Zacchya smiled.

"Oh that's wonderful. You know I've dabbled in psychiatry a bit so I can learn as much about humanity as possible. Always interesting to see the effects the brain has on us. Not always good, but interesting to say the least. It's always grabbed my attention that something we trust to work for us all the time, the brain, would turn its back on us and cause mental illness in some, depression or bipolar in others. I would love to figure out why. One of life's many mysteries."

"You're way too smart, Uncle Larry." Zacchya smiled at him.

"Oh heavens, no! Is there such a thing anyway?" Larry winked. "Here I brought you some lunch. I figured you missed real food." He unwrapped some Subway sandwiches and handed one to Zacchya.

"Thanks! Mmm... You know I love roasted chicken with ranch dressing. I sure do miss real food! Not that the cafeteria food here is awful, but it's not the same. I hope Mama brings me some home cooked stuff next time she visits. I miss her cooking."

"Hopefully she does! She was always a brilliant cook. Never understood why she didn't follow her culinary desires and went into being a CNA instead." Larry shook his head. "I also brought you something special. It's that tea from London you love. I flew over for a medical conference last week. I knew I had to pick it up for my favorite niece." Larry smiled and handed her a warm thermos.

"Awesome! That's the best stuff. There is nothing as good as tea from London." She poured herself some into the lid cup. "You want any?"

"Oh no, I got boxes and boxes at home. I wanted to make sure you had some. Drink up!" Larry smiled.

They continued to talk about numerous subjects, but also a bit about Marissa, which Larry found fascinating. Marissa had borderline personality disorder, which was a very complicated and difficult diagnosis for anyone to have. She told him about her recent good behaviors and getting better every day. They finished their sandwiches and Zacchya drank the whole thermos by the visiting hours were almost over.

"So how was London?"

"Oh the conference was boring enough. Just news about new drugs and side effects, also stuff about funding for the research committee I help, grants and such. Boring, smart people forced in a room together, trying to see who is smarter. I barely got to sightsee at all! I didn't even get to ride the London Eye! What a shame!"

"That is sad! Even though it seems too high for me, I'd have a heart attack at the top! You know me; I won't even go on a real Ferris wheel!" Zacchya shivered. "Well I'm glad you made it here to see me, anyway. It's always nice to know you guys haven't disowned me yet. Not that you wouldn't have reason for it..." she said quietly.

"You can't hurt someone who is going through a crisis. However will they get out of it? They need love and patience. Family should provide that. Hurting people hurt people. It's a part of life, unfortunately. We're your family and we won't disown you, I can promise you that," Larry replied and touched her shoulder softly.

"Thanks." She didn't quite know how to respond to that. Her head was feeling dizzy all of the sudden. "Oh man, I don't think I got enough sleep last night. I feel a bit light headed…"

How had the visit lasted over two hours? She wasn't sure. Maybe her nap earlier was messing with her head. The nurse came and said that it was time for Larry to leave. She hugged him goodbye and he promised to try and visit again soon. As Zacchya walked back to her room, her dizziness continued to grow. Maybe the warm tea had made her realize how tired she was. Hopefully Terrible Teresa would stay quiet for the night and she would get a full night's sleep. Apparently sleep was what she needed; either that or the sandwich was messing with her. She headed to Marissa's room.

"Hey I'm going to lie down for a bit. I think that sandwich or the warm tea is making me feel funny. If you have any more nightmares, you wake me up, okay?" Zacchya smiled.

"Yes Mama Zacchya, whatever you say." Marissa smiled back. "Go get some rest. If Terrible Theresa wakes up later and starts her shit, you'll need your strength to flush her head down the toilet!"

"HA! That's the truth. She needs it. Giving her a swirly would make me happier than I can even express. Watch out for cups of piss." Zacchya winked and walked to her room. She snuggled under the blankets, wishing it was warm and summer again. She was asleep before she knew it.

* * *

December 29, 2013

Zacchya was feeling full of anguish. She was supposed to be home with her family, but no, she was still at Sunnyvale. Her depression was wrecking havoc on her mind still. The week before, she had become overwhelmed with thoughts of self-harm again. She did all she could to fight it, but nothing helped.

Hollie and Trevor had come to see her on Christmas, bringing her some new clothes and snacks, as much that was allowed to bring in. They had a good day together, but it wasn't enough. She hugged and kissed them goodbye, to make sure they knew how much she cared. Somehow she knew in her heart that it was the last time she'd see them.

She and Marissa had been talking and planning for her suicide attempt. If the plan worked, maybe both girls might not survive. It seemed grim, but to Zacchya it was the only way out. Marissa had been extremely hesitant to help Zacchya at all.

"Zacchya, you can't! You're my only friend in here! Shoot, you're my ONLY friend. I won't survive this place without you!" Marissa pleaded, her deep eyes swimming with tears.

"I just can't do it, you know this. It's like the harder I try, the worse I get. Without him… I can't do it."

"I can't talk you out of it?"

"I wish you could… but no." Zacchya wiped a tear from her eye. They were alone in the reading room and she was glad for it. She didn't want people overhearing what they were planning. Marissa leaned over and hugged her tightly.

"Then I'll help you. You're my best friend. I have an idea anyway. What you need is a distraction…" Marissa looked at her and forced a smile.

So the plan was set to be put in motion during supper time. It was always a busy time around the unit. Zacchya glanced at the clock, 5:30. Supper should be ready at any time. She saw Marissa pacing the hallways, as Zacchya slipped into her bedroom.

The room was mostly bare: only a mattress, blankets, a desk that was bolted to the floor, and an open bathroom with no door. The staff didn't know, but she had a piece of broken metal from the desk, under her mattress. She had been slowly breaking it off for a few days. It was about four inches long and had an extremely sharp jagged edge.

"Supper is ready to be served on the unit. Please head to the cafeteria." A female voice announced over the intercom.

Zacchya's stomach began swirling nervously. It was almost time and she was beyond scared. What would happen when she died? Would she go to heaven? Would she see Jacob right away? Would she end up in hell for committing suicide? There were so many answers that she didn't have. Her heart pounded in her chest, her palms became sweaty. She had to focus on the plan and not questions, or she would chicken out.

She lay down on the mattress, pulling the blankets up to her chest and closed her eyes. She wanted the staff to think she was asleep if they came down to check on her. They were supposed to do location checks on her twice an hour, but she hoped that they'd be busy enough with Marissa's distraction they wouldn't come down. She tried to calm her breathing down so she'd appear asleep and waited for the cue.

Marissa walked determinedly to the cafeteria. She had two nails hidden in the palm of her hand, hiding them from everyone's view. She grabbed her supper tray and sat down in her assigned seat. Slowly, she took a few bites of her tomato soup, but didn't really taste it. She wasn't really that hungry. Her nerves were swirling inside, making her feel a bit nauseated. But it was all for show to blend in with the crowd, to make sure she didn't stick out. When no one was looking, she slipped the nails between her thumb and forefinger. With one deep breath, she forced the nails into her wrist and pulled as hard as she could. Blood poured out of her pale wrists and into her tomato soup and all over her supper tray.

"Marissa!"

A few screams of pain filled the air as soon as the girls seen what she had done.

"Call the doctor! Hurry!"

"Someone get me a towel!" An aide came to help Marissa as the color slowly drained from her already pale complexion. "Marissa talk to me! Look at me! Stay with me, Marissa!"

Zacchya heard the screams and knew that it was time. There was no more time for questions and answers about death. It was now or never. She'd only have a few minutes before the doctor would come, maybe less. Plus the aides had to check on her soon too, if they remembered or didn't have their hands too full. If one realized she wasn't there, it could be bad news for her plan. She jumped off of the mattress, lifted it, and grabbed the piece of metal. It stared menacingly at her, the jagged metal tempting her fate. Was she brave enough to do it? Was she strong enough? Could she even handle the pain?

She held the metal blade in her left hand, positioned it above her right wrist. Her left hand was sweaty and shaking from fear. Her breathing became quick and panic filled her. Never before had she tried to slit her wrist. It seemed much worse now that she was moments away from it.

Jacob's wide beautiful smile flashed in her mind. The overwhelming love and hurt filled her so much she thought her heart might burst open. She had to be with him again, it wasn't an option. She brought the blade down and cut.

The pain was unlike anything she'd ever felt before, completely overwhelming. Blood dripped down her wrist, faster and faster, red drops oozing all over her pant legs. She forced herself to make the cut longer, pulling the blade higher up her arm. The pain overtook her. Blackness overtook her.

"Zacchya, sweetie, it's time…" An aide creaked the bedroom door open and screamed. Zacchya was lying in a pool of blood. "Zacchya! Oh no! Not you too! Oh God, not you too!"

The aide rushed back to the hallway, panic overtaking her, "HELP! HELP! WE HAVE ANOTHER ONE!"

Chapter 6

NINE MONTHS LATER

September 3, 2014

"Can you believe it? It's our first day as seniors!" Bobby Woods exclaimed. He high-fived his best friend, Trevor Packers.

"Gonna be epic I think, Bob. I mean almost out of this shitty town. It sounds too good to be true."

"Yeah for real, man. Shit town. HA! So true… smells like shit too! I'm especially ready to get out of here after all the craziness this summer… Oooh, let's get this over with. Can it be May yet?" Bobby laughed.

"Totally wish it was, Bob. Wish it was!" Trevor chuckled. The summer had its ups and downs, but he was definitely ready to get the hell out of Larned. He never liked it much. It was just small enough to have nothing fun to do, and it always smelled like cows. There were two feed lots on the edges of town that with the wrong breeze, made everything smell like it was double dipped in cow diarrhea. Trevor hated that. Everyone hated that! But around July, Larned had gotten worse than normal.

"Yeah me too. Especially after Zombie One, God knows what's next. Maybe that zombie apocalypse they are always training us for. How many zombie movies have there been in the past year? Oh yeah, they want us prepared! You know I'm right!" Bobby laughed.

"I freaking hope not, one is enough." Trevor frowned. Of course there wasn't really an undead human trying to eat brains. No, just an undead human. He didn't want to believe it when he first heard the rumors. Jacob was alive? Jacob was a ghost? Jacob was a flesh-eating zombie? Whatever you called it, whatever it was; Jacob Track was back from the dead. He paced the railroad bridge outside of town, day and night, where he had jumped to his death the year before. If suicidal boys usually came back and haunted their place of death, Trevor didn't know. What he did know was that the town was slowly falling into chaos from it. Rumors filled the air of deaths and odd train accidents. Trevor didn't believe a word of it. The town was small enough to know if a train derailed. And he hadn't heard of any suspicious deaths, but he didn't really gossip or read the news either. What he did know was that if Jacob was a ghost, zombie, or whatever, and haunting the place of his death, there had to be a reason. It really messed with his head.

"Well let's get going to Trig, man. Teacher will kill us if we're late on the first day," Bobby said and they headed off to class. Thankfully they both found a seat next to Trina Johnson. Bobby had a crush on Trina, but hadn't made a move yet because of their long friendship. Also, Trina had been in a relationship with Jacob before he died and after it was over, she took a long time to get over the heartache. Then Jacob had died and she got worse before she got better. Jacob was now the walking dead and she seemed very affected by it. So Bobby was waiting for the right time. He flirted with her, tried to make her laugh whenever he could. She would come around eventually. He was always good with charming the ladies. With his tan skin and manly square features, perfectly offsetting his well-groomed, wavy, brown hair and brown eyes, he was definition of a "pretty" man. Girls usually found him very attractive and adored him. He had a wild summer night with a few college girls that didn't know he was only seventeen at the time. He enjoyed flirting and having fun with girls but a part of him wanted to give it a try for Trina.

"Bobby, I thought you were awful at math! Why did you sign up for this class?" Trina whispered, her blue eyes sparkling at him.

"Oh, you know need a math credit every year. So I decided to see if my brain knew anything about trig instead of just being sexy." Bobby winked playfully at her.

"You wish, weirdo." Trina smiled and lightly hit his arm.

At lunch, The Misfits found a table together. The Misfits weren't really misfits or outcasts at all. They just thought it was a fun name. Everyone in the group got along well and had throughout most of their childhood. After Jacob died, their small group just grew closer together. Jacob had been the leader of the group, the glue that kept them together. The girls: Trina, Zacchya, April, and Alicia had all dated Jacob sometime during their years, but it was surprisingly not weird for them to stay friends with each other. They knew that friendship was more important than letting a man tear them apart. The group consisted of: Trevor Packers, Zacchya Packers, Bobby Woods, Trina Johnson, Alicia Green, Tim Meadows, and April Walker.

"Physics was actually pretty fun today," Tim said.

"That's 'cuz you're a nerd, dude." Bobby laughed.

"Ha. Ha. Ha. At least I can spell my own name!" Tim joked.

"Now girls, let's all be pleasant!" Trevor smiled.

"You boys are so weird. I swear I need to find new friends." Alicia rolled her eyes and smiled.

"You'd miss my dashing smile! My sparkling green eyes!" Trevor winked at her.

"That's true... that's true. It is a dashing smile! I might be stuck! Oh, why did I have to date a weirdo?" Alicia brushed her long, wavy, brown hair out of her face, leaned over and kissed Trevor's cheek. They had been dating a little over three months.

"Oh romance! Ugh!" Zacchya rolled her blue eyes.

"What? You don't like people kissing?" Tim leaned over and kissed April's cheek. April's face went as red as Tim's hair.

"You're going to give the girl a heart attack!" Zacchya laughed. "You know she's too shy for PDA!"

"Yeah! Tim, sheesh, you SHOULD know this!" April smiled and playfully hit his shoulder, her cheeks still quite pink.

"I promise to never kiss my girlfriend again!" Tim smirked, his crossed fingers waving in the air. He and April had been dating for almost a month. April was still very shy and not used to having a boyfriend. Tim respected her and took things slow, but he did like teasing her to watch her cheeks get pink. He found her so cute when she blushed. Even though their relationship was new, Tim thought she might be the one for him. His mind wandered into daydream land at the thought of it. He had known April for about five years, since he moved to town. She was one of the few that befriended him right away. Tim had a lot of trouble making friends in past schools. He figured it was from his red hair and freckles, and his extreme smarts. He had been asked to join MENSA, but turned it down. He wanted his high school experience to be as normal as possible. He would let college be the place where he would overachieve.

He looked over at April's deep brown eyes. She was beautiful, even if the other boys only found her average. He knew what her potential was. She smiled sweetly back at him, and his heart melted. There was so much he wanted to tell her and share with her. But she wanted slow, so he went slowly. He was falling for her with every small quirk she showed him. He wouldn't tell her, couldn't scare her away by coming on too strong.

The bell rang and everyone said goodbye and separated toward their perspective classes. Zacchya had purposely tried to make a joke and fit in with The Misfits, but she still felt like such an outsider. They all knew her past. Most of the time, they looked at her like she was made of glass. *Don't upset Zacchya, she might crack and kill herself.* At least that's what she imagined their glances toward her meant. She had gone over six months without self-harm issues, but no one seemed to remember that. She was the girl that ruined Jacob's funeral. She was the girl who spent three months in a mental hospital. Broken glass.

She had done summer classes with a tutor so she could be caught up on all of her schoolwork. She felt better and her depression was nearly gone. She felt like her old self again. Happy-go-lucky Zacchya. Even when she heard the rumors about Jacob last month, she was okay. Upset that it might be true, of course, but adjusting. Her mom and brother watched her very closely after Jacob "returned."

Zacchya felt things about Jacob that she couldn't put a finger on. Sadness, being upset with herself, but there was something else. It was like a dark bubble in her mind and she couldn't pop it or see what was inside. So she did whatever she could to distract herself from thinking about him. She hid all the pictures from their year-long relationship in a box in her basement. No Jacob thoughts were allowed. But unfortunately, he was there. The harder she tried to forget about him, the more he was there. Everyone talked about him (in whispers when she was around) and wondered. Whatever he was or wasn't, she just wanted it to be over. She just wanted to move on. She wasn't even sure if she could move on, though. Her heart still loved him so much. It was more than a teenage puppy love. They had shared real emotional moments together, highs and lows. There had been passion and romance, more than she ever had expected to feel. She wondered if all couples felt like they did. A part of her hoped so.

But then she had ruined it. She started acting weird, not herself. She pushed him away and away he went. She wondered if they had gotten too close and pushed him away to protect her heart. She wasn't sure why she did it, but she had, and she deeply regretted it. Two weeks after they broke up, he went on a date with Trina again. Zacchya had been the furious, jealous ex and they had a huge fight. Both were in tears by the end. He stormed away and was dead within a week. She blamed herself. She pushed him too hard and he cracked. Broken glass.

She knew that when people died, the loved ones always blamed themselves. Humans do weird things in their constant search for answers. If the blame falls on them, then they have an answer to an impossible question. Especially when God can be so silent. But Zacchya really did feel the blame for Jacob's suicide. He loved her. She pushed him away. He killed himself over a girl he loved too much. How was it not her fault? Most of The Misfits thought his suicide was a lie. Zacchya thought they were hopeful dreamers. They were just looking for answers to an impossible question. Why would a seventeen-year-old boy with everything going for him commit suicide? Impossible question. No answer. Life was full of questions but not enough answers.

* * * *

Elizabeth Track hung up the phone and threw it on the chair next to her. She was disgusted with reporters. They called all hours of the day, no respect for privacy. They knocked on her door. They followed her to work. Did people have no decency anymore?

"Is your son a ghost?"

"How do you feel about the undead? Is your son the start of the zombie apocalypse?"

"Do you practice black magic? Or Hoodoo?"

"Was your son's death a farce? Is he really still alive?"

"Have you been to see if your son is really haunting the place of his death?"

The nerve! As if it hadn't already been the hardest nine months of her life as it was! She lost her son to a horrible suicide. She had to have a funeral without a body to bury, without a proper goodbye, which was horribly interrupted by a girl who tried to shoot herself in the head. Then without anytime to grieve, Elizabeth found out she was already two months pregnant. To make sure she didn't miscarry, she had to stay positive and strong. She wasn't allowed to cry, dwell on the pain, or scream at God for answers. No, she had a baby to nurture and he needed her calm. Thankfully, she had a safe pregnancy and Marcus Jacob Track was born July 10th, happy and healthy.

She headed to the nursery to check on Marcus. He was asleep, looking truly angelic. He had golden hair like his dad, Edward. Track boys were quite handsome. Marcus was truly a blessing she could never forget and would never take for granted. She did keep an extremely close eye on him, afraid for his safety. She couldn't bear to lose another child. After Marcus was born, she joined a local group for mothers of suicide victims. They met once a week and it was surprising how well it helped her cope. Maybe it was just knowing that she wasn't suffering alone. All of the ladies had gone through the worst thing, burying a child, but had somehow come out on the other side. Some were broken inside beyond repair, but some had strength unbeknownst to them and only grew stronger. Together they fought an unseen war on grief. The battles however happened on a daily basis. Elizabeth brought Marcus to a few meetings. His sweet innocence helped put a smile on the ladies faces and hope in their hearts. It was amazing how much a baby could help people. Something about the innocence and promise of a new beginning, sparked hope that was not always easily quenched.

Now if she could only get the reporters to see that! Elizabeth tried to push them out of her mind and see the positive, but sometimes it was a struggle. She constantly wondered if the stories were true. Was Jacob raised from the dead? Why would Jacob come back as a ghost? It didn't make sense to her at all. Weren't ghosts left behind because of revenge or refusal to accept death? Jacob was suicidal. What issues were unresolved or causing revenge? He had made his choice. Wasn't that enough to have eternal peace? It quite disturbed her. She believed in God and practiced Christianity. Jacob was saved by his belief in Jesus and that meant a ticket to heaven, not a ticket to eternal suffering on a bridge! Her faith was clearly being tested. She didn't appreciate it one bit. She liked to watch the Pastor Joel Osteen on TV some mornings. He was the best at explaining things that other preachers never seemed to see. Sometimes she had an urge to send a letter or email for prayer, but never did. She wasn't quite sure how to write it. *"Hi, I need your prayers. My son committed suicide last year and now he's back as a ghost... or some kind of undead. Thanks!"* It didn't quite have a realistic tone to it!

Liz's thoughts were cut short by the cries of young Marcus. He was probably wet and ready to eat. Thank God throughout this whole mess she had Marcus and Ed, of course.

* * * *

September 26, 2014

Trina sat on her bed staring at a blank sheet of lined paper that was supposed to have her math homework on it, but her mind was elsewhere. She had made it through September relatively unscathed. Rumors of Jacob appearances grew and grew. But she had tried to push them out of her head. She had turned eighteen a few days before, finally an adult. At her party, Bobby kissed her. They were laughing and flirting like always. Then the next thing she knew, he leaned into her, gently grabbed her face and kissed her. She thought about pushing him away, but his lips were amazing, so she kissed back. The kiss went passionate and then Bobby pulled away. He said, "Happy birthday, Sugar" and then left. She longed to know what caused the kiss. Was it just Bobby being his regular flirty self or something more? She wanted to ask him the next day in math class, but he was late to school. He didn't show up until right before lunch, and then he was weirdly quiet at lunch. She couldn't figure him out. Then he texted her as she was eating supper and "misfits meeting at the park. ASAP!" It didn't give any other details, other than the location. Why was he being so cryptic? Was he just pulling another practical joke?

Trina sent a text to Trevor and he replied back, "Got the same thing. Can't tell Zacchya though."

April texted Trina saying she had the same message. Alicia texted too. What was he thinking? Were they just supposed to follow him blindly?

Alicia texted again, "Leaving in five, want me to pick you up?"

Trina had too much curiosity about all of it, so she replied, "Yeah."

Trevor texted again, "You going?"

"Yes."

"Going. Why can't Zacchya come? Going to yell at him, I swear!" April texted.

"Don't blame you on that one..." Trina replied.

"April text you?" Tim wrote.

"Yep."

"Ok. You going?"

"Yep." So everyone was invited, except Zacchya, and heading to the park after Bobby's weird message. She might have to slap him. That was, after she kissed those wonderful lips one more time. He was messing with her head and she wasn't happy about it. Her hormones said to lick his face, her head said to kick him a bit. Being a girl was the worst.

Alicia showed up a few minutes later in her '99 yellow Jeep Wrangler. Trina loved that Jeep. It just felt like summer every time she rode in it. They drove across town to the park. The park was small, only a couple swing sets, monkey bars, and a few slides, nothing impressive. They noticed Bobby's black Mustang and parked beside it. A few minutes after they arrived, Tim, April, and Trevor all arrived. Trina and Alicia looked at each other and nodded. They got out of the Jeep and headed over to a swing where Bobby was sitting and not swinging at all. A very serious look was etched on his face.

Trina walked over to him, and suppressed her desire to kiss him again. Instead she asked, "Why on God's green earth did you call us out here for with that weird ass text?" She forced a hand upon her hip to appear stronger. She wasn't near as mad as she wanted to be.

"Glad you could all make it. Now, I'm sorry for sounding all weird and shit, but I didn't want Zacchya to find out."

"Hey man!" Trevor shouted. That was his twin sister, after all.

"No offense, man! You know I like her! She's a damn cool chick! It's just I've heard some things and I wanted you to all hear them and decide for yourself."

"Decide what?" April asked angrily. She wasn't happy about Zacchya's seclusion. That was her best friend.

"You'll see…" Bobby paused. "I have a good friend who isn't a Misfit, shocking I know. And he told me some interesting things last night over a few beers."

"Ok, so you're an alcoholic… get to the point," Trevor sighed.

"Ha ha… you're so funny, Trevor. Anyway, he said some buddies of his went fishing last week in the creek. Said they found some weird shit. Like dead animals who had been stabbed in the chest, lying on the shore."

"Ok, so we have some kind of animal serial killer?" Tim chuckled and rolled his eyes.

"No, asshole. They also saw something else. Something we've only heard rumors about." Bobby looked seriously around the group.

"Oh Lord! Not this Jacob shit again!" Alicia sighed loudly.

"You brought us here for Jacob rumors? Come on, man!" Tim stood up from the swing he sat on, annoyed.

"Shut up and listen!" Bobby began pacing the ground, his eyes wild with passion. "This ain't rumor bullshit! I wouldn't call you out here for hearsay!"

"Then get to the point please! Your dramatics are exhausting and I have homework." Trina frowned at him.

Bobby looked at her, feeling stung by her words. She found him too dramatic? He tried to push away his hurt and said, "The dude took a picture."

"Bullshit." Trevor huffed.

"Sure, sure, sure they did." April rolled her eyes.

"I have it on my phone. Friend sent it to me." Bobby reached in his pocket and pulled out his iPhone. He scrolled through and pulled up the picture of the creek. It was late afternoon, but enough light to see Jacob Track standing on the bridge clearly. He showed it to The Misfits.

"What. The. Fuck." Trevor was flabbergasted. He would notice Jacob anywhere.

"This isn't real. No," April shuddered.

"No. No," Trina could only whisper.

Alicia and Tim didn't say anything at all, just shook their heads in disbelief.

"You see why I couldn't have Zacchya here? She's been doing so well lately; I didn't want to upset her again," Bobby said quietly.

"It's hard to say really. She has been back to her old self, or close to her old self, for some time now. But this, man... this shit freaks me out!" Trevor shuddered. How was this even possible?

"Well it got me thinking. He is clearly back as a ghost or undead, or what-the-fuck-ever he is. We need to talk to him." Bobby was no longer sitting on the swing, but pacing slowly in front of the group.

"NO! NO! That's a horrible, horrible plan, Bobby!" Alicia shouted.

"Horrible plan!" April spoke.

"If he is some undead creature, he could try to kill us! He already serial killed those animals, right? He could eat our brains or something!" Tim squeaked.

"Serial killed, is that even a real phrase?" Bobby rolled his eyes. "Honestly, are you even listening to yourselves? Jacob was the nicest fucking dude I ever met! And you all fucking know that! Whatever he is, Jacob's still in there! Maybe we can help him pass on..." Bobby was pacing fast now, his heart was racing.

"Or he could kill us," Trevor said.

"Jacob isn't a killer! He's probably just after..." April's voice trailed off.

"What, April? Don't get quiet now! Your face says you know something!" Trevor said, staring at her.

"Nothing. Just forget it." April shifted nervously on her swing.

"You're not telling us something! Spill it!" Bobby walked briskly over to her swing. He wasn't trying to appear threatening, but April was clearly scared.

"Chill out, Bobby!" Tim stood up to April to protect her, standing between her and Bobby.

"Tim, it's okay. I just... I..." April's voice trailed off again. Tears were forming in her brown eyes. Tim put his arm around her. She fell onto his shoulder, sobbing.

"Look what you did!" Tim shouted angrily.

Bobby tried to apologize, but no one would let him talk. Alicia and Trina both headed toward the Jeep. Trevor was standing by Bobby, defending the right to know the truth.

Finally, as Alicia opened her Jeep door, April shouted out, shooting up from the ground, "Wait!"

All of The Misfits stopped walking and stared at her. Her long brown hair was sticking to her face from the tears. Her eyes were sad, but wild. She tried to muster up courage. "Jacob… well… he… he didn't kill himself."

Chapter 7

So there it was. April had finally spoken aloud the truth she'd hidden for almost a year. Her heart should have felt relieved and less stressed, but it was quite the opposite. She felt panic rising in her chest. She knew who killed Jacob. She saw the murderer's face. That murderer was a Misfit. As her pulse continued to rise, she knew she had to play it cool. Tell them she never saw the face. *Play it cool, April,* she thought to herself.

"Wh… what did you say?" Trina stuttered, her feet no longer worked and she stopped walking toward the Jeep.

"Murdered. I … I was there, sort of," April said quietly.

"You were there?" Trina screamed and ran back to April's side. "How were you there?" Trina's hands were on April's shoulders, shaking her, her eyes wild.

"Trina! Let her go!" Trevor came and split the girl's apart. "Chill the fuck out! April will explain herself. Won't you, April?"

"Yes. I will. I just want everyone to sit down and chill out. This isn't CSI." April focused on her breathing, trying not to panic. She waited until everyone was back sitting in a nearby swing or on the ground, looking up at her expectantly.

"It was by accident really. My parents were arguing, which they rarely do and it upset me. I just had to get out of the house. So I walked down to the tracks and just lay next to a tree for a bit. Trying to calm down and focus on the prettiness of nature. Well I guess I dozed off for a bit and woke up right after sunset. I sat up, grabbed my iPod and went to leave. It was getting cold, dark, and threatening to storm, so I needed to get out of there before I was soaked.

"I heard a scream as I turned to leave. Thinking someone was in trouble, I headed toward the sound." April was sweating. Her heart raced, her speech was quick. She couldn't face them now, staring at the dirt on the ground. She was playing it as cool as she could.

"And?!" Trevor asked. He was so confused. Jacob was murdered?

"Well I made it close to the bridge, and heard screaming again. I was scared now. I didn't know what was going on. Then I saw Jacob heading towards me, but he was still a ways off. I was going to call his name, but someone was chasing him. Then he fell and I heard another scream." April's eyes filled with tears. It was so hard to relive it. So hard to believe it even happened the first time.

"Then the... person leaned over him. Stabbed him... I think." Her eyes still focused on the dirt below her feet. "Then they pushed him over the bridge, I think, and he was gone," April said quietly. Tim was beside her, wrapped his arm around her. April welcomed the embrace and cried into his shoulder.

"You... you didn't see who it was?" Alicia asked loudly.

"N... No... nope. Just like a shadow. I... I couldn't tell. Think it was a girl."

"Oh..." Alicia said.

"So actually murdered! Wow... that makes so much sense!" Bobby said, scratching the scruff on his chin.

"Makes sense? What planet are you living on, Bob?" Trevor asked.

"Yeah, dude! Jacob wasn't suicidal! He was the happiest guy I ever met. He was emotionally sound, more than all of us. He would NEVER put his parents through that. He loved them too much."

"That is true. My gut always told me something was off about the whole thing. Never knew what though. Holy shit, man, it's crazy." Trevor nodded.

"You realize whoever did it... covered it up! That's some pretty sneaky shit!" Bobby gasped.

"I... just want to go home. Too much. Just too much." Trina shuddered and pulled on Alicia's sleeve.

"Ya. I need a weeklong nap," Alicia agreed.

"What? You're leaving? NOW?" Bobby asked.

"Yeah," Trina whispered and she and Alicia walked quickly to the Jeep. They sped off and were gone before anyone could protest their leaving.

"Weird... I guess everyone processes different." Bobby shook his head. "But this shows us! We have to go see him now! We have to catch his killer! That's probably why he came back! It's our duty as his friend!"

Trevor sat quietly for a minute, thinking hard. Then added, "Definitely."

Tim wanted to say yes as well, but he didn't want to upset April. She had stopped crying, but he enjoyed comforting her too much. "Well, I'm going to get April home. Let's just talk about it another time."

"Yeah, we will later for sure," Trevor agreed.

Tim and April got into his Pontiac Grand Prix and he drove slowly to her house. He kept a hand on top of hers; he hated seeing her that sad. Going through something as traumatic as seeing your friend murdered, he couldn't even imagine what that would be like.

"No, Tim. Don't go home just yet. I want to stay with you a bit longer. Just go park somewhere in the country and hold me," April said. She was still scared. The Misfits knew now. She felt the hours of her life ticking by. Speaking the truth out loud for the first time seemed to start a horrible chain of events. Maybe she was overreacting, but she felt her time was short. She knew her days were numbered now. She just wanted to spend her last days, weeks, and months unafraid. She had spent her whole life afraid of something. She never took chances, always played it safe. She kept her mouth shut and stayed proper. She was tired of playing it safe. Who knew how much time she had left? She had fallen for Tim but kept him at a safe distance, so she wouldn't get hurt. He hadn't even done more than kiss her, and they had been dating almost two months. It wasn't long, of course, but it wasn't that short either. But after bearing her truth, she felt as if it was enough for her. She wanted to give him all that she had kept away hidden inside of her.

Tim found a dirt road, drove a few miles so they weren't near the town, and parked. It was dark and the stars shone above them. He put his arm around her. "It will be okay. I promise, baby."

"Tim, will you kiss me? Kiss me like you never have before," April pleaded, her hands touching his face. She was inches from his face, and loved the feel of his warm breath on her face.

Tim smiled and held her face gently in his hands.

"Anything for you." He kissed her softly and sweetly. Then the passion overtook them both and the kiss grew harder, more passionate. April let her hands fall over his chest, trying to memorize every inch of it. Tim was well built, but not that muscular. She already loved the small squish in his stomach area. She was glad he wasn't built like a movie star. He was just Tim.

Tim's hands caressed her sides, her arms, passionately but still being respectful. April moved his hands under her shirt. The fire inside of them grew. Instead of being afraid for once, she let herself feel nothing but passion and love for Tim.

* * * *

October 17, 2014

It was almost three weeks after April confessed to witnessing Jacob's murder. None of The Misfits had time to meet up since then, except at lunchtime, but Zacchya was always there. At school, they were usually busy with the large amounts of assignments. Their senior year was a little harder than they expected. Alicia was usually busy after school with cheerleading practice and football games. Trevor and Bobby were both on the football team, so usually busy as well. Trina was usually watching her younger brother, Kent, after school while her mom, Betty, worked a second job. April and Tim did all their homework together and spent all their free time together as well. Their relationship had grown closer since that night.

So when Zacchya was at home sick with the flu, no one was surprised when Bobby decided to bring up the subject again at lunch.

"So I know we've all been busy, but next week is the one year anniversary of Jacob's death, October 28th. I think we should go see him."

"That's a school night, Bobby," Trina said.

"I know that. I meant we should go see him on Halloween."

"That's just cheesy as hell, Bob." Trevor rolled his eyes.

"Eh, it is a bit. But I don't want to go on Halloween for that reason. I want to go because it's a Friday. It's a holiday and we can easily get away from the house for a night without too much question from our parents. Everyone is out that night. We won't look out of place, whatsoever! Especially when we go sneaking off to the woods. They'll just think we're dumb teenagers off to sneak a few beers or something," Bobby explained.

"That actually makes some sense. You're smarter than I gave you credit for." Tim smiled.

"Thanks, Tim. And between football games and homework, it really is our only time until God knows when! It's now or never, really," Bobby said.

The Misfits looked around at each other. The group still didn't think it was a good idea to even bring it up to Zacchya yet. They couldn't have it on their conscious if she tried to kill herself again because of seeing Jacob again. Bobby was right, and they knew it. If they wanted answers, they had to go on Halloween.

"I need the truth. Let's go," Alicia said quietly. She had been more quiet than usual since April's confession. No one knew why, but guessed grief and confusion. Bobby secretly had a feeling that Alicia was the murderer. He hoped she wasn't, of course, as she was dating Trevor. And he didn't want Trevor dead too. But he kept his suspicions to himself. In case she was, he didn't want to be the next victim either.

"I guess so," April agreed.

"Totally, let's go," Trevor nodded.

"Let's go, then," Tim said. Trina only nodded.

So it was set. The Misfits continued to plan their trip to the tracks and their cover stories for their parents. Trevor worried if he could hide it from his sister. They had always been so close. It really bothered him to lie to her. But he didn't want her heart to break all over again. He wouldn't be able to live with himself if Zacchya hurt that much ever again, or his mom, Hollie. Hollie had taken it so hard after the funeral when Zacchya had been hospitalized. And Zacchya had been at the hospital for over three months. The twins' dad died when they were very young and Hollie never remarried. She was raising the kids on her own, working a lot of extra hours as a CNA at the nursing home. Trevor had a lot of respect for his mom and only wanted the best for her. So he would keep the trip to see Jacob a secret to keep Hollie safe, and Zacchya too. It was the only right thing to do, a little white lie to save them both.

Chapter 8

October 31, 2014

HALLOWEEN

Zacchya stood in the bathroom staring at her reflection. Her long wavy blond hair framed her heart shaped face just right. Her large blue eyes and small features made her look like a beautiful doll. Numerous people throughout her life told her that she needed to get out of Kansas after high school and become a model.

"No one that beautiful should ever be sad!" A surprising number of people had told her that. As if being beautiful was the only key to ultimate happiness. But Zacchya didn't feel beautiful. She felt guilty and dirty. It was like the stories she heard from Marissa after being molested. Something inside of her wanted to disappear from existence, but it didn't make sense to her. She felt awful and ugly. Her hope was fading again, and there was no reason for it.

She had been spending extra time with her Uncle Larry after school. They would talk about everything that bothered her. He always promised to listen "like an uncle and not a doctor." She appreciated that. It was hard to get someone to listen to her when she needed to get things off of her chest. The kids at school talked with her, but they didn't trust her. They treated her different than before the funeral. She didn't know if the reason she felt so awful was just the rehashing of the old hurts she confided in to Larry or something else. But she felt miserable. She tried to hide it from Trevor and Hollie, but it was so hard to do. Hollie had noticed something was off and they went for a special girl's day to buy new clothes and splurge on ice cream. It was nice spending time with her mom, but it didn't help. She was too far gone again.

No, it's a rough patch. I can get over this, she told herself. As she stared at the glass in the mirror, she realized how easy it would be to break it and cut her wrist. Too easy, really.

Broken glass cutting someone that everyone treats like glass. How ironic! But I am broken. God, why am I so damned broken? She sobbed. No one was home to help her. No one would find her if she did something stupid. Trevor had gone off with Bobby for a boy's night, as he told her. April had called her days ago telling her of The Misfits going to the bridge to see Jacob. April was her best friend and was trying to trust her. Zacchya loved that about April: she could always see the good in people.

Zacchya wanted to confront Trevor but decided against it. He was just trying to be a good brother and protect her. He didn't want her to see Jacob, and she didn't want to see Jacob. She couldn't punish him for that. She didn't want to know if Jacob was real or not. He was real enough in her heart, and that was already too much for her to bear. How could she see him in person and not completely crack in half?

Just the thought of Jacob's name pierced her heart. Why had she grabbed that box of pictures from the basement? Salt in the wound. Everything she did reminded her of Jacob. It all came back to him. Maybe her depression was returning because his death anniversary had just passed on the 28th. Then his funeral was on November 2nd and when she was committed for a suicide attempt and depression. It all was connected to Jacob. Part of her wanted to run to the tracks and throw her arms around his neck, if he was there, and kiss him until her lips fell off. The rest of her just wanted to die. It was all of her fault. She should end her life in a way to tribute her undying love for him.

"Break the glass. Cut the vein and be reunited. Just do it," she told herself, tears pouring down her pink cheeks. Why did they leave her home alone? She wasn't to be trusted. The pink scar on her right wrist tingled. She remembered the pain from the suicide attempt at Sunnyvale. What if she lived through it again?

"Think of Trevor and Mom. Don't do this to them. They can't handle it. Fuck! Why did they leave me alone?" she screamed out to the empty house. The tears wouldn't stop pouring down.

Before she knew it, she punched the mirror and it smashed into sparkling, sharp pieces into the sink below. Too easy.

* * * *

Across town a man wearing all black was pacing in his kitchen. He slipped on a black ski mask as he put down his coffee cup. Two days earlier he had found that those stupid brats were going to see Jacob. *"Had to know if he was real,"* they said.

"Of course he's real, you fucktards!" he thought to himself. He could feel his blood pressure rising. He had someone wiretap all of the kids' cell phones. He also found out that April Walker knew Jacob was murdered. This was information that the man could not allow. He had tried too hard to cover up that murder! Too hard! He wasn't going to let some know-it-all bitch ruin it. How the hell did she find out anyway?

April and her boyfriend Tim weren't going to the bridge to see Jake. He had found that out from the wire taps yesterday. April was scared and begged all the other "misfits" to reconsider.

"Can't you see how bad this is? My gut says we can't go! It's too dangerous!" she had begged them. Tim loved her; *stupid teenage love bullshit,* the man thought. The two were planning on running away and getting married in Vegas. While the rest of the "misfits" were planning on going to the bridge, April and Tim were leaving town tonight.

He only hoped he could catch them, ask the bitch how she knew the truth, and then cut her throat open. There were only two things he loved more than killing someone: one was power, and the other... well he'd never tell anyone. He'd rather just kill or watch them all kneel to his power. And they would one day. Oh yes, they would.

* * * *

Zacchya sat in the bathtub, knees to her chest, hugging herself. She was shaking from the cool water flowing over her from the shower nozzle above her. She had turned the water on to mask her tears. She hated crying, it made her feel so weak and useless. She held a large shard of glass in her left hand. If she did cut herself, she wanted to make sure Hollie didn't have to clean blood out of the tub; it would just wash itself down the drain. The thought of her mom cleaning her blood stains disturbed her so much. She couldn't do that to her mom, or anyone. But that didn't stop her from planning to cut herself. She had made one tiny shallow cut on her arm. She stopped because of the pain and she was crying so hard she couldn't see.

She had grabbed her iPod putting it on shuffle. Music always calmed her down. The song "Broken Glass" by Three Days Grace came on, which she loved. She sang quietly through her tears. The song was comforting to her. To know that someone else felt like her, broken and alone, helped. She was tired of being seen as the victim, the fragile girl, where everyone was so scared to talk to her, afraid she'd crack up. The song wasn't necessarily happy or sad, but it was honest. She respected that about songs, especially in country or rock music. They sang about real life. There were so many songs that perfectly captured thoughts and emotions that people couldn't always express themselves. She loved that about songwriters and musicians, the gift to express emotions raw and real. It was one of the most important gifts God handed out. Music helped people get through things they would never be able to. It was a supporting hand to hold in a time of need. The right song at the right time could save a life.

"Amsterdam" by Coldplay came on next and she broke down crying even harder. The song had always been one she tried to avoid if she was sad, as it was too heartbreaking to deal with. The pure emotion, haunting piano, and content were too much for her.

She tried to keep singing to herself, but soon she was starting to doze off. Her eyes were too heavy from crying. Her soul felt too broken to stay awake.

* * * *

April Walker woke up in a haze, as if she was stuck in a dark foggy tunnel. She was so exhausted that she couldn't open her eyes, but she was awake. Her body had never felt so heavy before, as though she weighed 1,000 pounds instead of her 180. She tried to lift her right arm, but it wouldn't budge. She tried her left arm, and it didn't move either. She then tried to lift her legs, also with no luck.

Oh, God, am I paralyzed? she thought through the fog. What day was it? Better yet, what year was it? Was she paralyzed? Where was she? Nothing was making sense in her foggy mind. She wished she could open her eyes, at least.

"You awake?" a quiet voice asked, slurring the words together.

April tried to nod her head, but it just weighed so much. She wondered if she was really awake at all. Maybe it was all a dream.

"April?" the voice asked, still quiet and slushy sounding as if it were underwater.

April tried to open her mouth and say yes. She didn't know if it worked until she heard the voice reply, "Good."

"Sleep?" She got one word out. She wished her mind and body would do something at all. She couldn't handle this heaviness and confusion.

"No. Drugged. Bad man," the voice said. At those words, the fog tried to lift from her mind. She remembered a bad man. A man dressed in all black. Flashing lights. A gun.

"Gone?" she asked.

"Away. Be back," the voice replied. She finally recognized the voice; it was Tim. He was somewhere near her. Slowly she was regaining her memory.

"Paralyzed?"

"Rope. Tied down."

So she was tied to a chair, not paralyzed. Not a dream. She wished it was a dream. And she wasn't sure if being tied to a chair was better than being paralyzed. Whoever the bad man was, he would be back.

Flashes of Halloween night were starting to return to her. She remembered going to the entrance to the tracks, she met up with The Misfits and begged them not to go. They didn't listen and she and Tim left. She had an awful feeling someone was about to die. No one listened to her. She wondered if it was still Halloween at all. She had no concept of the time that had passed while she was unconscious.

"Are we..." her mouth was so dry and hard to move, "gonna die?" Her mouth felt like a cotton ball. She wished she had a drink.

"No. Baby. No," Tim said.

April wasn't so sure. She and Tim had packed the car with clothes and various other items to leave town. The group ignored her, and they weren't going to stay and watch their friends get slaughtered. So they left their parents notes and headed west for Vegas. They planned on getting married in two weeks after she turned eighteen. They were in love and wanted out of Kansas. She could feel the evil brewing and she wouldn't be its victim. They planned on coming back to visit their families but that was about it. They were ready for a new start.

As she remembered more and more from Halloween, the fog slowly lifted. She finally opened her eyes. Tim was right beside her, tied to a wooden chair, less than three feet away from her. It was dark wherever they were, but just enough light to see. It was a very large room, painted in a light color, but she couldn't tell what color. The walls were lined with books and boxes. There were numerous tables around the room, covered in what looked like science equipment, but she couldn't tell for sure. There were a few empty metal tables also. It looked like a weird office or laboratory to her. She wondered if they were in a hospital or something. She looked over at Tim, who was looking back at her. His eyes were puffy and red. She wasn't sure if it was the drugs or from crying, or both.

"I love you," she creaked out. Her mouth was still so dry. Her voice sounded like it belonged to a stranger.

"I love you," he said.

"Now isn't that sweet!" A deep masculine voice filled the room, echoing off the walls. The lights above came on, filling the room with a blinding light.

April squinted at the man, still dressed in all black head to toe, as he walked in front of them. She could only see his eyes and teeth through the ski mask. He was grinning widely.

"Who are you?" Tim asked. His voice was much clearer than hers. His drugs were apparently wearing off faster.

"Oh who I am isn't important to you. Who you are, is!"

"What?" April asked, confused. The sight of the man scared her. The ski mask took away so much of his features, reminding her of death or a monster.

"April Walker! You've been a bad, bad girl. You told all of your friends something no one needed to know!"

The man's deep voice seemed to echo off the concrete walls. It was loud and chilled her to the bone. He sounded upset, but trying to pull it off as a joke.

April swallowed hard. She knew exactly what he meant. How did he know? She didn't want to know. She just wanted to leave this horrible place and get away from this evil man.

"You took something so perfect and planned out, and abused it! You're no better than a sexual predator! The exact same as a child molester! Disgusting!" The man spat on the floor.

"Hey!" Tim shouted.

"Shut up, Tim. One smart person speaking at a time, please." The man walked over to Tim's chair and slapped Tim across the face. Hard. Tim's lip began bleeding almost instantly. "I am talking to April now. You can wait your turn."

The man walked over to April, leaning his face close to her, only inches away. She felt his cool breath on her face, which smelled like wintergreen tobacco. She hated that smell. He touched her lips softly, his fingers lingering.

"Now, you are going to tell me WHY you know Jacob was killed! And you're going to tell me WHO it was! Understand?"

April nodded. Her eyes stared at his mouth. It was vaguely familiar to her, but she had no idea why. She wished the man wasn't so close to her face. Between his breath on her face, and the sheer evil that seemed to drip from his pores, she felt nauseated. She could hear Tim sobbing quietly beside her.

"Why do you know, April?" the man asked again, more polite than before, but her fear stayed strong.

"I was there."

The man began shaking angrily, his eyes wide. His hands reached around her throat.

"What the fuck else did you see? What? Fucking bitch! Tell me what you saw!" He squeezed tighter around her throat. She began to feel her oxygen level dropping quickly.

"She can't breathe!" Tim shouted at the man strangling his girlfriend in front of his face. Tears poured down his freckled cheeks.

The man stopped choking April and stepped away.

"I lost my cool. I'm sorry." The man paced lightly in front of them, his voice was collected and calm. Tim, however, noticed his hands were still shaking slightly. "Explain all of what you saw. All of it." The man was nervous, but he tried to hide it. This could be fixed. He would kill them once he knew what they knew. Just get the information and let it die with them. Then the plan could move onward, easily.

April coughed and gasped for air until she could breathe again. She was going to die. She knew it. The man wouldn't let her live, that was clear. It didn't matter if she cooperated with him or not. The small piece of hope she held on to so tightly, slipped right through her fingers. She swallowed her fear and began to tell him exactly what she told The Misfits. She didn't take a moment to pause through the details, as she knew she'd break down and cry and never stop.

"And?" the man asked impatiently when she was done.

"Nothing. That's it."

"Liar. Who killed him? I know you saw it, April."

"I didn't see. Too dark, I swear!"

"Do you want to watch poor, sweet, Tim get his throat slit?" The man walked back to the empty metal table, about ten feet away from them. He brought back a large hunting knife.

"NO! Please no!" April screamed.

"Tell me now. Or I'll gut him. I swear on that, bitch. I swear on that!" The man held the knife to Tim's throat. Tim cried helplessly. He was tied to a chair, ready to be murdered by a madman. What a horrible way to die. He prayed it would be quick and painless. He prayed April wouldn't suffer either.

"NO! Oh God, no! Please! I'll tell you! Don't hurt him!" April screamed through her tears. She struggled in her chair. She wanted to help Tim, anything to help him. She would rather die than have Tim die. Tim was a great man. The best man she knew.

"Smart girl. Go on, then." The man didn't lift the knife from Tim's throat. The blade shone under the fluorescent lights. It teased her, holding Tim's life in its sharp hand

Chapter 9

October 31/ November 1, 2014

Bobby was furious at himself, and scared. April and Tim had been so right. Coming to the tracks was a horrible idea. He and Trevor stood at the entrance of the tracks by the side of the road, waiting. He was sure one of the girls was dead. Bobby shook his head, fighting back tears. What if it was Trina? He never even got to tell her how he felt about her. They were waiting for the girls to meet up with them. It had been about fifteen minutes and there was no sign of them anywhere. He was sure that Alicia was the killer, and that's why Jacob had chased them. He never hoped she would get murdered too though. *You don't know they're dead,* he thought to himself.

Earlier that night, they had met up where he and Bobby were standing now. Trina was smart and brought a backpack with flashlights to navigate through the dark trees that surrounded bridge. They all stood there, scared to enter the bridge.

April and Tim drove up, parking beside them. "Thank God, we didn't miss you! I was so worried!" April said as she jumped out of the car.

"April, I'm sure it'll be fine, don't worry about it," Bobby said.

"Come with us, then! The more people there, the less likely he is to grab one of us, if you're that worried about it," Alicia replied.

"You guys, I've had a horrible feeling since we talked about this. I tried to push it out of my mind, thinking I was just overreacting. Or maybe I was just scared to see Jacob again. Maybe I was just scared the killer would find us... I don't know. But that wasn't it! I'm telling you; my gut says to leave him alone. Whatever brought him back from the dead... it couldn't have been something nice. Happy, peaceful people don't return from the dead. They just don't!" April pleaded.

"We know that, April. It's not like we're going to walk to Jacob and do something stupid. We'll keep a safe distance in case he... in case he's violent," Trevor said.

"Guys, we're leaving town tonight. I don't know how you can't feel the darkness over this town right now. If we don't hurry, we'll get sucked in too. You can feel the evil in the air, almost." April shuddered. "Don't look at me like I'm crazy, man. I'm serious. Something bad is going to happen. I know it. I know it."

"April, the darkness over the town is the shit cloud from the feedlot. It bothers me daily too…" Bobby smirked.

"That's so not funny, Bobby." Tim glared.

"We wish you weren't leaving, April, Tim, but I don't feel the pressing evil like you do. Maybe I'm blind to it, or maybe it's far enough away still. I'm sure we'll stay safe. I know I'm standing in the back. This whole thing scares me, that's for sure. But not enough to skip on getting the truth. You know I…we all cared about Jacob," Trina said, trying to reassure April.

"I want the truth too, Trina. I do. Just not enough to do something stupid about it," April sighed.

"We'd better go, baby," Tim finally spoke out, touching her hand lightly.

"You're right. We're leaving for Vegas, getting married as soon as I'm eighteen in two weeks. I wish…" April's voice trailed off.

"Be sure and call us. We'll miss you. Tell us you're going to come back!" Trina said.

"We'll keep the phone off for a few days, just to be alone. We'll miss you. And we're not sure… eventually we might be back," April replied. She hugged each one of them tightly, hoping it wouldn't be the last time she seen them. She didn't want any of them to die; it was too horrible to think about.

Tim and April drove off, waving goodbye one last time. The group stood quietly for a few minutes.

"I guess we better get going..." Trevor said.

"Yeah, I guess so," Alicia replied quietly.

They headed slowly toward the bridge. It wasn't a long walk, about a half-mile. The further they got along, the more trees surrounded the area, and you could hear the Arkansas River slowly running near them. It had been a dry past few years, so the river wasn't very high, and it looked more like a small, winding creek.

As they got closer to the bridge, Bobby was happy that Trina brought the flashlights. It was quite dark with only a quarter moon shining above them. The moon was always bright in Kansas though. There weren't a lot of city lights in Larned, so you could see hundreds and hundreds of stars. Bobby loved astronomy and he had to force himself to look ahead of him, and not up at all the sparkling constellations. He had always wished he were smarter at science and math so he could be an astronomer. But it wasn't the time for daydreams.

They made it to the bridge, staying back about twenty feet from Jacob. He was there, the flashlight beams and the sliver of moonlight was shining on him, but not through him. Not a ghost? Bobby had never seen a ghost, but he had thought they were supposed to be transparent. Shit, he'd never seen anyone undead before! They stared at him for a moment before anyone spoke. Jacob had his back to them, lost in thought. He was wearing a heavy sweater and jeans. His blond hair was a bit longer than they remembered, but still cut the same. He was still Jacob.

"Jacob. Do you… do you remember us?" Bobby finally choked out the words.

Jacob turned around quickly, staring at them angrily. The beautiful goodness he once had was gone. His eyes looked different in the darkness. He didn't answer Bobby's question, just glared at them.

"Jake, can you talk to me? Please. It's Bobby. Don't you remember me?" Bobby pleaded, unable to remove the sadness in his voice.

"Get out of here!" Jacob screamed at them, his eyes wild.

"Jacob, please…" Trina pleaded, holding on to Bobby's shoulder, barely able to look at Jacob.

"GET OFF OF MY BRIDGE!" Jacob screamed even louder.

Trevor tried to take a step closer, but it was as if his feet were glued to the railroad ties. "We were best friends, man. Best friends."

Jacob turned toward Trevor, taking only one step closer. His eyes were full of anger and hatred. "I have no friends. Unless you know who killed me, get the fuck off of my bridge."

"What happened to you, Jake?" Alicia asked quietly.

"I died. I'm here looking for my killer. The end," Jacob growled, barely looking at the group. His focus was on something else. "Now get the fuck off of my bridge, before I MAKE you leave."

The Misfits were frozen with fear and sadness. They wanted to help their friend, but he was refusing all help. Jacob wasn't the same person. He was different, angry, and full of hate. He wanted revenge against his killer and that was that. He didn't even seem to remember them at all. Trina was sobbing quietly, hiding behind Bobby.

"Are you HER?" Jacob stopped pacing in front of them and screamed suddenly, pointing toward The Misfits. He broke into a run toward them. The Misfits turned and ran for their lives.

Bobby didn't turn around once until he reached the street. His lungs were burning. Why had Jacob suddenly charged them? Did he see the killer? Was it one of The Misfits?

Trevor soon was behind him, panting hard, a look of confusion and fear etched on his face.

"Where are the girls?" Bobby asked.

"They were just behind me. Give them a minute..." Trevor said breathlessly. Bobby and Trevor had been waiting for over fifteen minutes, as Bobby checked his watch every few seconds.

"They aren't coming, man. We need to go back and find them!"

Trevor was pacing nervously in front of him. He breathed warm air over his hands, as the temperature had dropped to 40 degrees, the wind making it feel much colder.

"I know. It's not that big of an area, but it's not that small either. They could be anywhere, dude. Anywhere."

"Yes they could. Stupid woods. We got to go look for them, though."

"Yeah, Alicia is my girlfriend! We can't leave them alone to be murdered by Jacob! Fuck. I thought we would be able to talk to him!" Trevor sighed.

"Yeah. We have these flashlights, let's go search a bit. Call out for them and see if they fell or something. Probably just tripped and slowly crawling to us..." Bobby said, trying to reassure himself and Trevor.

"Yeah... probably," Trevor nodded.

The boys headed toward the bridge again. They stopped every little bit, shouting for the girls, listening for any kind of reply or sound they were alive. They never heard a reply. The wind was picking up and the temperature was dropping quickly. Kansas had a history of snowing on Halloween for many years; they hoped this night wouldn't be part of that tradition. If the girls were injured and couldn't call out, the boys had to find them fast. Time was running out before they might freeze to death. As they reached closer to the bridge, they still had no luck. They didn't see Jacob on the bridge ahead of them, which was good, but it didn't mean he wasn't still around somewhere.

"Bob! I found something!" Trevor yelled. Bobby ran over to find Trevor holding a pink shoe in his hand. It was Trina's shoe.

"Shit, man…" Bobby said quietly, his heart dropping in his chest.

"Yeah…shit. We need to get to the cops!"

"Cops?"

"Yes, we need more help on this search!" Trevor exclaimed.

"But don't they have to be missing for over twenty-four hours for it to matter? That's what always happens on TV and such unless they are little kids. What if they think we did it?"

"Hell if I know!" Trevor stared at the shoe. "But I swear I see drops of blood!"

"Blood?" Bobby swallowed hard. His heart was beating too fast to think clearly. He grabbed the shoe and looked closer. He definitely saw some dark liquid drops on the shoe, but it was too dark outside to see if it was blood or not.

"Could've tripped and scraped a leg or something. Doesn't mean they're dead," Trevor said, his hand on Bobby's shoulder trying to reassure himself and Bobby.

"Yeah, tripped..." Bobby said quietly, nodding. A sick feeling grew in his stomach. He never got to tell Trina how much he liked her. What if she was dead?

"Let's just run back into town and get some supplies. Then we can search all night and not like freeze to death or something," Trevor said.

Bobby stared at him for a second, unable to shake the sadness from his face. "We will need heavier coats, food, and a first aid kit too."

"Exactly. Let's go." Trevor smiled and they headed back toward town. They walked back to the road and down six blocks to Bobby's house from the entrance to the tracks. They grabbed gloves, flashlights, batteries, hats, a bag of food, blankets, and a first aid kit that they shoved inside a large duffel bag.

The boys set out again for the tracks. They would find Trina and Alicia alive and everything would be okay. At least they thought it would be okay until they saw a police car rolling slowly towards them.

"Should we tell them? You thought getting the police involved was a good idea," Bobby asked quickly.

"No, I change my mind. Either they will think we hurt the girls or we're making up stupid Halloween stories! They won't believe us, man. You know they won't," Trevor said, shaking his head.

"Damn it, you're right. What should we do?" Bobby asked quickly.

"Make something up!" Trevor whispered as the car pulled up next to them.

"What you kids up to tonight?" Officer Nick Walker, April's dad, rolled down the window.

"Oh you know, just finishing some trick or treating, sir." Bobby forced a smile.

"You know it's after midnight. Curfew is at eleven even on holidays." Officer Walker stopped the car and stepped out. He stepped toward them, knowing that both boys were friends of April's. And everyone knew Trevor Packers because of his sister at the funeral. Nick hated to be a stickler for the rules, but if he bent them for one, he had to bend them for everyone. And that just went against his whole nature.

"Is it after eleven already? Wow!" Trevor shook his head. He really had no idea what time it was. He had other things on his mind. He hoped that Officer Walker would let them go; they needed to start the search as soon as they could.

"I promise we're not causing any trouble! Really we're not! We just have somewhere important to be," Bobby said quickly.

"And I'm eighteen, sir," Trevor interjected. "And Bobby's turning eighteen in like a month!"

"Almost isn't the same as actually being an adult."

"No! Please listen! Our friends are missing in the woods! We have to find them. ASAP!" Trevor shouted, unable to keep the urgency from his voice.

"Is this a Halloween prank, son?"

"No! Of course not! We went to see Jacob…"

"Oh not this Jacob nonsense! Now boys, get in the car and I'll take you home. Don't give me those stories, please. You're old enough to know better than that!" Nick shook his head. He was really quite tired of the rumors surrounding Jacob. It was just fantasy and people's imaginations running wild.

"But it's true! We saw him! He chased us and we got away, but our friends didn't. We have to save them!" Trevor shouted. His heart raced with urgency. He couldn't help shake the feeling that their time was running out to save the girls.

"Enough! Get in the car! It's too cold and past curfew. Come on, now." Officer Walker opened the back door, waving his arm for them to get in.

Bobby looked at Trevor, wishing he had words to explain what he was thinking. If Trina and Alicia died, it would be their faults. It was his idea to visit the bridge; all of the responsibility was on his shoulders. They left them behind to die. He couldn't have that on his conscience. He couldn't let the girls die.

Trevor let out a huge sigh of defeat and shuffled slowly toward the car. Bobby, however, stood still.

"Whatever happens, sir, just know that I'm so, so sorry," Bobby said sincerely, the guilt and fear had taken over his mind.

Officer Walker turned around to ask "What?" but never got the words out. Bobby came at him fast, hitting Nick in the face hard with a heavy-duty flashlight. There was a loud thump and Nick shook, his mouth agape in surprise, falling to the ground. His vision was fading, his head pounding. Before he could even try to get up, Bobby and Trevor began kicking him in the ribcage. Nick's consciousness faded away.

"Bobby! Stop! I think he's dead!" Trevor screamed in horror.

Bobby didn't realize how far they had gone. What had he done? He assaulted a cop! He bent down to Nick's body, bleeding on the ground, to feel for a pulse. It was faint but still there.

"Not dead! Call 911," Bobby exclaimed. They were so foolish. How could he have thought that would help their situation? He knew Nick; Nick knew him! There was no doubt he and Trevor would face jail time. He hoped that he didn't make the wrong decision. It felt so wrong. Why had he made such a rash, stupid decision? He had let his panic and fear take over. There was no way they would get out of this without consequences.

"Someone just beat up Officer Walker! I was walking home and found him! 203 Broadway! Hurry!" Trevor said into the phone and hung up before anyone could ask him any questions. He gave Bobby a panicked look. "What the hell did we just do, Bob?"

"I don't know… but it's bad. Shit. Shit. Shit." Bobby sighed as he paced in a small circle.

"Let's go before we're too late!" Bobby said quickly, frowning. He gave one last glance toward Nick's unconscious body, whispered, "Sorry, we're so stupid, but we have to save our friends, if it's not too late already. Sorry." Hopefully they could save the girls before it was too late, because if not, they would go to jail, and possibly prison, for nothing. Bobby ran as fast as he could to the tracks, barely feeling the burn in his lungs. His stupidity and recklessness had to be for something.

* * * *

Hollie Packers arrived home at 12:30am from her double shift as a CNA at the nursing home. She had changed too many elderly diapers, gave too many showers, and just felt gross. She only wanted to sleep. Her shoulder-length blond hair was greasy, and she felt like she aged twenty years overnight. She wanted a shower and a nap before she had to return to work at seven. She grabbed some clean clothes from her bedroom and headed down the hall to the bathroom. She could hear the water running inside.

Hurry up! I really want to sleep! she thought to herself. She stood, well leaned against the door, too tired use any more energy than she needed to. After about five minutes, she decided to knock.

"Hey who's in there? Can you hurry it up? I would like to sleep before I have to get back up!" she shouted at the door. There was no reply. She sighed. The walls weren't that thick. She banged on the door again, her exhaustion making her very impatient. There was still no reply. She was tempted to just walk to her room and collapse on the bed, greasy and dirty. But her gut sharpened and she thought of Zacchya. She had felt awful leaving her alone on Halloween.

Hollie ran up the stairs to Zacchya's room and pushed the door open. The bed was empty. She checked Trevor's room. Empty. She ran back downstairs, feeling breathless and panicked. She pushed the bathroom door open, thanking God it was unlocked.

"Zacchya!" Hollie shouted out. Her head turned right then left and saw Zacchya sitting in a tub, leaning against the shower wall, running water from the shower pouring down on her. She looked so pale.

"Zacchya! Oh God. Zacchya!" She shook her daughter's shoulders. Zacchya was so cold. "Please don't be dead!" Hollie cried as she noticed a small cut on her wrist.

Zacchya's eyes opened slowly. "Mama?"

"What on earth? Oh my God!" Hollie turned off the water, which was now quite cool. She helped Zacchya out of the tub, wrapping her with a soft towel. Zacchya was shivering with tears in her eyes.

"What were you thinking, honey?" She held Zacchya tight in her arms, crying.

"I didn't want you to clean up my blood." Zacchya leaned into Hollie's arms, crying.

"What?!"

"Wanted to hurt myself. Didn't want you to clean my blood. Couldn't do it. Sorry. So sorry."

Hollie wasn't sure how to respond, so she just held her daughter close. She didn't know what was wrong with Zacchya, and why she couldn't get better. Was she a bad mother? What caused depression like that? She didn't know how to deal with her daughter hating her life. Hollie felt like breaking down, but she couldn't. Her daughter needed strength and support.

"Please don't send me back. I promise it's the last time. It was just a bad day. I promise, Mama," Zacchya cried.

"No. You're staying with me. We will figure out something together. Somehow, we'll figure it out together." Hollie squeezed her tighter.

"Will I ever stop loving him? Does it ever stop hurting? It's the most horrible thing I've ever felt," Zacchya said, shivering and pleading for the right answer to her question.

"Yes. One day down the road, the hurt will stop. You'll never forget him and you may never stop loving him. But the hurt will stop when your heart runs out of tears. The broken pieces never heal right, and they are so easy to re-break… but it does get a little better. No one ever knows how long that will be, but it does happen."

* * * *

Tim sat quietly in his chair, wishing desperately to stretch his legs. The ropes were cutting into his wrists and ankles. His lip was swollen and oozing blood from where the man slapped him. The man in black was clearly evil. Tim knew in his gut that as soon as he had the information he wanted, they would both be dead. How?

He didn't want to know that just yet. He closed his eyes, half listening to April, half praying to God for a quick escape or a quick death. He had just turned eighteen in September and lived so little. He was two weeks away from marrying his first and true love, April. Too young to die. They were both too young to die. And whoever this man was, he was involved in this mess more than he let on. Why would this man in black care who killed Jacob? Unless he was Jacob's dad. Tim almost burst out laughing at the thought. Edward Track was one of the most kindhearted men he'd ever met. So who was this crazy man?

April was almost at the end of her story. Tears were filling her brown eyes. Tim wished he could hold her and make all the hurt and sadness go away.

"So we're finally to the point when you tell me who you saw," the man said impatiently. He had been pacing slowly in front of her as she spoke. He was standing in front of her, less than a foot from her face.

"So she stabbed him and pushed him over the bridge. I was scared and disgusted. I made sure I was hidden behind a nearby bush, frozen in fear. I couldn't be seen. I didn't want to be killed as well. I was too scared to even cry or run, just frozen there behind that bush," April paused. She was so scared. Scared as soon as she said the killer, the man would kill her. She never told anyone who she saw and never planned to.

"The lightning was flashing so much as she ran past me. I couldn't believe it. Still don't believe it to this day." April swallowed hard.

"Just fucking spit it out already!" the man screamed in her face. He wrapped his hands around her throat. He wished to squeeze the name out of her stupid throat. But he needed information. Then he would kill them both. First he needed the name.

April was coughing for air when he finally let go of her throat. She had no doubt that he would kill them. Tim screamed next to her. The man punched him in the face again, hard. Blood sprayed out of an already broken lip. Tim struggled in his chair. He cursed quietly under his breath. He wished he was strong enough to break the ropes from his wrists and ankles. He wished the situation wasn't so hopeless.

Chapter 10

November 1, 2014

ELIZABETH TRACK WAS PACING THE floor. Marcus had been up all night with a high fever and she couldn't get it to stay down. He was crying and miserable, but she had no idea why. She contemplated taking him to the ER but she didn't want to jump to conclusions if it was an easy fix. She grabbed the phone and called one of her best friends, Larry Rumsfield, who was a doctor.

"Hello, Larry, I'm so sorry to bother you."

"Oh, Liz, dear, it's no bother!" Larry replied politely.

"I just… well Marcus has a fever, had one all night. I didn't want to go the ER for nothing…"

"Say no more! I'll be over in ten minutes."

"Oh bless you, Larry!"

"Anything for my precious godson." Larry smiled and hung up.

Larry was a doctor at the hospital and the smartest man she knew. He was probably one of the smartest men ever, and had some awards to prove it. He had achieved so much with research on Alzheimer's and could work anywhere in the world. But he stayed in Kansas to be near his family, and he said he loved working with every day patients too. He was one of her best friends, had been since high school.

They actually dated during their junior year and part of the senior year. She had loved him so much. That dark wavy hair, green eyes complimenting his beautiful olive skin, had won her over. And even when Larry was seventeen, he had such a respectable air about him. He carried himself tall and proud. She loved that about him, always so confident. She was crazy about him and he about her. She had been sure they would end up married with beautiful, smart children. They seemed so right for each other.

But then Edward moved to town, halfway through their senior year. In Liz's eyes, it was like he rode in on some magical perfect white horse, except it was a white Camaro. His shaggy blond hair, blue eyes, and strong arms gave her the quivers. She had never seen anyone as beautiful as Edward. He was what she had always been looking for and never knew. When she was around him, instead of feeling flustered and clumsy, she felt peaceful inside. It was unlike anything she ever felt. She found herself making excuses to be around him and spark up a friendship. Slowly her relationship with Larry suffered and ended. They promised to stay friends, and unlike most couples, they actually did. Even when Larry went to college in New York City, they wrote letters and called at least once a week. She had been extremely blessed to have a friend like Larry. He would drop anything for her when she needed him, and he was a very busy man.

Larry had even been there for them when Edward was shot by a stray bullet in Kansas City in 2000. Larry was the first person at the hospital and had later, secretly, paid their bill. He was Jacob and Marcus' godfather, and would get custody of Marcus if anything ever happened to Liz and Edward. Larry had split with his wife of ten years, Alberta, two years before and had no kids of his own. He loved Marcus like his own son, which he told Liz all the time.

Larry showed up on time, exactly ten minutes after their conversation. He was always prompt and a man of his word.

"It's so good to see you, Larry!" Liz hugged him close.

"And you too, dear! You're looking too beautiful for a woman who has been up all night with a sick baby! I think you might be pulling my leg!" Larry chuckled. "You women and your strength just flabbergast me! I don't know how you do it."

"You and your flattery, sir, if I didn't have a husband…" Liz laughed. "You've always been such a charmer!"

"And quite a looker, the ladies say." Larry winked.

"Of course! We need to find you a good woman now. Can't let all that charm and handsomeness go to waste! It'd be a crime!"

"Ha! I've been off the market since you broke my poor heart," Larry snickered. Liz playfully punched his arm and they walked to the living room and sat down on the couch.

"Oh I'm sad this isn't a social visit. I miss all of our talks together."

"Definitely! Work has been so busy lately. People keep getting themselves hurt left and right. And then I have my monthly conferences in Kansas City with the Alzheimer's Foundation, but we are making amazing progress. Once we have a cure, it will be worth it in the end, really."

"You do so much for everyone else, Larry. I hope you're finding time for yourself too."

"Helping my friends is good enough for me. It's all the fulfillment I need. Now where is my baby boy?"

Liz led him into the nursery where Marcus had finally fallen asleep. Larry checked him for swelling and signs of infection. He listened to Marcus' lungs and heart with a stethoscope.

"Hmm I'm not seeing any swollen organs or signs of infection. Is he urinating and having regular bowel movements?"

"Yes, he's going fine. He's eating well too."

"You're giving him the right dose of baby Tylenol?"

"Yep, I followed it just as it said on the bottle."

"Well he sounds good in the lungs and heart too. And the fever went down a bit, you said? It's probably a run-of-the-mill cold. Any runny nose?"

"Well maybe a little, actually." Liz remembered.

"I say keep at the baby Tylenol and if the fever doesn't go down by tonight, go the ER for x-rays and tests. I don't think it's an infection, but I could be wrong."

"Good, I hope it's not. He's too young to be getting infections," Liz sighed.

"Unfortunately babies get infections all the time. But if the fever goes to 102, take him in. Keep him cool and keep on the Tylenol. He should be okay, though."

"Thanks Larry, I really do appreciate this." Liz grabbed him and hugged him tight.

"You're going to make me blush, dear!" Larry smiled and held onto her tight. He loved her hugs; they were always so sincere. "I really must go, though. Some hood-lums beat up… oh this is a secret, Liz…"

"My lips are zipped," she said as she walked him to the door. She would always keep Larry's secrets, she respected him too much.

"Nick Walker was beaten last night and left on the street. Goodness knows by whom!"

"Oh no! I adore Nick!"

"Yes, me too. He's going to make it, but he's definitely in a bad way right now." Larry frowned.

"That's so sad; his family must be worried sick!"

"I contacted Patty this morning and apparently April had run off in the night for Vegas to get married! She has no idea about her dad. Apparently left her cell phone on her bed! Such a shame she has no idea about her dad."

"Oh goodness! That doesn't sound like April at all! That girl is the most sensible teenager I've ever met! Patty is probably near a nervous breakdown! I should send her some flowers and maybe some chili." Liz shook her head. How could April leave without a proper goodbye?

"I'm sure Patty would appreciate anything you gave her right now. Call me if you need anything else. I love you, Liz."

"Thanks, Larry, I love you too. Whatever would I do without you?"

"Die, I suspect! See you later!" Larry smiled and hurried back to his pearl Escalade. He wished he didn't have so much work to do at the hospital. He wanted to spend all day with Liz. He wished to sip tea and laugh at old movies with her. Actually, he wished he could spend every day of his life with her. His love for her was real, and more than just a friendship.

Even when she ended their romance in high school, he loved her. She was his angel, his soul mate. But she had thought otherwise and fell in love with Edward. His heart was crushed, as if there was nothing left but a fine powder. He hid his feelings and decided if he wanted her in his life, he would have to settle for friendship. So he did that. Even twenty-three years later, his feelings for her never ceased. He loved her more every day.

He married Alberta in 2002 in hopes that he could cover his love for Liz. It worked for a while, as he forced himself to get lost in the attraction and sex. But after a while, it was just sex. There was a small part of him cared for Alberta, but never as much as Liz. In the end, he and Alberta became strangers. The divorce in 2012 wasn't as bad as it could've been. He cried for a few days, got wasted for a few more, and then he was fine. For a ten-year marriage, he thought it would hurt more for it to end. But he had moved on and became so encompassed in his work that it had been over for a long time. He had moved on and decided not to try another relationship. Love was hard. Relationships were harder. Why make it worse when you were secretly in love with your best friend? He quit wasting his time on lies and relationships. He had waited this long for Liz, what else could he do? His heart only knew how to wait for her to realize where she belonged. One day he would tell her, but it had to be perfect. Only perfect would be good enough for her. She deserved the earth, the sun, moon, and the universe. He had a plan on how he would tell her… but until it was perfect, he kept quiet.

Larry pulled into the hospital parking lot, hoping the emergencies would be few today. He had barely slept the night before and Liz was stirring his emotions. A quiet day would be just what he needed. Little did he know that his day was about to get very busy.

* * * *

Around nine in the morning, Roxanne Snow was driving towards her house on the edge of town. She was in a hurry because her co-worker, Hollie, had called in sick. Roxanne had been at work since six and had forgotten to pack a lunch, and she still had nine hours of work to go. She was driving home to pick up a can of soup and a sandwich on her fifteen-minute break. She was glad it was cool outside because it meant little traffic. She pulled into her driveway and stepped out of the car. After about three steps, she stopped. There was a body lying in her front yard. All she could see was that it was a female, in ripped clothes and caked on blood.

Roxanne was scared. Why was this girl in her front yard covered in blood? Was she dead? Roxanne bent down and felt for a pulse. It was faint but still there. Not dead! She let out a sigh of relief and lightly tapped the girl on the shoulder.

"Hey! Are you okay? What's your name?" she asked, hoping for a response. The girl lay perfectly still, unconscious. Roxanne grabbed her phone and called 9-1-1. She told them her address and that she found a girl in her yard.

"What's your name, ma'am?" the female operator asked.

"Roxanne. Roxanne Snow."

"Do you know the girl in your yard, Roxanne?"

"No. No, I don't think so." Roxanne's hands were shaking.

"Have you been home all morning?"

"No, I just got home for a break. I was at work. I just came home and found her covered in blood."

"It's okay, Roxanne. I have help on the way to you. Can you tell me if she still has a pulse?"

"She did a minute ago. I'll recheck." Roxanne bent down and double checked for a pulse. "Yes, still there, but pretty faint. Should I cover her up? It's so cold out here and her clothes are all ripped up."

"The ambulance is almost there. You can cover her with a jacket."

"Okay, I will."

"Can you tell me if there is any blood on the ground around her? Or is it just on her body? Is the blood still flowing?"

"Um… I don't see any, unless it's underneath her. She's face down. I shouldn't turn her, should I?"

"No, leave here there. In case there is spinal damage, it's best to not move her. You're doing really great, Roxanne."

"I don't feel so great at this…" Roxanne shivered. She wondered if it was from the cold, as her jacket was atop the unconscious girl, or if it was fear. She guessed it was probably a combination of both. She was a CNA and had been for ten years. She had seen elderly die numerous times, but they were old and it was their time. This girl was young, maybe sixteen or eighteen years old, and something awful had happened to her. She had crawled from God knows where to find help and collapsed in Roxanne's yard. It wasn't something that Roxanne was comfortable with.

"You're doing great, really. Can you hear the ambulance now? They should be almost to you."

"Yes, I do! Thank God. Here they come!"

"I'm going to let you go. Thank you for calling and helping this girl. You did a great job, Roxanne," the operator replied and hung up.

The ambulance pulled up and the EMS crew came quickly over to the girl on the ground to assess her. It all happened so fast. Roxanne tried to stay back out of the way as the EMS crew rushed in an orderly chaos. Soon she was on a stretcher and moved into the ambulance, as two men tried to start an IV. They were gone as quick as they came. The only thing she thought she heard was "stab wound" or at least something that sounded similar to that.

She knew in her gut that that the girl had been through trouble, but she didn't expect she'd been stabbed. She hoped that justice would come to the culprit. Who would try to take the life of a young girl? It was such a violent world when even teenage girls in small town Kansas were getting stabbed and left for dead. As she grabbed her food inside the house, she knew that she was going to be late for work. She didn't care. There were more important things. Everything seemed to happen for a reason in this world. If she wouldn't have forgotten to pack a lunch, the girl might have not been found. Work could wait. Life was too short to be worried about such trivial things. She took a moment to call her family and make sure they knew she cared.

* * *

Nick Walker had a concussion, numerous lacerations and bruises, and a broken jaw that was wired shut, but he was alive. He had an IV drip of morphine and was currently in a painless sleep. Larry looked over Nick's chart and was sure there was nothing more to be done for the man at the time being. He was badly injured, but there was no doubt that he would live.

Larry also had just gotten a new patient, a female, approximately eighteen years old, no identification, stab wound to the chest. She was sent straight to the OR where they would try to stitch up the wound in her chest. He had seen her before they wheeled her to the OR and recognized her immediately. He called Betty Johnson to identify the girl, as he was sure it was Trina Johnson. There were numerous lacerations on her face, which was bruised and swollen, but he was positive it was Trina. He had known her for a few years. Apparently there had been quite a struggle before she was stabbed.

"Dr. Rumsfield to the ER. Dr. Rumsfield to the ER," the overhead intercom announced.

"Damn it! Here's another one!" Larry put down Nick's chart and headed speedily to the ER.

"What do we have?" Larry asked the RN as he headed into the ER room.

"Female, stab wound to the chest."

"Good God! Another one?"

"Yes found three blocks from the other victim actually. Similar wounds and lacerations to the body," the nurse replied.

"Well let's hope it's the last one! Prep another OR room. I'll take this one myself," Larry said as he headed in the room to look at the victim. The RNs were trying to wash the dried blood off of her body, but he recognized the girl immediately. Alicia Green, the girlfriend of his nephew, Trevor, was lying on the table.

"Her vitals are dropping quickly. Get me the OR Room! Start her on morphine and anesthesia, stat." Larry rushed out of the room to scrub up for the surgery. The clock was on to save yet another teenage girl's life. Did it ever stop? Three hours later, Betty Johnson was sitting next to her daughter's bedside. Trina had made it through the surgery fine and was now asleep in ICU. They wanted to keep a close eye on her in case there were complications. Betty's eyes were red and puffy from crying. How did this happen? Trina never came home after an evening with her friends. Trina always called if she wouldn't be home on time. There had been no calls, no messages, nothing. Betty was beyond confused. She wished Trina wasn't asleep so she could ask her questions, but she knew that she needed the time to heal. So Betty cried and prayed next to her bedside.

Betty tried to call her soon-to-be ex-husband, Mark, but he hadn't answered yet. He was probably in some important meeting or banging his twenty-two-year-old girlfriend. The thought made her sick. Mark was a terribly selfish man. She had loved him once when she was young and dumb. She knew better now that he was nothing but a selfish asshole who loved fucking younger women. When he got a girlfriend, he left Trina and Kent, who was six, in the wind. They longed for a relationship with their father, but he was too distant to care.

Trina had a hard time dealing with the break-up of the marriage and had a small wild phase of drinking and partying too much. It lasted about six months. That had also been around the time that Trina and Jacob had broken up, too. Trina eventually realized that no amount of drinking and partying were going to bring back her father back. Deep down, Trina was a good girl; she just had to have a moment to rebel against an absent father who didn't love her. Mostly she stayed home after school to watch Kent now. She loved Kent too much to not do all she could to help out.

No matter what mistakes Trina made in the previous year, no one deserved what happened to her. Betty wished she could take all the pain away from her baby girl but nothing helped yet. She prayed that whoever hurt Trina would pay the price.

* * * *

It was Halloween night, about eleven o'clock and Tim and April were tied to their respective chairs. April was moments away from saying who had killed Jacob. She had broken down in tears after the terrible man dressed in all black had tried to choke the information out of her again. The fear was overwhelming for her, and for Tim. Tim wished he could close his ears and not hear the name. It was just too much to bear. It was tearing April apart inside and he didn't want to deface a friend. One of his friends was a murderer! How could he deal with that?

Tim shook his head, trying to let the thought roll out of his mind. Didn't that happen only in movies? The characters were friends with villains and never knew it. Always the last person they expected was a psychopath. But no, this was real life and he was just like those blinded characters. He felt so hopeless and worthless. He said another prayer to God that he would go to heaven. He knew the man would kill them, he could feel it in his bones.

"I will fucking choke your ass one more time if you don't give me that name!" the man screamed at her, his eyes wild with rage. His eyes and mouth were the only visible parts on him and it made it even scarier for them both looking at his wild eyes.

"Ok! Fine!" April cried, tears pouring down her pink cheeks. "Zacchya! It was Zacchya!"

"And you're one hundred percent sure of this?" the man asked, a smile creeping on his face.

"Yes, yes I'm sure," April wept. She wanted to hide her face, her shame, and her fear within her hands. Having her hands tied to the chair was making everything so much worse.

Tim had his eyes closed as tight as he could when she said the name. He heard Zacchya's name and felt a shiver in his spine. How was that possible? Broken Zacchya, a murderer? It made no sense at all. He peered his eyes open slowly, facing his head toward the man, expecting to be stabbed any moment. To his surprise, the man in black was smiling. Then the man began laughing!

"Why are you laughing? I don't see the humor…" Tim asked, scared to get a response.

"Oh, Tim! Don't you see how wonderful this is?"

"I guess my friend being a murderer isn't that wonderful to me, sorry," Tim answered quietly.

The man stepped closer to Tim, and then surprisingly put his arm around Tim's shoulder.

"If you could only see the bigger picture! So many things I can't divulge yet, Tim. The bang at the end of the story will blow everyone away!" The man waved his arms wildly with excitement, laughing.

"That doesn't even make any sense…" Tim shook his head in confusion.

"You're not going to kill her, are you? She's grieved so much. I think she's paid her dues," April asked, tears still glistening on her cheeks.

"Oh, April you don't know how right you are. She has grieved so much. And no, I'm not going to kill her." The man paused. He didn't want to tell them too much. Just in case the plan worked better than he expected.

"Good, because despite what she did, I still see her as my best friend. There was a while that I was scared of her, because I didn't understand how she could do that. I still don't. But after Jacob's funeral, I saw how much her guilt affected her. It's done enough damage to her."

"Her guilt? Oh April, you are so naïve!" The man laughed cheerfully again.

April looked at Tim, so confused. How was she possibly being naïve? Zacchya killed Jacob and her guilt drove to her to try and kill herself. It was as simple as that. She never forgave herself for the apparent crime of passion that happened a year ago on that railroad bridge.

"Before I say another word, I think we should celebrate with a shot!" the man said, eerily cheerful, and walked out of sight into an adjoining room.

Tim glanced at April, shrugging his shoulders. Clearly they were missing something important. Why would this man, who had already tried to choke April twice, bring them a shot of alcohol? Were they now bosom buddies? Tim was beyond dumbfounded.

A few moments later, the man returned carrying something in his hands. But it wasn't alcohol or shot glasses. It was a small bag, about the size of a woman's handbag. He was smiling widely again. April stared at his bright white teeth, shining against all of his black attire. It was the only feature visible to them except for his cold eyes. A shudder passed through her, thinking about those eyes. It was as if they were void of color. She guessed if it was the shadows of the room playing with her, or if the man was really so evil his eyes appeared glassy.

"So," the man said as he unzipped the small bag, "Before I get to the fun parts, there are some things you both need to know."

April swallowed hard. He was going to kill them with whatever was in that bag. She wanted to cry and break down again, but something in her stayed strong. She looked at Tim, trying to convey all of the love she felt for him. Tim seemed to know too that they had reached the end. His eyes were full of love and fear.

"Now I've been working on something extremely confidential. And just in case… I can't tell you what that is. But what I will tell you is that in a few moments you will be dead." The man smiled widely again.

April's eyes filled with tears. She was right that he planned to kill them. Her heart ached for sunny days, growing old with Tim, having babies, and a million other things she would never do. In only a moment her whole future passed in front of her eyes. It was the most beautiful thing she'd ever seen. Her heart was so full of hope and love for a moment, she could barely stand it. It was a future she'd never live, a future stolen from her, but it was beautiful and perfect. No matter what this evil man did to her next, he could never take that beauty and love away from her. She sat up straight and the tears stopped flowing from her eyes. No more tears for this horrible man. This monster would get nothing more from her.

"Perfect love casts out all fear. I love you, Tim," April said, looking at Tim, who was weeping quietly in a chair next to her.

He smiled at her through his tears, and said, "I love you too."

"Oh hush it, kids. The adult is speaking now," the man spat. "I was saying… You will die. But that might not be the end of your story."

"Huh?" April asked surprised.

"Tsk! Tsk! I can't ruin the surprise now! Before I kill you, I will give you one nugget for your last thoughts." The man stepped closer to April with a syringe, full of green fluid, in his hands. He smiled widely with his bright white teeth and whispered softly in her ear. "This is going to hurt. And Zacchya…" he paused dramatically, "doesn't know she killed Jacob."

April's eyes widened with curiosity and wonder. She felt a sharp jab in her chest from the needle and winced.

The man walked over to Tim and used another syringe, this one filled with a blue liquid. The man then walked away for a few minutes, letting the drugs take effect. He grabbed a knife on a nearby table; the blade glistened even in the dimly lit room. He walked back in front of April, grinning madly.

She tried to find words to explain how she felt about what he whispered in her ear. "How?"

The man held the knife gently to her throat, his pulse racing with excitement. "How does she not know that she killed Jacob? Did she just forget about the whole thing? Did the grief push it out of her mind? Is it some psychological block in her head? Or is it something else, something no one could even think to ask.…" The man smiled widely. "Now that is the right question. Honestly, it is the only question." He grinned again, as he quickly slashed the blade across her throat.

Chapter 11

Trina was running through an open field. The wind was whipping her long blond hair around her face. She giggled as she pushed it away from her blue eyes. It was summer and everything had a radiant golden glow. Flowers were blooming, the sun was warm, and it was a beautiful day. She softly collapsed on the green grass, trying to soak up every sound and feeling. It was a wonderful day. She had never seen such a beautiful sky, full of puffy cumulous clouds. She heard a soft plop next to her that made her smile. She knew just who it was.

"My, my! You run faster than I imagined, gorgeous!" Jacob leaned over her, smiling.

"My mom ran track in high school. It's just good genes, really. Blessed I am!" She winked at him. The sun was shining behind his head, making him appear to have a glowing halo. It was a great light for him, enhancing his stunning good looks. She could look at him for hours and hours and never get tired of his face.

"Did you get those pretty pink lips from your mom too?" Jacob asked as he gently caressed her lips with his fingers.

Trina could only sigh. She loved his hands; they were like magic to her. The goose bumps covered her arms and legs. Jacob slowly leaned down and kissed her gently, but passionately. When he finally pulled back from her, she said, "Do we have to go back to real life? I want to stay here… for like ever."

"Real life isn't so bad, you know. The bad things come, of course, but they never stay. You can make anything beautiful if you try," he said, smiling at her. He was always so wise beyond his fifteen years.

She could only smile at him. Deep down, she already loved him. It was too easy to love him. He always said the right things, made her laugh, made her feel truly alive. It was too good to be true.

"Do you think we'll be together after high school, Jacob?"

"Sure, that's only two years away. Sophomore and junior years will fly by and then we'll be seniors kissing in hallways, getting in trouble by the principal. It will be freaking awesome!" Jacob suddenly jumped and did a goofy break dance. He loved to randomly break out his bad dance moves to make her laugh.

"Oh Lord! Call the Dance Police! Wahoo! Wahoo!" She laughed and stood up next to him.

"Don't leave me busting my sexy moves all alone, Trina! You've got to dance away the Dance Police before they get here!" Jake laughed and continued wiggling, waving his arms around like he was trying to do some unknown dance moves from 1973.

Trina giggled harder, but danced along next to him anyway.

"Whoa, shake those hips, baby! Shake away the Dance Police!" Jacob laughed as he disco danced next to her. Trina could barely stand from laughing so hard. She really did want to stay in this field outside of town, dancing like an idiot with her boyfriend forever. There was no one like Jacob. And she knew no one would ever compare to him. He was perfect.

* * * *

Trina awoke, unsure of what time or day it was. She was lying in a hospital bed hooked up to IV's in her right arm. She tried to piece together her memories to see why she was in the hospital at all. All she could see were flashes. Railroad tracks. Running. Crawling on a road. Pain, lots of pain. Then nothing.

She tried to sit up, but instantly realized what an awful decision that was. Pain shot through her entire body, but radiated mostly from her chest. She looked under the right side of her gown and saw a large bandage. What had happened?

She squeezed her eyes shut, trying to force the memories out, but nothing came. It hit her that whatever was under the bandage would probably scar her chest. She didn't want to be vain but a girl's chest was important to most people. In society, image was unfortunately very "important." All teenage girls longed to be perfect and beautiful, even adult women constantly tried to achieve perfection. Society pressured females to have it all: long legs, perfect hair, large breasts, curvy hips, skinny waists, and no imperfections. The human race wanted Barbie dolls and God didn't make dolls. Trina sighed at the thought of being scarred. She tried to push the thought out of her mind. She was stuck in this hospital bed, too painful to move, so she better try and focus on the positive or she was going to lose her mind. At least, she had to give herself some daydreams.

She remembered having a dream about Jacob sometime. Was it the night before? She had no concept of time. It hadn't even been a dream at all; it was a memory from the summer she dated Jacob. They dated for three months. It had been so awesome and perfect to her. Jacob was her first love and his too. But school started and Zacchya had blossomed practically overnight. Jacob had broken up with her after summer's end. At the beginning of school, he began dating Zacchya. Trina had liked Zac-chya as a friend, but she learned not to trust her.

Once their relationship started, they were insepa-rable. If Jacob's hand wasn't holding onto Zacchya's, it surprised everyone. It made Trina a bit sick really. Her first love had moved on and she was stuck in her own sadness, forcing herself to remain his friend. But all she longed to do was hold him, kiss him, and never let him go. All the while, Jacob was kissing on Zacchya right in front of her. Every touch they made was a dagger to Trina's heart. She had hoped that they would break up and Trina could win him back.

By the end of the sophomore year, Jacob had bought Zacchya a promise ring. They talked constantly about eloping after high school. Trina tried to play off that everything was ok and she was happy with it all. She did everything she could to move on and act like it didn't bother her. Trina hoped their relationship wouldn't last.

Then junior year started, Zacchya began acting weird. She wouldn't wear her promise ring. They broke up at the end of September. Trina had gone on a "date/ not date" with Jacob a few weeks after his break-up with Zacchya. Jacob had kissed her but couldn't commit. He was dead barely a week later.

Seeing him on the tracks had stopped her heart all over again. She remembered looking at those beautiful, blue eyes again, except they weren't the same, colder and emptier.

Suddenly a shiver went down her spine. It was like her memory was trying to fill the holes and not telling her what they were. All she could see when she closed her eyes, was Alicia's long, wavy brown hair and blue eyes looking over her. Something was very wrong with Alicia's eyes... Trina's body was covered in goose bumps. Something scared her, deeply and she couldn't put her finger on the cause. The memory of Alicia's eyes made her question everything about that night. Trina wished the holes in her memory would be filled with the truth, but she wasn't sure the truth was best.

* * * *

November 2, 2014

Patty Walker had been sitting by her husband Nick's side for almost two days straight. She was exhausted, barely able to sleep from worry. April had run off the night of Halloween with her boyfriend Tim to Las Vegas. Patty was hoping she would have at least gotten a call or message from April saying she was okay, but nothing had come. It was the same night that Nick was beaten and pretty much left for dead. Thank goodness for the anonymous 9-1-1 call. Nick had been on a lot of pain medication and very sleepy most of the time. He had awoken a few times but could only communicate through notes, from his wired jaw. When he tried to talk, he could only get out a few words, before it caused too much pain. He had written down that the beating was not an accident. Patty was hoping that he would wake up soon and tell her if he knew who the attackers were.

She was sitting in a chair next to his bed, crocheting a hat for winter, to keep her occupied. Crocheting kept her busy when her mind just wouldn't stop thinking. She had started the hobby when she was thirty, over ten years ago. She had even sold a few blankets here and there for extra money. She loved crocheting, so it was great when she could make some of the money back she invested.

Nick was slowly stirring next to her. She reached for his hand and he squeezed it back. Her heart stirred with love and hope. He was on the road to recovery. He pushed the button on the bed to raise it to a sitting position.

"Hello sweetheart. Hope you're feeling better today," she said.

Nick slowly nodded and pointed to the notepad on the table nearby. Patty reached it and a pen for him. He wrote slowly on it and slid it over to her.

Patty read the note: *I know the attackers. In April's class.*

Patty gasped. "In April's class? How is that possible? Was it an accident?"

Nick shook his head no.

"They purposely hurt you? Why?" Patty couldn't wrap her head around the idea. Nick was a very beloved man; it made no sense that one of April's classmates would ever purposely hurt him. He was too good of a person.

Nick reached for the paper again, wrote something and slid it back to her. *Trevor Packers, Bobby Woods* was all that it read.

"Well let's get Dr. Rumsfield in here and have him get the cops to press charges!" Patty replied, flabbergasted that those two boys would ever do that to her husband. They were good friends with April and decent boys. It didn't make sense.

Nick nodded slowly. He had a feeling he couldn't quite explain. Part of him wanted the boys in jail, but part knew there was more to their story. Nick always was in search for the truth.

Patty had already hit the call light for the nurse. When the RN arrived, she said, "Can you please get Dr. Rumsfield in here as soon as you can. Nick has identified his attackers and would like to press charges."

"Very well, Mrs. Walker. I will get a hold of him." The RN left the room. Larry Rumsfield had left very specific instructions to be contacted when Nick identified or wanted to identify his attackers. Getting to the bottom of the attack was very important to him.

Chapter 12

November 2, 2014

ZACCHYA HAD SPENT THE MORNING with her mom, Hollie, shopping at the malls in the nearby town. After a filling lunch at Applebee's they returned home, tired and happy. Hollie was trying as hard as she could to keep Zacchya's spirits up. After the Halloween scare in the bathroom, she was almost afraid to let Zacchya out of her sight. She also knew that she had to try and trust her daughter, though. Zacchya was trying very hard to fight the depression. And Hollie knew all too well that losing the man you loved changed you forever.

When the twins were only two years old, Hollie's husband, George Packers, was murdered. George had a gambling problem for many years, but he was overall a good guy. He had loved Hollie and the twins very much, but he couldn't stop gambling. Larry, her brother, warned her that George was bad news, but she didn't listen. She was twenty years old and sure she could save George from all his faults with just the love in her heart.

However, one night she returned home from grocery shopping with the twins to find George was shot in the head, lying in a pool of blood on her living room floor. She would never forget that image as long as she lived. It took all she had not to drop a sleeping Trevor in her arms. With her hand still holding Zacchya's small hand, she raced out the door and called 9-1-1. Everything after was a blur. The incident changed her for life and she was never the same again.

Larry offered to watch the kids as much as he could, between all of his schooling. Larry and she had been so close growing up. They had an abusive father, Frank, growing up. Larry had been the older child, by two years, and Frank always favored Larry for the abuse. Larry never mentioned it to Hollie, but she was sure some of it had been sexual. The thought of her father doing that made her skin crawl. She could never understand how a father could hurt his child, physically or sexually. Hollie tried to jump in whenever Frank was hitting Larry, but it never helped much. She would get hit and then Frank would turn even more aggression to Larry for not "taking it like a man."

When Larry turned eighteen, he and Hollie moved out of the house. Larry held a job as a waiter, supporting them both, while they finished high school. After high school, Larry went to the local community college and then realized he was made for more than the life he'd been handed. Hollie kept the apartment, got her CNA license, and Larry moved to New York to start his doctorate. They kept in touch, calling at least twice a week. Larry had always tried to send her any extra money he had for bills. Life had not always been good to them, but they always had each other to lean on.

Hollie still had trouble believing Larry had grown into the man he had. He graduated at the top of his class, became a doctor at twenty-five with a minor in Chemistry. He was working with different hospitals and an organization for Alzheimer's, trying to find new medications. He was by far the smartest man she knew. She was so proud of him. And she was so glad that he continued to be a large part of the twins' life. He always spent a lot of time with Zacchya, trying to help her understand the depression and finding ways to cope. He was a good male role model for both of the twins, and she couldn't be more appreciative.

As she and Zacchya walked into the house, Hollie thought that maybe a visit to Larry would be a good for Zacchya. She was having such a hard time. It was the one year anniversary of Jacob's funeral. They heard about Trina and Alicia who had been injured on Halloween as well. Plus, her best friend, April, ran off to Vegas to get married, so she was without a best friend to lean on.

Hollie was sure that Zacchya was trying, but barely keeping it together. Maybe she needed a little family time and a good talk with her uncle. She definitely needed all of the support she could get.

* * * *

When Alicia Green woke up in the hospital, she was beyond confused and scared. She barely remembered what happened to bring her there. She could only remember crawling on the tracks, cold and bleeding, wishing for enough strength to reach the street. Apparently her wish had come true and she was saved. Alive. The nurse told her that she had surgery for a stab wound to the right side of her chest. She also had numerous cuts and abrasions, and a badly sprained ankle.

"If the object would have been even an inch to the left, you wouldn't be here with us." The nurse told her, smiling.

Oh yes, thanks for that bright info! Alicia thought to herself. No one wants to hear they almost died, especially when she was only seventeen years old and had a whole life ahead of her. It was too scary to even contemplate. She wanted to hold onto the fact that she had a life to live. *Let me feel immortal a little longer, lady!* Her inner monologue was more sarcastic than she was in real life.

When she first woke up, she was happy to see her mom, Chelsea, sitting at her side. Chelsea had obviously been crying all night, her eyes red and puffy. They hugged lightly to not cause Alicia any more pain.

"I'm so glad you're okay, baby! I was so worried about you. When I got the call…" Chelsea's voice trailed off.

"I'm okay, Mom. Please, it'll be ok." Alicia caressed her mom's hair. She hated seeing her like that. "Where's Dad, anyway?"

"Oh he thought he would feel less stressed at work. I'm supposed to call him when you wake up. You know how your father is. He'd rather work through the problem."

"Well go call. I'd sure like to see him," Alicia said. She was a bit of a daddy's girl.Alicia had seen her mom over the past day quite a bit. Her dad, Clarke, had been able to visit as well. Alicia was glad for the visitors. It got so boring in a hospital with nothing to do except sleep and watch the *Price is Right* or crappy daytime TV. She was naturally social and needed all the interactions she could get. She loved having people around to adore her all the time. She received a bouquet from her cheerleading team too. So far, she had just been waiting to see Trevor.

She and Trevor had been dating for over four months. She really enjoyed talking to him and was thinking she might be falling in love. The idea of it quite scared her though. Romantic love messed with your head and your heart so much. People went crazy in love. She didn't long to be some doe-eyed girl in love who couldn't think of anything except her man. She liked to keep her senses about her. She didn't mind getting occasionally buzzed or drunk at a party, but that was different, just a bit of fun. Otherwise, she loved to stay in control of her mind and actions. Even when Trevor and she were deep in a passionate kiss, she felt a part of her still holding onto control. A small part of her wished to lose her inhibitions, let loose. It was like nothing she did could turn the switch off in her brain that constantly repeated, Control. Stay focused. Don't ever let yourself go, too dangerous. It was quite frustrating. And she really did miss Trevor. She was missing his face and wishing he would visit. Didn't he care that she was injured and had almost died? She needed to be nursed back to health by her boyfriend.

* * * *

November 2, 2014

When Trina woke up from her afternoon nap, she was surprised to see Bobby sitting at the edge of her bed. She rubbed her eyes, trying to get a clearer picture, but he was still there. She began to feel very self-conscious. There was no way she could look pretty after the past few days. Oh, why did she even care? The kiss from her birthday was reliving in her mind, though.

"Morning, beautiful, I didn't wake you, did I?" Bobby asked sweetly. He really was very charming.

"Oh, no of course you didn't. I didn't even know you were here. Were you here very long?" Trina blushed, smoothing some hair behind her ear. Did he really think she was beautiful?

"Not very long. I'm glad I didn't wake you. Me and Trev were so worried about you and Alicia. I just had to see you. Make sure… make sure you were going to be okay," Bobby stammered.

"The doctor said I should be fine. How… how is Alicia?" Trina swallowed hard. She still felt very uncomfortable thinking about Alicia.

"She's good, from what I hear very similar to your injuries. I think Trevor was going to see her."

"Oh, good. You didn't see her yet?"

"No, I came here first." Bobby smiled.

"Well it's good to see you. Thanks." Trina smiled back, happy that he came to visit her first.

"I need to tell you something important. I don't have a lot of time… " Bobby didn't look her in the eye, but focused on the blank wall behind her.

"Time?"

"Yeah… um… Me and Trev, well… we beat up April's dad," Bobby stuttered, staring at the floor.

"You what?" Trina sat up too quickly. Sharp pains spread throughout her chest.

"I know… I know! But he tried to make us leave and we thought you were dead. We had to find you! We had to! I reacted stupidly. I was so stupid. And look, it didn't even matter. You were still hurt. It's my fault really."

"Oh, Bobby! What on earth were you thinking?"

"I had to save you, Trina! I had to! And look what good it did me? You still almost died! If I were… I am just stupid." Bobby had tears forming in his brown eyes.

Trina was so mad at him, but she could see that he was really feeling guilty. It broke her heart to see him in this state, even if she was mad at him.

"I just wanted to, you know… before I turn myself in…" Bobby paused. The thought of jail scared him so much.

"It'll be okay, Bobby." She leaned toward him slowly, putting her hand on top of his.

He looked up at her, his brown eyes still swimming with tears. She could barely look into his eyes, she felt like she would explode. They were so beautiful and broken.

"I just… it's stupid, really… I just… wanted you to…" Bobby stared into her eyes. She was beautiful, even injured and disheveled. He leaned over and kissed her lips.

Trina was surprised by the kiss, but didn't reject it. She actually welcomed it. Maybe it was a near death experience that told her to live a little. She only had the now. And now, she was enjoying Bobby's soft lips.

When he finally pulled away, Bobby's eyes were sad and leaking tears.

"What's wrong?"

"It's hard not knowing how long I will be in jail for. Would you still have me... after I'm a criminal?" he asked sincerely.

Trina smiled and wiped a small tear from his cheek. "You know, I never thought you'd be a good choice for me. I think you are though. Underneath your tough, goofy exterior, you're a softie, Bobby," Trina paused. She was never good at expressing her feelings into words. "I'd love to have... to be your... girlfriend, if that's what you want. Doesn't every girl want a bad boy?" She blushed as she spoke, barely able to look into his eyes.

Bobby gently placed his hand behind her head, pulled her close and kissed her again. "Awesome."

Trevor had visited Alicia around the same time Bobby was with Trina. He expressed his feelings for her and told her goodbye. She was angry with him for hurting Nick, but claimed to somewhat understand why he did it. She wasn't happy about it though. Alicia was happy to see him but she didn't tell him that. He kissed her goodbye and she hoped Nick would heal and Trevor wouldn't spend too much time in jail. She wondered if she could date someone who had been to jail though… she wasn't sure if she could. She didn't feel right about it; the whole situation just sucked.

* * * *

About an hour after Nick and Patty called for Dr. Rumsfield, he made it to the room to see them.

"Sorry about the delay there, Nick, been a busy afternoon all around. So are we making progress?" Larry asked as he came into the room.

Nick nodded and handed the paper with the names on it over to Larry. Larry examined it, his eyes widened with surprise. His own nephew!

"This will be dealt with immediately, Nick. Thanks for your cooperation again. I will make sure this is passed along to the authorities immediately." Larry took the paper with him, nodded, and exited the room quickly. He rushed to his office on the third floor, sat at his desk with his hand on the phone.

"Yes, Nick Walker had identified his attackers: Trevor Packers and Bobby Woods," he said. The other line replied to him.

"Yes, yes. I understand you will need more information. He can give you that within the day. Let him rest, please." Larry ended the conversation, hanging up the phone.

He wasn't surprised about Trevor. The boy had been bad news for his mother since he was born. Larry knew he'd end up just like his father, George... it was only a matter of time. Both kids were really damaged seeds. There was no fixing them.

Larry had hoped when he killed George, all those years ago, that the trouble would stop for Hollie. He hoped he had snuffed out the bad role model for the children so they would grow up properly. But no, the kids continued to show signs of trouble. Hollie deserved better than that. He was always the one to protect her and take care of her, make sure she had the best.

Larry already had set plans in motion for his niece. Her death would come soon enough. He had been trying hard to think of a way to dispose of that trash, Trevor, but with no success yet. Now, this beautiful opportunity had arisen. Trevor would be arrested for battery. The only way to make it better than that was to up the charges. It would be such a terrible shame if Nick Walker succumbed to his injuries... Murder was a hard charge to shake off, especially when the victim was a respected police officer. What a shame it would be. The community would suffer from the loss. Trevor would never be able to move on.

"Bye, bye Trevor. Have a good life in prison, asshole." Larry smiled widely, unable to contain his good luck.

Chapter 13

November 3, 2014

TREVOR AND BOBBY HAD BEEN in jail for a whole day. It was amazing to Trevor how much guilt he felt with each passing minute. He should've stopped Bobby. He should've been smart enough to find a better way to handle the whole situation. But he didn't… and was willing to pay the consequences. Hell, he deserved the consequences!

He was secretly glad his Uncle Larry hadn't posted bail money. Larry was rich from all his careers, but there was always something about him that put a red flag in Trevor's mind. Sure, he loved his uncle, never had been wronged by him. But Trevor found him "too nice" and charming, and it came off as insincere. He really didn't want Larry's help this time. He deserved to be punished for his crimes.

Bobby had thought his dad, John, who was a lawyer, would bail them out but hadn't yet.

"He'd love for us to sit and stew in it. You know my dad has the emotional range of a teaspoon! He wouldn't want his image tainted by a son in jail, either," Bobby sighed.

"But he's a defense lawyer, dude. All he does is help people in jail!" Trevor said.

"Yes, but they aren't related to him!" Bobby frowned.

"True. True. But really we only have another two nights in here before we're out. We can wait."

"Yep, then just a court appearance.... Who knows when that will be, either," Bobby sighed.

"Yeah, since it was a cop, I'm sure they will hurry it, just to punish us faster."

"Yep, man I bet April will never forgive us when she gets back. Never forgive us…"

"Hard to say, man. I wouldn't blame her if she didn't. Fuck, I wouldn't forgive us!" Trevor sighed.

They stopped talking for a bit and Trevor just stared at the floor. He could have visitors, but was sure his mom and Zacchya were probably too pissed to visit yet. How could they not be? Trevor didn't even go home after Halloween, just sent his mom a text the next day saying he was fine. She had begged him to come home, but he couldn't face her. He stayed at Bobby's because his dad was never home. They said goodbye to Alicia and Trina before going to turn themselves in. On the way to the police station, they were pulled over and arrested.

Trevor used his one call to tell his mom not to worry and he loved her. He would explain it all later. He didn't get time to talk to Zacchya. Bobby called his dad and told him the news. John never answered, so he had to leave a voicemail.

Since then, they had been in a cell together with a man clearly high on drugs, probably meth. The man stunk horribly and muttered to the walls a lot, scratching at his arms constantly. It wasn't a very big cell, but enough for three bunks and a toilet with a small walking space. Bobby asked the guard for a pen and paper, but wasn't allowed. He was a criminal now—goodness knows he might shank someone!

Jail pretty much only gave them time to think and watch the walls. Bobby was sick of both. He had regretted his decision to beat Nick and lived with that guilt. He was willing to accept his consequences, yes, but over thinking it wouldn't help at all. He just wanted something to do! Sometimes he'd try to daydream of Trina and their future relationship. That helped pass the time quite well until his imagination went too far and he'd have to hide an inappropriate erection. Nothing worse than having wood in a small room full of guys! So he would try to stop himself from daydreaming too long, or at least keep them PG-rated.

"Woods, Packers, you made bail," a grumpy overweight guard hollered at them.

"What? Oh, thank God!" Bobby said and they both were led expectantly to see who bailed them out. Bobby felt like skipping! Jail was too boring. However, his joy left when he saw his dad John waiting for them. John had an angry scowl on his normally handsome face.

John said nothing to them as they grabbed their belongings. He walked silently to the car. Bobby sat up front with John; Trevor was in the back seat. As they drove away, John finally spoke.

"Robert, I am beyond ashamed! You know I'm a criminal lawyer! It is my job to prove people's INNOCENCE! And to... have a son purposely BATTER a police officer! Do you know the scrutiny I will face?"

"I know, Dad... I..."

"I do NOT want to hear your excuses or apologies! I should have left you there! You will pay me back EVERY CENT of the five thousand dollars I paid to release you both! EVERY DAMN CENT!" John's face was boiling red with anger.

"Yes, sir."

"And I will not be representing you when this goes to court, either."

Bobby sadly nodded. He expected nothing better than this. Trevor shuffled uncomfortably in the back seat.

"I will drop you off at your house, Trevor. After that, I wish you to please not converse with Robert again."

"Yes, sir," Trevor nodded. He was trying not to be ungrateful about getting bailed out of jail, but he hated John. John was an egotistical man who never loved Bobby. Trevor didn't know how Bobby kept sane living with that man. They reached Trevor's house shortly after. Once Trevor was out of the car, Bobby's insides squirmed. He knew the real John was soon to emerge.

When they reached their home, a beautiful two-story stone home, John grabbed Bobby's hand and escorted him inside. Once the door was shut, John slapped Bobby in the face, hard.

"I have spent my entire fucking life on this career, Robert! You have been nothing but a burden since your mother left us. NOTHING BUT! I raised you as best as I could. But you know that I never wanted children! And then I end up with you! Disgusting!" John's face was red and full of hate. "And then you have the fucking nerve to hang out with Trevor Packers! His sister's a complete fucking psycho! How on earth do you expect him to not end up in a giant pile of shit?"

Bobby stood silently. He knew reacting to John's rage was never a good idea. You stood there, took it like a man, and it would eventually end. He was surprisingly starting to miss jail at the moment, however.

"I hope for all of this ridiculous trouble you've put me through today, that you know you will be finishing your jail sentence."

"Dad…"

"Don't you fucking 'DAD' me! You know I do not have the patience or the kindness to put up with you. I tolerate you, at best!" John spat.

Bobby had heard most of that before, but the words always stung. Parents were supposed to love you. John hated him. John couldn't love anyone but himself and Bobby knew that. But damn it, he was supposed to love his only son! He fought back tears so John wouldn't see his pain.

"You know I was in the military as a teen, explosives and more. Don't ever forget that." He was near whispering in Bobby's face. "If you don't pay me back my money and leave this house before graduation, I will find a way to dispose of you. Fire is easy to start, Robert, damn easy… *Boom*."

John then grabbed Bobby by the hair and dragged him down the hall to a doorway leading to an underground wine cellar. He pushed Bobby down the stairs, hard. Bobby rolled down the set of stairs, praying for no broken bones. He landed on the concrete with a soft thud.

"Enjoy your new jail! I'm going to Wichita for a few days. I met a hot sexy 20-year-old begging for me to fuck her. Mmm!" John licked his lips. "Watch out for spiders, especially the brown recluse. You know they come out most in the fall and winter!" John laughed and slammed the door. Bobby heard the clicking of the door lock.

Bobby sat up and quickly assessed his body for injuries, he couldn't find any. Probably nothing more than a few bruises, thankfully, even though he did feel quite sore. He had been locked down here a few times in his life and had hid a light once somewhere; he just had to find it. Searching in the ten-by-ten, nearly empty room, helped distract him from the pain he felt in his heart. He found the small lamp he hid, and the bucket. Oh, he hated that damned bucket. Of all the horrors of this entrapment, the bucket was the worst. He had gotten used to no food or water, well not used to it, but tolerated it. John never kept him imprisoned long enough to actually hurt his health. But the bucket made him feel like an animal. Having to use a plastic bucket to relieve himself was beyond horrifying. The smell of urine and feces were his constant companion. How could anyone do this to their own flesh and blood?

He found a corner on the opposite side of the room from the bucket, and curled up next to the wall. His emotions finally came flooding out. He longed to understand humanity and those that lacked a compassion gene. Tears poured down his face. He vowed to himself to never end up like his father. He even hated calling John his father!

The world looked at John and adored him. John was tall, athletic, tan, handsome, charming, smart, etc. All the ladies adored him; everyone did really. No one knew the man behind the pretty smile. No one knew that he abused his son and only cared about his appearance and money. John was soulless. He didn't care about other humans at all, only pretended to in public.

Bobby realized that his dad, John, was a villain. Not in the sense that he was the worst guy, the one that kills people or anything like that. John was an every day villain. The one that hid in the shadows, smiling brightly in society, unnoticed. John was charming and likeable by everyone who knew him. It was almost worth a chuckle thinking of his dad as a villain, but he wasn't in the mood for laughing. His life wasn't a book or a movie where he was the good guy and would prevail against any enemy. No, he was just a regular guy and that was the worst part. He was just another one of the regular kids that live with abusive parents and can't find a way out; kids that are too scared to leave, and too scared to stay. He was trapped.

Chapter 14

November 4, 2014

ZACCHYA REALLY NEEDED SOME GOOD news. She was happy, of course, that Trevor had come home the day before from jail. She actually slapped him for being so stupid and reckless! And then she hugged him tight, saying "You leave me for jail again, I'm going to kick your ass, bro!" She loved him too much to stay mad at him. She was a pretty forgiving person in general, and definitely understood his point of view after he explained it all. She was mad that he was stupid enough to go to the tracks to see Jacob. Furious that Jacob was actually there and that it was not a rumor. Mad that Nick was abused, but sympathetic to their "hero" wannabe moment. Sad that Trina and Alicia were injured.

Then she had to deal with April and Tim being gone as well. Trevor was friends with both, so he was saddened too, but not as much as she was. April was her best friend. It really hurt she hadn't even said goodbye. All of her texts to April were returned as "undeliverable." April had completely turned off her phone, no service.

And to make it even worse, she got a call from Sunnyvale that her friend, Marissa, was dead. Marissa had a long history of self-abuse, so she knew that the call would come eventually, but she never expected it so soon. But knowing someone will die if they continue their destructive behaviors, and them actually dying, is quite different. Marissa had made it numerous times where she shouldn't have lived, but always pulled through. Apparently that wasn't one of those times.

Between the grief, sadness over April, worrying about Trevor, and her depression all combining together, she was a bit surprised she hadn't lost it yet. Her emotions were running too high and she was having a lot of difficulty keeping it together.

As she sat at the lunch table, she realized how bad things had gotten over the past week. Alicia and Trina were gone in the hospital. Bobby was apparently grounded or faking sick, as he wasn't there either. It was just her and Trevor alone. She picked at her ham sandwich and chips, but she didn't feel that hungry. Trevor wasn't eating much either.

"You think everyone knows I was in jail?" Trevor asked quietly.

"Who cares if they do? Don't let them judge you. They don't know your true intentions."

"I know. I just am so full of guilt from it all, I feel like it's a beacon on my face." Trevor sighed.

"I know. You are glowing a bit." She smiled.

"Ha ha..."

"I can't imagine you'd not feel guilty. I think I'd disown you, if you didn't!"

"You probably should anyway. You realize I could do prison time for this…" Trevor sighed again. He wanted to make a joke and forget his troubles, but they were too heavy on his shoulders. He wanted to be a good brother and comfort his sister, but he didn't have the strength. That alone made him feel even worse about himself.

"Trevor I would never disown you and you know that! We're womb-mates! I love you!" Zacchya smiled, trying not to focus on the thought of her brother in prison.

"Womb-mates! Oh you've been watching 'Jack and Jill' haven't you?" Trevor smirked.

"You know I love Adam Sandler movies. They help cheer me up! I watched it the other day."

"Maybe we should watch it together after school. I need a good laugh and a good twin movie."

"Yes, definitely we should!" She smiled. Her life might be in a bad spot, Trevor's too, but she always had her brother. Just Trevor being there beside her, not even trying to help, helped. They were twins and best friends.

She couldn't make it without him, and she surely didn't know what she'd do if he did go to prison.

* * * *

Patty had been to visit Nick numerous times in the three days he'd been hospitalized. Nick was really starting to make improvements. He was slowly getting better at talking. She could actually understand a few words through the wired jaw. Nick was being especially quiet as he watched Family Feud on TV. She could see something was bothering him.

"Sweetie, you okay?" She asked as she reached over, lightly touching his hand.

Nick looked into her eyes and shook his head.

"What is it? Can I help you?"

Nick reached for his notepad and began to write:

"*I want to talk to the boys who attacked me, dear. They apologized to me before the attack. Told me a story about their friends being hurt. I want to hear the whole story. Please.*"

"Nick... I... I hadn't told you yet. Two of April's classmates are here in the hospital too. Trina Johnson and Alicia Green, both were stabbed the same night as you. I talked to their mothers in the waiting room." Patty stared at the floor.

Nick sat up quickly and regretted it, a sharp pain radiated from his ribcage.

"I didn't want you to worry! I didn't think it was connected!" Patty replied.

"Call them..." Nick mumbled through his wire.

"If you really think it's a good idea… I'll get a hold of them." Patty leaned over and kissed Nick on the forehead. Even when he was injured in the hospital, he was still looking to do the right thing. She knew if those boys were trying to save Trina and Alicia, Nick would find a way to drop the charges. It was just the man he was. Always striving to help and be the better man, a man that believed in justice and dignity. She admired that quality about him deeply, one of the things that made her fall in love.

She reached for the phone out of her purse. Before she dialed the number, she placed her hand of top of Nick's, looked into his brown eyes, "You're the best man I know. I can't believe I got lucky enough to have you. I love you so much." Her eyes misted over. She had never loved him as much as she did in that moment. Nick was sacrificing his own health to do the right thing. Even after a twenty-year marriage, her heart felt like it would burst from the love she felt for him.

"No. I'm lucky," Nick said back to her, gently touching her cheek.

By one o'clock in the morning of November 5th, Nick was asleep in his bed. Patty had gone home earlier in the night. They hadn't been able to get a hold of Bobby or Trevor. Trevor was at football practice and couldn't visit. They couldn't reach Bobby at all. Trevor did say he would try the next day. Nick had fallen asleep, feeling more peaceful knowing that he was doing the right thing. He believed in justice and fairness. As angry as he was for their actions, he could understand if it was to save someone's life. He had gone into the police force hoping to be that hero for someone. Save a life and do the right thing all the time, be an honorable man. He was slumbering peacefully when Larry entered the room.

Larry had made sure the RN's and aides were nowhere near Nick's room. He had to be careful. He had too many plans. Plans that could save lives and even help the military. He couldn't end up in jail for murder. He pulled out a vial of potassium chloride and injected it into Nick's IV tubing. If it worked correctly, as it should, Nick's heart would stop. And without an autopsy, people would think he'd succumbed to his injuries.

Larry put the empty vial back in his pocket and left the room quickly. Within a few minutes, Nick would flat line and the room would be full of nurses. He'd have to come back to help with CPR when the Code Blue was called, of course.

He just made it to his office by the time the Code Blue was called. He walked briskly to the elevator, then to Nick's room. Even though he was in excellent shape, he had broken into a sweat. A large group was performing CPR on Nick. Larry stepped in and took over.

Ten minutes later, Nick was pronounced dead. Larry wiped the sweat from his brow.

"1:20 a.m. on November 5, 2014, time of death. I will call the coroner. If you could please contact his wife," Larry said solemnly.

"Of course, Doctor."

Larry left the room, heading back to his office. He could still feel the small empty vial in his chest pocket. There was a small part of him that was sad Nick had to die. Nick was a good man, an innocent man. But the rest of Larry smiled deeply. The bigger picture was too grand. Trevor would go to prison. His poor sister's burden would be lifted, especially after he finished his plans with Zacchya. And that made Nick Walker dying, perfectly okay with Larry.

Chapter 15

November 5, 2014

"How is Trevor doing?" Larry asked.

"Oh, not good. Not good at all. He was worried that Nick….well that it was all his fault. He couldn't get out of bed today. He's just sick with worry," Zacchya replied somberly.

"Oh that is a shame. It's up to the family whether to do an autopsy or not. But under the circumstances, I would think probably not. I'm afraid Trevor might have to do some real prison time."

"Oh, Uncle Larry!" Zacchya frowned, tears forming in her blue eyes.

"I know, it will be rough on all of us. But I just can't see a positive outcome, dear. Manslaughter at the very least…"

"But Trevor wouldn't! Oh, God…" She sobbed over her plate of food, tears landing on her biscuits.

Larry reached over and touched her hand. "I know, sweetie. Drink some tea. You came here for a good time, not sobbing!"

"I know. I'm sorry Uncle. I've been having such a hard time lately!" She squeezed his hand.

"Well after supper we can play some games and talk, if you want. Get you feeling better and put a smile back on that pretty face." Larry smiled.

"Smiling would be very welcome at this time," she replied and sipped on her cup of green tea.

* * * *

When Zacchya woke up, she had no idea where she was, yet she had a feeling she'd been there before. She was strapped down to a chair with an IV in her right arm. If her mind hadn't been so groggy, she would have surely been panicking. She tried to focus her blurry eyes, but wasn't having any luck.

"Oh, good! You're awake! That sedative had you out for over an hour!" Larry walked toward her smiling.

"Larry?"

"Yes, I called your mom and told her we were busy watching a movie." Larry paced in front of her, the smile left his face. "You know I hate lying to your mom." He leaned close to her, his green eyes blazing.

"I … don't… understand." She gulped. Her stomach was swirling with nausea.

"Oh, I swear! I hate this damned part! I drugged you. I am going to redirect your thought process," Larry replied angrily. "You always forget! It is the point, but I fucking hate repeating myself!"

"What?" The confusion in her mind was trying to clear but hadn't yet. She was scared and confused, but the déjà vu she felt wouldn't leave. How many times had she been here?

Larry was still pacing in front of her, clenching his fists. "Before I record this, I want to say again the one thing I don't mind repeating: I fucking hate you!"

"Uncle? Why!?" Zacchya gasped.

"You're a piece of trash and a burden on my sister. I would kill you, but it's too bloody obvious. And… I like to play with my food." Larry leaned his face close to her, barely an inch away from her, licking his lips.

Zacchya suppressed a gag. Fear was creeping up on her faster than a bullet. She didn't move, partly from being tied down, but she could sense the evil in him. An evil she'd never seen before. Fear overtook her, froze her whole body.

Larry reached his hands over her neck, squeezing lightly. A small laugh escaped from his mouth, his sticky breath right over her mouth. He forcefully stuck his tongue in her mouth, deep.

She fought the urge to bite his tongue off or puke. She couldn't tell which one she wanted to do more.

Larry's hand slowly moved down her body, stopping at her breast, squeezing a bit too hard. "You sick bitch. I want to hear you moan. Scream if it hurts! I love it when you scream!" Larry kissed her even harder, his teeth pressing against her lips. He moved his hand lower, sliding it over her jeans. His other hand found the buttons and undid them.

"You're nothing but a disgusting slut. You deserve this. I should tear it apart. Claw at it! Fuck you so hard, you rip right in half." Larry's breath in her face was so hot; it was making her even sicker. His eyes were more evil and full of hate than anything she'd ever seen in her entire life. She wanted to scream. She wanted for God to save her. How could this happen? Why would anyone do this to their family? Tears began streaming down her cheeks. She couldn't even fight… tied to a damn chair, helpless and abused.

"Fuck you," she said through her tears, so angry and disgusted that she was surprised she could even talk.

"Oh, dirty little whore has a dirty mouth! I should break your fucking jaw! Don't you talk to me like that! EVER!" Larry spat in her face.

He removed his hands from her jeans and slapped her hard against the face.

"I'll show you what to do with that fucking mouth, bitch!" Larry unbuttoned his pants. He was full of rage and power. "Fucking cunt!"

Zacchya began gagging, turning her head, anything to try and avoid the situation. She had never felt so sick, so shamed in her entire life. And she couldn't fight back. She was a victim, another hopeless number in the never-ending war on sexual abuse. She felt like she would never recover. Zacchya sobbed. *Please, God, no... Oh God, please let it end. Please. Please.* She prayed repeatedly in her mind.

When the indecency was over, Larry turned and left the room. Zacchya shuddered silently in her chair. Tears pouring down her cheeks, praying that he wouldn't return. Praying he would die and she'd never see his face again. She couldn't take any more abuse.

Larry returned a few minutes later, with a vial of blue liquid. He pulled a camcorder out to the middle of the large room they were in, putting it about fifteen feet in front of her. He turned it on to adjust the angles.

"Before I hit record... know this part is science. You mention ANYTHING about the actions before this, and I will kill you. I promise you that. Don't ever fucking forget that." He glared at her. She knew he wasn't kidding, even though she was wondering if death wasn't really all that bad.

Larry hit record and stepped in front of the camera, standing a few feet in front of her. "I have Test Subject Number One here. This is her tenth dose of the 33X serum. Because of the previous amount of injections, she responds very fast to the serum. As I have learned with her and Test Subject Number Two, the more times the serum is used, the quicker and better results given. It should take less than five minutes before I can activate new commands."

Larry turned toward her, giving her one more promising glare, and emptied the vial into the IV tubing. "I'm injecting the 33X serum now into an already placed IV in the right forearm."

Zacchya sat silently, tears still leaking from her blue eyes. Inside she was furious and sick. Larry who had just... molested her, his own niece... was now talking like his regular Mr. High Class, charming, smarter than everyone else self! It took all she had to swallow down the bile in her throat.

As soon as Larry emptied the vial into her tubing, and stepped away from her, she began to change. Her mind cleared, her fears began to dwindle away. The bile in her throat settled down to her stomach. What was this drug?

Larry faced the camera again. "As you can see from her expression, it is already taking effect. Her sadness is fading and her tears drying. She said in a previous test that she feels calm and perfectly clear-headed, which in my hypothesis, it's the synapses of the brain turning off and on in the proper areas. The drug mostly affects the memory section of the brain, especially the temporal lobe. As you already know, the temporal lobe is also involved with auditory perception, which is why the auditory commands help the information stick. Along with working in the hippocampus and medial temporal cortex to help the memories stick in her brain. Creating new memories from the auditory commands that I give her.

"I also believe that with further study of the 33X serum, we can find a way to work with the Alzheimer's patients, helping them lock into their memories for good. This drug can revolutionize science studies and leap us forward many years! The lives that can be helped and saved will be insurmountable!" Larry exclaimed. He always got very excited talking about his inventions. They made him a god amongst men. The power to hold life or death was in his hands... he loved it.

"I believe Test Subject Number One is ready." Larry turned toward Zacchya, pulling a nearby chair to sit in front of her. "As you know you have given me free reign to command Number One to do whatever I wish. I have taken a kind girl and made her into something different.

She is still kind, yes, but her personality is completely different from when I started the 33X. Which I know sound terrible on paper or film, but honestly I believe that it shows the power and ability that 33X has on the brain functions! You could make the perfect soldiers or keep peace in violent countries. The possibilities are truly endless!" Larry had become almost breathless with excitement. He was truly going to change the world.

"Also, as you know, I also gave her severe depression with suicidal ideations. She has attempted suicide approximately five times in the past year, since the start of the testing. One of them was very recently on October 31st, 2014. I have also implanted and hidden the murder of Jacob Track in her mind. If the drug were able to leave her system long enough to be reset, she would actually remember killing Jacob.

"I had also been slowly dosing her with an ingestible form of 33X for quite a few months. I used a particular tea she enjoyed and prepared it during our visits. Ingesting the serum does work, but not as quickly. It takes about a week for the serum to react to the neurons in the brain. So visits must be frequented within the allotted time. It does help to ingest more, as my study has found. I will send the documentation along with the video. And as I said before, the more the patient has been dosed with the drug, the better it works and the longer it lasts." Larry paused to catch his breath.

"As you know with Test Subject Number Two, with whom I've done more long term studies on, the serum will wear off in approximately four to six weeks on a low dosed person. Over time the effects will last longer, Subject Number Two can now last eight to twelve weeks without a dose before his previous memories return. Not all progress is lost, however, if you re-dose immediately. If you cannot re-dose, memories will slowly begin to reform and return. The patient will make a full recovery and possess all memories as real and no longer leave them as implanted commands. All test subjects will different of course, because of DNA and body chemistry, but so far the results have been similar.

"Now I'm going to implant some commands into Number One that are brand new to her. Recently her brother assaulted a police officer. The officer eventually succumbed to his injuries. She and her brother have always been close; they are twins actually. I have never found him to be a worthy candidate for 33X, however. I am hoping to implant a deep mistrust and hate for her brother." Larry glanced at Zacchya's slack face and frowned.

"Now I know it seems harsh to give these commands to cause hate instead of love, but I have already shown that love can be emphasized by 33X and need to prove the opposite effect. To be completely accurate in these studies, both sides must be shown. Let's begin."

Chapter 16

November 5, 2014

PATTY SAT NAKED IN HER shower; the water had turned quite cool long ago. She hadn't even noticed the drastic temperature change. She had been crying so hard, the pain overwhelmed her. She found a song on her iPod by Little Big Town, "Lonely Enough," and it was now on repeat.

The song was about praying to God to send back the one she loved because she'd been lonely enough. Her love died and didn't know how to cope when she already lost so much. Patty could relate to those lyrics too well. Within a week, she had lost her daughter and her husband. She prayed that April would return home or at least contact, eventually. With no contact at all, it felt like April was too far gone, as if she was dead too.

Patty shook as she held her knees to her chest. She wished she had someone to comfort her, hold her. She wanted Nick to tell her it would be ok. But he was gone, dead. How could her precious Nick be dead?

Just yesterday he was feeling better, alive and healing. He was going to help causes that he found just. That was Nick, always fair and honest. How could God let someone that good die? Patty began to slowly sing along to the song. Maybe singing would quench the hole in her heart.

Patty sang through her tears until she couldn't sing anymore, breaking down. She curled into a ball on the tub floor, crying too hard, barely able to catch her breath, the cold water was pouring over her. She didn't know how long she had been there in the shower, naked and crying. She really didn't care that much either. Little Big Town kept singing to her, and she kept wishing she would grow the strength to turn the song off. It wasn't helping… at least it didn't seem to do anything except make her cry harder.

"Patty? Patty, dear, where are you?" A female voice called from a nearby room.

Patty had cried herself to sleep, curled up, the water still coming down on her.

"Oh God, Patty! Are you okay? You look so pale!" The woman reached into the tub and turned off the cold water. She grabbed a nearby towel and wrapped it around her. "Oh, God, sweetie!"

Patty's eyes slowly began to open. "Tiff?"

"Yes, it's me. What are you doing? You're going to get hypothermia!"

"I didn't feel it," Patty whispered through her shivering.

"Well you're ice cold. Come on, I'll help you warm up. You NEED to warm up!" Tiffany reached down, putting her arms around Patty, helping her out of the tub. She found her some warm pajamas. Tiffany helped Patty to the couch, where she wrapped her arms around her sister, holding her close.

"You know I love you, sis. I can't imagine how bad it is losing Nick after April left. So awful." Tiffany's brown eyes filled with tears as she caressed her sister's hair.

"I can't do it," Patty cried into Tiffany's shoulder.

"You will find a way. If I lost Brendon... oh God, I can't imagine. It's going to take a long time. But I'll be here. You always have me... always."

"Don't leave me. No more leaving..." Patty looked up at Tiffany, her brown eyes swimming in sad tears. She couldn't bear to lose anything else. It was too hard. She didn't know if she'd survive it.

"Never! Never!" Tiffany squeezed her sister tighter, both girls sobbing together.

Tiffany was Patty's younger sister, thirty-seven. She had long brown hair, dark brown eyes, was very pretty and a freelance artist. She didn't make a lot of money, but her and her husband, Brendon, always found a way to make it. Patty and her were always close growing up, which is something not all sisters are good at. But family was important to them and they always found a way to work out their differences.

Tiffany had been in her home art studio when she got the news about Nick's passing. She wanted to rush right over, but her two-year-old daughter, Clara, was being extremely fussy and she didn't have the sanity to deal with a fussy two year old while comforting her grieving sister. Brendon came home an hour later, and Tiffany finally headed over to check on Patty. She was glad she made it when she did as Patty had been so cold and pale from the cold water running over her for however long. Tiffany guessed it wouldn't have been too much longer before Patty's body went into shock or hypothermia.

"I'm going to make us some hot cocoa to warm you up. You want me to put in a movie to distract you a bit?"

"No. I think I wanna lie down," Patty sighed. Her body was so weak with grief.

"Okay, hot cocoa and then bed. I'll call Brendon and tell him I'm staying all night."

"Good... I..."

"Don't mention it. That's what sisters are for." Tiffany smiled. Patty almost managed a smile back. She wondered how long it would be before she could smile again. She didn't know, no one could know. Grief was a horrible monster that sucked away your hopes and dreams, leaving you with nothing. It clung to her like a wet blanket over her mouth, slowly suffocating her. If there was hope for a future, she couldn't see it. If there a light, it was lost in an endless night of blackness. Grief was truly a horrible monster.

* * * *

November 6, 2014

Surprisingly, John returned home around seven in the morning to unlock the basement door without a word to Bobby. Bobby was awake and snuck up to his room to grab fresh clothes for a shower. John was already gone again. Bobby was extremely grateful John hadn't stayed home for any amount of time, which would have ended in abuse, verbal or physical. He made it to school, only five minutes late with a fake sick note to be excused for the past few days.

Bobby made it to his classes but couldn't focus on them. His mind was clouded with the recent seclusion and he had to make it stop. He couldn't live another day like that. His only dilemma was running away from school. He didn't want to abandon his education and be-come another dropout. He knew he couldn't make it too far without a diploma, not in today's society. The best job he could hope for would be a fast food restaurant for the rest of his life, and while there was nothing wrong with working at fast food, he had bigger dreams. He would miss his friends too much and Trina. He wished to find a way to leave with her. Their relationship was too recent for her to run away with him… barely started. Bobby knew he had a lot to plan and figure out before the day's end. Hopefully Trevor would help him decide at lunch. Oddly, Trevor never showed up to his math class, which made Bobby worry he wouldn't show up at all.

Bobby found Zacchya sitting alone at a table in the corner of the lunch room. She looked especially moody.

"Hey girl, how you doing?" Bobby smiled.

"Eh, not that great. I'm just so mad at Trevor right now I can't stand him!" Zacchya huffed as she poked her mashed potatoes.

"But you and Trev never fight!"

"I know. I just can't look at him since Nick died."

"What!? He died?" Bobby gasped.

"How did you not know?" Zacchya almost shouted at him. She was quite in a sour mood.

"I … I was grounded. Couldn't leave the house or anything." Bobby's eyes shifted to the ground.

"Oh yeah? That's must be a damn strict grounding."

"You can say that…"

"But honestly, I don't know why I'm being chummy with you, either! You hurt Nick too! April's dad! Are you nuts?" Zacchya whined.

"Listen, I know it sounds and looks awful. And I'm beyond upset that he.... well he...he's gone." Bobby shook his head sadly, unwilling to cry in front of her. "And I'm okay with whatever consequences, Zacchya. I am. We thought we did the right thing. We were going to save lives and be heroes for a day. But we were wrong. So damned wrong." Bobby stared at his meatloaf. If only they could've saved Trina and Alicia. He would feel less guilty about it, made it at least almost worth it. But now a man was dead. His family was grieving. April was without a dad, and that was his fault. He would never forgive himself for that. Never.

"This isn't a David Bowie song, Bobby. It doesn't change anything, though. You'll both probably go to prison for manslaughter or murder. Murder! There's no happy ending here." Zacchya frowned. "Shit... here he comes. I'm out." She left her untouched tray on the table and marched angrily out of the cafeteria.

Trevor walked slowly to the table, eyeing his sister as she left. He slumped down in the seat across from Bobby.

"We're having a bit of a row," Trevor sighed.

"A row?" Bobby chuckled.

"Oh sorry, I've been watching too much British TV lately, a fight. She's never been this pissed at me, though."

"Sucks. She was telling me a bit about it. I … I didn't know about Nick, man."

"Oh… yesterday. Mom told me. We've all been so torn up about it," Trevor said quietly, "Don't know what that means for us, Bob. Scares me."

"Ditto, dude. Fucking ditto."

"Sucks wish we could go back and do over."

"Yeah time machine this bitch upright." Bobby half smirked.

"Exactly! Hot tub time machine!" Trevor smiled.

"Ya…" Bobby's face sobered up. "I do want to ask you something important for real."

"Sure, go ahead."

"I need to leave my house."

"Your dad being a dick again?" Trevor frowned.

"You don't even know the half of it! Don't wanna talk about it really." Bobby stared at the meatloaf again. "I'm not going back there. Never. And I don't know where to go. Or how…"

"Well I'd like to tell you to get in that car of yours and drive and drive. But if you leave the state it'll look suspicious."

"Yeah… I have a few hundred bucks saved up my dad doesn't know about. Thought about staying in a hotel or finding some really cheap apartment, but I don't have enough to turn on the electric and gas unless I find one that's all bills paid."

"That would be nice. You're only seventeen now, Bob. Just go check with low-income housing. Give them a sob story and tell them you have to move right away."

"Good idea… good idea." Bobby smiled. Maybe there was still hope for a future without John.Later that night, Zacchya was still avoiding Trevor at all costs. He had tried to talk to her at home, but she refused to acknowledge his existence. He tried to see it from her point of view, and could easily, but it didn't make the hurt any less. She had been so supportive of him since hearing about the attack, and then she suddenly couldn't handle it. He could see she was dealing with a lot of internal stress about all her friends. Then her friend from the hospital died. She was clearly near a breaking point. He wished he knew how to help her, but he was at a loss. It wasn't helping that she was refusing to talk to him, either. He found it hard to believe that just two days ago he was watching an Adam Sandler movie, laughing and joking with her, bonding over being twins. It felt like a lifetime ago. He was in his room, trying to forget about their fight, doing his math homework when his cell phone rang.

"Hello?" he said.

"Trevor Packers?" A woman's voice asked.

"Yeah, this is he."

"Oh, good. I got the number from April's… address book." Trevor knew instantly it was Patty Walker. Guilt turned his stomach into a lava pit.

"Oh, hi Mrs. Walker."

"I just wanted to tell you… Nick wished to talk to you before…"

"I remember…" Trevor replied quickly.

"Well, he wanted to know why you attacked him," she said quietly.

"Oh… our friends were in danger, ma'am. We tried to tell him that. He thought we made it up."

"Will you tell me, please?" she begged quietly, her voice barely more than a whisper.

Trevor couldn't imagine how hard the call had been for her to make. To call the person that killed her husband, even if it was on accident.

"Well I'm sure you heard the rumors about Jacob being back from the dead. Well we all were really stupid kids and decided to go and see if it was true. Jacob was a good friend of ours. Well we made it to the bridge, and he was there. I swear on my life, he was there. We all got scared and ran for it, but Trina and Alicia were missing by the time we hit the street. We looked for them. Found nothing. So we went to get supplies to search all night.

Officer Walker stopped us; it was after curfew. He tried to take us home and we couldn't go… we just couldn't." Trevor paused, tears filing his green eyes. The guilt was overwhelming him again. "We were stupid, Ma'am. Boys thinking we were going to be heroes saving the girls we loved. We never wanted him hurt, I swear! It just went too far too fast. Bobby was desperate and made a dumb decision… and I was just as dumb, because I thought he might be right. I'd take it back a million times. And now you…" Trevor was bawling now, gasping for words. "Your husband is... gone. I'm responsible for that. April's dad is gone. I don't think I could ever forgive myself for that. Never."

There was a long pause from Patty. She listened to Trevor sob uncontrollably, tears rolling slowly down her cheeks. It felt like ages before she grew the courage to speak.

"I believe in doing the right thing, Trevor. I believe in justice and fairness. I believe my husband is… was… the best man that I ever knew." She fought back the tears welling viciously in her eyes. "I may never… forgive you, Trevor, or your friend Bobby. But Nick was willing to. And it was his last living wish to drop the charges on you."

Trevor sat upright, wiping his tear soaked eyes. What did she just say? "Ma'am?"

"Unfortunately it is not possible because he was an officer of the law. The legalities won't let me drop the charges. I have suspicions in my heart that I can't express. I ordered a full autopsy. If it was something other than his injuries that …. well, you know… then you will be off the hook. I don't know you well, Trevor… but know this; I do not do this lightly. I am without a husband because of your actions. But two mothers have safe daughters because you cared enough to try and save them, even if your actions didn't pan out correctly. I can at least respect that you tried to save them, and so could Nick." Tears slowly began rolling down her cheeks. "I pray that you consider all of your actions from this day forth. I would appreciate it if you would pay your respects at the funeral on the 9th at two p.m. You owe him that much."

"Yes, ma'am… I don't… know what to say."

"No words can fix this, ever. I just want answers. The truth is the most important thing here. Nick was getting better, doing fine… and then he was… I feel in my heart that there's more to it. And if it was something else that… killed him, Trevor, I'd still suggest finding a lawyer," Patty swallowed hard. She still couldn't believe it was a reality that Nick was dead.

"Thank you. I understand if you never forgive us. We don't deserve it. I'll never forgive myself." Trevor saw a small of light of hope that they might get off the hook and not have to do prison time. He couldn't imagine a world where someone would actually kill Nick Walker, but apparently Patty had a feeling about it.

"Yes, well I must go. Please tell your friend for me. I do not wish to, nor do I think I am capable, of making this call again," Patty sighed; her energy was zapped.

"Of course, I wouldn't ask you to." Trevor replied and the call was ended.

Part of him wished so much for them to be off the hook. That someone, whoever, killed Nick so he and Bobby could be free. Was it wrong to wish someone to go to prison so he didn't have to? He wasn't sure, but he knew that prison was not a place he or Bobby would do well in. He wasn't cut out for it. The other part, a much larger part, could only think of Mrs. Walker planning a funeral with a missing daughter, calling to tell him that there was a chance he could be free. It was completely unfair world that they lived in. He was free and a man was dead. He texted Bobby giving him the news.

"Are you serious?! She called for an autopsy?" Bobby replied.

"Yep, just called me."

"Crazy. She thinks someone else did it?"

"Yeah, I guess so. So nuts to think we might not have to do prison time. You at the hotel?"

"Yeah. Even if we're not guilty of… murder or manslaughter or whatever, would we still have to do prison time?" Bobby gulped hard. "Hope Dad doesn't find me here. I won't go back, dude."

"No idea, man. I hope he doesn't find you there. I'm going to lie down. Tired."

"Thanks for telling me bro. Night."

Patty was staying at her sister Tiffany's while she planned the funeral. She had called and asked for an autopsy to make sure she was doing the right thing. She wasn't sure if it was just the grief playing with her mind or not, but something felt wrong. She had watched him heal, they told him he would be leaving soon. And then he was dead, overnight. They never mentioned internal bleeding or heart problems. People didn't usually just die without reason, even if they were beaten, unless it was caused by some kind of blood clot or aneurism. But hospitals always give shots to patients who have an extended stay to prevent blood clots. Getting blood clots while being less mobile in hospitals was quite common. So she figured it was probably not a blood clot. She didn't know if the boys were innocent or guilty of killing Nick, and part of her didn't care. Even in her extremely deep hole of grief, she needed answers and truth.

* * * *

November 9, 2014

The past three days had passed without much incident. Trina and Alicia were released from the hospital, but told to limit their activities as much as possible for at least another week. Trevor brought Alicia all of her books and assignment lists from school for when she had the energy to work on them. He even let her copy some of his homework so she wouldn't be overwhelmed. Alicia was healing quite a bit faster than Trina, though. Her wounds were not as deep as Trina's.

Bobby called Trina every day since he had been out of his dad's homemade jail. He told her about the hotel he stayed at, and a low-income apartment he should be getting soon. He offered her to stay with him, but she declined. She wanted to stay with her mother and little brother for family support. Plus, she thought it was too soon in their relationship to be moving in. They hadn't even had a proper date.

Both couples, along with most of the town, showed up for Nick's funeral. It was bigger than even Jacob's had been. A lot of other cops spoke very highly of Nick during the funeral. April had not showed up, which tore Patty apart even more.

Trevor was sobbing, holding Alicia's hand very tightly. Zacchya was still refusing to talk to him, even after the charges were dropped, so he needed support in whatever form it would come in. Alicia tried her best to be supportive, but when she closed her eyes at night, it wasn't Jacob she was seeing. It was Trevor beating Nick. She wanted to believe Trevor was better than that, but she didn't fully trust him anymore. He had killed a man, sure accidentally, but still dead. She wasn't sure she could date a killer. She was thinking of breaking up with him, but knew it had to be after the funeral. He was much too distraught to do it before. She was scared for him, and it hurt her a bit to let him go, but it felt like the right thing to do. She had a future and a reputation to uphold. She would have to let him go, but just not today. She squeezed his hand tighter, giving him one last chance to lean upon her for support.

Nearby, Trina and Bobby were holding hands as well. Bobby was leaning on her shoulder, too full of guilt and sadness to sit up on his own accord. Trina caressed his cheek with her free hand. She had also been unsure if she could date or care for someone who unintentionally killed a cop. But the moment she seen Bobby's brown eyes, swimming in tears, his face twisted with grief and guilt, she knew she could. She had seen that he was beyond sorry for his actions. Accidents happen, even horrible ones where someone ends up dead. What was there to do? People would disagree with her, but she didn't care. Even the bad decisions in life can be made by genuinely good people. He had done that to try and save her life. It hadn't worked exactly, but the gesture meant a lot to her. It wasn't fair that Nick was dead. Oh, God, it was downright awful. But inside of her soul, she forgave Bobby, and knew that the more she held this sobbing man, the more she cared for him. Bobby, the eternal joker and class clown, showing his emotions raw and uncut, impressed her. She felt her heart was growing towards him. Somewhere, ironically at a funeral, she was falling in love, and it was something she didn't think was possible to do again.

As the funeral ended, Zac Reynolds found a place next to Patty before she left.

"I just want you to know how truly sorry I am for your loss. You know I looked up to Nick," Zac said with tears forming in his dark eyes. Zac was the youngest cop on the force at twenty-two, and had deeply admired Nick.

"Thank you, Zac. I know he cared for you like a son." Patty said, grasping Zac's hands, looking up at him.

"Thank you. I looked up to him like a father figure as well." Zac squeezed her hands lightly. "But that wasn't the only reason I came over here, Patty."

"Yes?"

"Well I wanted you to know that I put a rush order on that autopsy report."

"Good, it's been weighing on my mind," she sighed.

"Mine too and I agree with you… Patty, I put in a favor and told them as soon as possible, which should be another two to three weeks."

"Good. If only it were like TV and done in a day!"

"Yes I know. But toxicity reports take much longer. And you need those for a full report. I promise I will let you know as soon as I know anything." He smiled.

"Thank you, Zac. You're a good man." She patted his hands lightly. "If I had the energy in me, I'd find you a good woman. You need to settle down, you're too handsome to be single."

"The right girl will show herself eventually. I'm more worried now about the autopsy and crime on the streets." Zac was a very good looking man. He was tall, just over six feet, with dark, soulful eyes, broad shoulders, and masculine features. He had distinctive dark eyebrows that shaped his face well, and short brown hair. Most women found him very attractive, but he just never found the time for dating.

"Very true. Let me know as soon as you hear something, Zac."

"Absolutely. If you need anything at all, ever, you let me know. I'm here for you." Zac hugged her tightly. "And please don't worry about me. I want you to focus on you. You're the most important person here."

Patty hugged him back, feeling comforted by his strong embrace. She really respected Zac as a person. She couldn't help but think of him like the son she never had.

Patty went to head to Tiffany's car, and was stopped yet again, this time by Larry.

"Oh, Patty! I'm so sorry for your loss!" Larry reached out for her hand.

"Oh, Larry!" She squeezed his hand and reached for a hug. "I know you did all you could."

"Of course, Nick was a wonderful man. I wish we could've stopped… whatever caused his heart to stop…"

"I know. I know you're tried, Larry." Her eyes swam in tears again. She hugged him tightly.

"If you need anything at all, just say the word," Larry said.

"Thank you, that means a lot to me. I really need to go. Tiffany is waiting for me."

"Of course, I'm so sorry. But I do mean it, Patty, anything at all… you just call me," Larry said.

She hugged him again and headed to Tiffany's car. It had been such a long week and she was hoping for brighter days. She hoped it would be soon, but hope and good days felt so far off.

Larry left the funeral, heading back home. He had too many tests to do, plans to make. He had been extremely surprised to see Trevor and Bobby at the funeral. That meant they hadn't been re-arrested yet for manslaughter. He figured the time would be coming soon, though. He just had to wait. And Larry was a very patient man when he wanted something.

Chapter 17

November 9, 2014

Around eleven o'clock p.m. on November 9th, Larry was sitting in a black car he owned, on an empty street that was not his own. The lights were off and he was dressed entirely in black, including a ski mask. He was waiting patiently, but angry, for the medical examiner, Tyler Hampton, and his wife, Marie, to go to sleep. After the funeral, he stopped by his office to grab something. While he was there, he overhead a police officer mention to a RN that Patty had ordered an autopsy. If it came back Nick didn't die from his injuries, she was going to try and drop the charges on Trevor and Bobby.

"If you ask me, she's damn lost her mind. Those boys killed her husband and a damn good cop. Stupid!" the cop said.

"Oh my! She must be completely blinded by grief or something! Shit, most people get angry, not want to let the killers go!" the RN replied, clearly angry.

"Reynolds mentioned an autopsy. Apparently she thinks it's all fishy! Ha! Autopsy, that's ridiculous! Those boys beat the shit out of him and he died. Makes perfect sense! Nothing fishy about it! Only fishy thing would be letting those boys go! It don't even seem legal, does it? I swear if I can find a way… I will see those boys rot in prison!" the cop spat.

"Yeah I surely hope you find a way!"

Larry's face grew hot with rage, his cheeks turning a deep shade of crimson. All of his work was for nothing? He wanted to choke as many people as possible! He tried to calm himself to still hear the conversation.

Larry stood up from his desk so fast, the chair fell to the ground with a loud boom. An autopsy? How on earth would she ask for an autopsy and not tell him? He was her damned doctor! The autopsy would ruin everything! It would show Nick didn't die from his injuries, but poisoned from potassium chloride. Oh, he had been stupid! His one mistake could ruin everything! He had never expected her to ask for an autopsy!

Larry grabbed the files from his desk and rushed from his office. He barely noticed anyone in the hallways trying to say hello. He was too busy, too angry to see anything but his white hot rage. If he couldn't stop the report, he was doomed. He would be arrested and in prison forever. Murder always had a long sentence, a life sentence, usually. He had to find a way to stop that report. Shit! His life and his work depended on it. He was too close to be stopped. Too damned close!

He rushed home, speeding the whole twenty blocks back to his house, surprised he didn't get a ticket. His plans of working on side projects were put aside. He paced furiously through his study. There were only two options: Find the file and destroy it… or kill the medical examiner and ruin the file. And he was running out of time. It had already been four days that Nick was dead. There was a good chance the file had already been sent off to Kansas City to be read. Larry's hope was fading fast. But he couldn't let this go, either. He had to do something and fast.

He ran through his house, looking for items to help his situation. He grabbed a gun and a silencer from his bedroom upstairs. Then he ran to the garage, grabbing some empty gas tanks. If everything worked correctly, it'd never come back on him. The gun he had bought on the black market in Kansas City a year ago, never used, no serial numbers. Good.

He worried about a fire, as it looked suspicious, but hopefully it would burn hot enough to destroy all evidence. If he was a praying man, he would've prayed. But Larry believed more in himself and the power of science than God. Larry saw himself as a god; he didn't need outside help.

He grabbed his black clothes and a ski mask, and waited for the sky to turn dark. None of the autopsies were done in Larned, but in a town nearby, Hays, which was about sixty miles away. He took all the items to his black Jaguar, put them in the trunk and set off. He would grab some supper from a fast food restaurant and wait.

He reached Hays at about seven p.m., grabbed some Burger King (not wearing his ski mask, obviously) and found the name and address for the medical examiner through a contact he had. Since it was late fall, the skies were almost dark, which helped him quite fine. He found the address easily through GPS. It was a very nice two-story stone house in the "rich" part of town. The street was near empty with only a few scattered houses throughout the two- to three-block area. He found a good hiding spot and parked with his headlights off. He was less than a block from the Hampton's house. He used binoculars to peer into the windows, watching them as they did their nightly activities. Tyler Hampton was not young, but not old either. He was forty-three, had dark hair with a speckling of grey, was well built and healthy. His wife, Marie, was thirty-eight, blond, busty and Larry guessed enjoying her nicely paid small city life. Larry didn't know the wages of a medical examiner, but guessed it must be good to afford such a nice house, or one of them had family money.

He waited for them to sleep, wishing they'd stop watching the damn news. Finally around eleven, Tyler kissed Marie and headed upstairs. Marie went to the kitchen, then followed. Larry knew his time was getting closer. He watched them make love in the upstairs room and then the lights were off. He gave himself another thirty minutes to assure they were asleep. In all his watching, Larry never noticed them to check doors or windows. He suspected, like most small town Kansas people, their doors were unlocked. He hoped anyway.

At 11:45, Larry, gun in pocket and mask on his face, walked slowly to the Hampton house. He stayed in the shadows as best as he could. He was surprisingly light and quiet. As he suspected, the front door was unlocked. He opened it quietly and headed upstairs. He had watched them enough to get a general layout of the house. He headed upstairs.

He quietly stepped into the master bedroom. Tyler and Marie were asleep on their backs. Larry pulled out the gun and silencer, shot them both once in the head. Neither woke up nor knew anyone was in their house. They died instantly.

Once dead, he replaced the gun back into his jacket and began rummaging through their belongings. He wanted it to look like a robbery, but he had to be quick. He didn't have a lot of time. He found a large wad of cash in a sock drawer and grabbed some necklaces and rings from a nearby jewelry box. Larry headed back downstairs, broke a few small items to look as though he was rushed and dangerous, and strewn papers around the living room. He found a few more small valuables on a coffee table and shoved them into a jacket pocket. Seeing that it was clear outside, he left the house as quiet as he had gone in. He walked slowly as to not cause concern to anyone who might have been peeking out a window. Once he was in the car and moving again, he kept the headlights off until he was far enough away to not be a suspect.

Using his contact again, he found the address where Tyler worked. It was a small concrete building on the south edge of town. He was a bit worried about cameras and other security measures. He knew the building was empty but had to plan how to get inside without notifying the police. He had only one choice. He dialed the number, as he drove past the building.

"Larry, this is the third call of the night!" a man said angrily.

"I know, sir. I wouldn't call if it wasn't an emergency."

"How is it an emergency?" the man asked impatiently.

"Sir, if I do not take these actions tonight, I will not be able to continue my research and finish the LZ Virus. And we both know that you do not want that."

"I've just about had enough of your troubles, Larry. I do not pay you for your personal choices, however awful they are!"

"Yes, sir, I'm sorry to be a burden to you. But you know that I am close to finishing it. I need to finish it!"

"What do you want? I don't have all night."

"I need you to hack the security cameras and doors to the address you last gave me," Larry said.

"Are you fucking serious, Larry? The protocol I will be breaking!"

"I need to destroy a file, sir. It is beyond important!"

"A file on the LZ Virus?" the man asked.

"No… no, of course not!"

"Then I don't see how I can be of much service to you. I've given you enough of my time for one night. Good…"

"Sir, please!"

"Good night Dr. Rumsfield." The man hung up the phone.

Larry punched the steering wheel. He would have to find a way to do it himself. He couldn't stand that man, whatever his name was. Larry usually did his job without much trouble, but the past six months had been very hard for him. All of his life tests were coming at him at once, and it wasn't always easy. He had to make a lot of hard choices that weren't always considered "moral" by most standards, but they were for the greater good.

Larry found a deserted road, changed into normal clothes and then headed back into town. He stopped at a gas station and bought a six-pack of beer, then headed to Walmart for alcohol and a few cleaning rags. He had a plan that he hoped would work. Before getting back to the ME's building, he changed his clothes again, removed his license plate, filled the beer bottles with gasoline and soaked the rags in alcohol. He drove slowly back as to not spill his new Molotov cocktails in the car.

Larry knew he had to be as quick as possible to not be caught. He couldn't afford to get caught.

He pulled slowly into the parking lot, easing close to the building. Larry pulled out the gun, shooting frantically at the front door to break the glass, also aiming at the visible camera. The glass door shattered, the camera fell to the ground with a crunch. Larry pulled out the Molotov's, lit one and threw it inside. He watched the fire slowly creep through the doorway, flames licking the entry way.

He lit another and tossed it. The fire on the ground helped ignite the new cocktail. Flames began growing through the building. Larry lit another and tossed it. Fire ball. Glass windows were breaking. He could smell the burning of the gasoline. He quickly lit and threw the last three bottles. The whole thing was over in under two minutes. He sped away as the flames and smoke filled his rear view mirror. He had five to ten minutes before the police would show up and he'd be long gone. Larry couldn't help but smile.

He had done all he could for one day. They'd never catch him now. He was a free man. Hopefully, that report never went any further than Hays. The computer would be ruined. Any paper or audio recordings would be ash. Everything except the concrete walls would be left standing. Nick's murder would be nothing but a memory now.

PART TWO: TRUTH

Chapter 18

November 24, 2014

ALL OF THE MISFITS WERE crowded comfortably in Bobby's new apartment for his eighteenth birthday party. Bobby had managed to find some secondhand furniture: an ugly, ragged brown couch, some mismatched plastic chairs, and a twin sized mattress. He borrowed a small dorm-sized fridge from Trevor, who had one in his room, and the apartment was already furnished with a stove. He was happy with the place, no matter how small it was. There was nothing better than being away from his abusive dad, just being free.

He and Trina had been spending a lot of time together, really letting their relationship grow. Bobby had offered to throw himself a birthday party so that everyone could come over and hang out. They were always so busy with school and things, it was hard to get time to just be friends and enjoy each other's company. Trina made a cake, chocolate with whipped cream frosting. Zacchya brought some DVDs to watch that everyone wanted to see. Trevor brought hot dogs and Alicia brought chips and pop.

Even April and Tim, who had been back since late November and living with her mom, came to the party. April had been absolutely devastated to learn of her dad's passing. She was angry and confused but chose to stay civil as her dad wished. Patty had never been as happy as the day she returned. April explained that they were having such a good time in Las Vegas, they couldn't bring themselves back. They had gambled and won just enough to stay longer. Their wedding was great, but sadly no pictures were taken. It had been very private. They both enjoyed the freedom of Las Vegas.

April felt extremely guilty of all the good memories she and Tim made, after finding out about Nick. She wished she could take it all back, but there was nothing to be done about it. The past was unfortunately in the past.

Alicia and Trevor were no longer dating, but were trying to stay friends. However, it was a little harder for Trevor, as Alicia had recently gone on a date with a basketball player in their class, Kevin. He tried to hide his jealousy and be a good friend but mostly he thought, *Fucking Kevin. Fuck him.*

Zacchya was there, but she was still having a hard time getting along with Trevor. No matter how much he apologized, she was still angry with him. Sometimes so much so that she could barely look at him. She gritted her teeth for Bobby's sake and played nice.

Bobby and Trina were snuggled on the couch, next to Trevor. Alicia and Zacchya were in some plastic chairs, April and Tim were covered up in a blanket on the floor, leaning against the wall. The group of Misfits were together again, happily munching away on chips, watching *X–Men: Days of Future Past*.

"That speedy kid is pretty fucking sweet, dude." Bobby smirked.

"Totally! I like that girl that makes the pretty teleport holes, or whatever you call them." Trina smiled.

"Pretty teleport holes! Oh, gosh… I'm dating Barbie over here!" Bobby laughed and kissed her cheek.

"Puhhhlesse! Barbie ain't got shit on me!" Trina giggled, flipping her hair.

"Oh, lovebirds, I'm going to puke. Can't I watch Magneto in peace?" Trevor sighed.

"Magneto, huh? Oh, so Mystique's name changed? I missed the memo! You know you're checking out 'dat ass, bro!" Bobby laughed.

Trevor winked and kept watching the movie.

"Jennifer Lawrence ain't that hot. Mystique is okay… I like Storm myself. Make all the thunderstorms I want!" Alicia chimed in.

"And no more damn snow!" Zacchya said.

"Exactly!" Alicia laughed.

"Glad that last bit of snow melted. So sick of that!" Tim replied.

"Well you know what they say, Tim…if you don't like the weather in Kansas, give it five minutes!" April joked. Everyone laughed. Kansas' weather was always changing.

Toward the end of the movie, Magneto's character lifts and entire baseball stadium with his mind. "See? Magneto, Bob. He's fucking cool as hell!" Trevor said, pointing at the TV.

"Oh, he's alright. But Professor X, the good guy, that's where it's at!"

"Storm," Alicia said.

"Kitty's cool. And Mystique," Zacchya chimed in.

Tim coughed, which sounded a lot like "Wolverine." Everyone laughed again. It was so nice to have the group back together again, just being like normal high school students. Their luck seemed to slowly be changing. By the movie's end, everyone was ready for another, except Zacchya.

"Oh guys, I'm just tired. Think I'm going to head home. Trevor do you need a ride later?" she asked.

"Nah, I'm sure I'll find one."

"We can drive him home, Zacchya." April smiled.

"Thanks. Bobby, thanks for inviting me. I hope you have an amazing birthday! You're like a brother to me!" She walked to him and hugged him.

"Aww… my sissy!" Bobby laughed.

Zacchya waved goodbye to everyone as she threw on her coat. She got into her 2002 Dodge Stratus and drove away, except she didn't drive home. She drove to the west side of town, past the city limits, to the cemetery and parked. She just needed some time alone to think. She kept the car running for music and the heat. It was quite cold, about twenty degrees, and she didn't want to freeze. She had just been so overwhelmed. She was angry at Trevor, for almost no reason, but she was beginning to hate him. It didn't make any sense to her. Trevor was her twin brother; she loved him. How could she just despise him so much that she couldn't stand to be around him? She was always mean to him, near disgusted when she spoke. It made no sense. She was also fighting every day to stay positive and get rid of her depression. Her anti-depressants helped some, but not enough. All she wanted was to feel normal again, to be the girl she was before Jacob died— happy, peaceful, loved to be around people and make them smile. That girl was dead, wasn't she? There didn't seem to be much hope for a full recovery. She suffered too much.

Her eyes caught on a stone angel in the cemetery, the moon glowing on it serenely. She loved angels; they made her feel peaceful inside. It was like someone was watching out for her. As she was distracted by the glowing angel, a car pulled behind her and stopped. She heard a light tap on the window that made her jump.

"Can you roll down the window?"

Zacchya said, as she rolled down the window, "Oh, gosh you scared me!"

"Sorry, ma'am. I just wanted to make sure you were okay. No one is supposed to be in the cemetery after dark." It was Officer Zac Reynolds. She remembered him as the cop that pulled her away from Jacob's casket.

Zacchya's cheeks flushed pink. "Oh, sorry! I…just needed some air."

"I understand. I won't give you a ticket. I was more concerned… I mean, about your safety," Zac stumbled.

"Oh… thanks. Just having one of those days." She sighed.

"We all do. I get off duty at midnight, in an hour, if you need a friendly ear. I'm quite a good listener."

"Really? I …"

"You look like you need a friend, that's all. There's a little diner that just opened, Café Bean, where the old Dairy Queen was. They have wonderful pie that fixes all your problems." Zac smiled at her. She found him to have such a sincere face and smile. She also found him to be quite attractive.

"Sure, that would be nice actually. Thanks." She smiled. She was glad it was dark and he couldn't see her blushing red cheeks.

"Good. See you in an hour. Bring an appetite, the pie really is amazing." Zac gave her another toothy grin, and then walked back to his car.

Zacchya was already feeling a bit better. She hadn't talked to Zac much before, but always sensed he was kind and genuine. He was one of the few people that didn't seem to judge her for the funeral or look at her like she was broken. She always appreciated that. No one wanted to be seen as damaged goods. She left the cemetery, deciding to cruise the empty streets listening to music. She had on The Killers album, *Battle Born*. She loved it so much. She sang along to the songs, trying to forget about her problems, as she waited for midnight. She was actually looking quite forward to meeting up with Zac. He was such a good looking guy, tall, sensitive eyes and muscular. She would have a hard time not getting a crush on him. It was weird to think of having a crush again, even if it never was anything more than that. The last guy she liked was Jacob. She wasn't sure if she was ready to move on, but maybe she was.

At midnight, she pulled into the diner. She went inside and ordered a French vanilla cappuccino. She texted her mom to tell her that she would be home later and was still okay. Hollie would worry about her if she didn't text at least. Zac showed up about ten minutes after her. He pulled off his coat, revealing a tight black T-shirt and jeans. Zacchya blushed as he waved, walking toward her table.

"Sorry I'm late. I ran home to change clothes." He smiled. He had the most wonderful toothy grin, wide and cheesy, that she already swooned for.

"No problem, I was quite enjoying my cappuccino." She smiled.

Zac looked at her in the eye when he spoke. She didn't know if he did that to everyone or just her, but it was like he looked into her soul. She felt her almost-crush growing. "Good. You know… I've been wanting to talk to you for a long time…" he said, still looking into her eyes.

"Oh?" She purposely took a drink to avoid his deep brown eyes.

"Yeah, I know you've been through a lot this past year. It can't have been easy. I know what that's like." Zac sighed. "My girlfriend, Rachel, committed suicide when she was eighteen. I was nineteen at the time."

"Oh no, that's awful!" She fought the urge to reach for his hand on the table.

"Yes it really was. It took a long, long time before I felt normal again. I still miss her. You never forget that pain. No matter what they tell you. You never forget," Zac said, his voice quiet and sweet.

"I can't see how anyone could forget. I really, really cared about Jacob. A part of me always will. It's hard to recover from that shock."

"Absolutely. That was three years ago and some days it feels brand new."

Zacchya leaned her hand onto the table towards him, he gently grabbed it. She felt so connected to him in that moment. There were no words to say what that small genuine touch had. She looked into his eyes; she knew he was feeling the same way.

"You two ready to order?" a short, curly haired waitress asked.

Their hands separated quickly, both replying, "Sure."

"I'll take a mocha and a slice of blueberry pie," Zac said.

"Blueberry sounds great, I'll take that too," Zacchya said.

"Okay, I'll be back in a jiffy." The waitress scribbled on her notepad and left.

"I'm impressed. Most people order apple or cherry." Zac smiled his adorable toothy grin.

"Well, I almost said lemon, but there is something special about a perfect piece of blueberry." She chuckled.

"Couldn't have said it better myself. So tell me about yourself, Zacchya. What's your plans after high school?"

"Oh... I don't know. I've always been drawn to music. I think it'd be the most amazing thing to help artists that are just starting out, like the ones that need to get signed to a record label. I do love making people's dreams come true. Is that cheesy?"

"No. No way. I wouldn't have gone into law enforcement, I would have been a drummer in a band. Music touches people in a way that nothing else can. Speaks without words, that's powerful stuff." Zac smiled.

The waitress brought their pies and they continued to talk about nothing and everything. It seemed as though they were destined to be friends. They had a lot in common and Zac was so easy to talk to. She'd never met a man she was so comfortable expressing herself to. And goodness, he was attractive. She knew her crush had started and would only grow. Every time he laughed, his brown eyes would almost disappear, and she found it so cute. He also had a wonderful, loud, infectious laugh. Everything he did just felt so sincere. People always hid themselves behind walls to stay safe from pain, but he wore it all outside. She respected that about him already.

It was almost 2:30 a.m. before they finally left the diner. They stood bundled up in coats and hats by her car.

"I had a great time tonight, Zac. Thank you."

"So did I. We need to do this more often. I think you're a great person, Zacchya. I really, really do." He stood close to her, barely a foot away. He wanted to kiss her, but didn't know if he should.

"Yes, that would be great," she said, staring into his eyes, nervous and excited. It had been an amazing night.

Zac turned to leave, but stopped in his tracks. He turned to face her again. "Um… can I… kiss you?" he asked shyly.

Zacchya's face was beet red. She wanted to kiss him all night. She never expected he would try though. She hoped he couldn't see the redness of her face under the yellow streetlight. "Yes," she said softly, looking at the ground nervously.

Zac lightly touched her chin, lifting her face, looking in her eyes, then gently leaned into her lips. Zacchya kissed him back, just as gently. His full lips felt wonderful to her. She forgot about everything except his lips and his strong arms wrapping around her waist. The cold December air was a memory for the moment they were together. When they finally pulled away, even then being a gentleman, they were both a bit breathless.

"Can I see you later? Before I go to work?" he asked, his hand still gently wrapped around her waist, his warm breath on her face.

"Yes, please," she replied quietly. She didn't feel like there was enough air to speak. Her heart was beating so fast, she was sure he would hear it.

He leaned into her again, his full lips so warm and gentle on hers. "I will definitely call you." He smiled again. "I really have to go. I'll call. Promise." He kissed her one last time and turned to leave.

As he walked to his car, he was overcome with but-terflies. He had almost forgotten what they had felt like; it had been so long. But Zacchya had something special about her. He could barely resist her. She was a few years younger than him, eighteen, but he didn't care. "When you find someone special, you grab a hold," his mom always told him. Zac drove home smiling the whole way. Maybe things were finally changing for him, and for Zacchya.

* * * *

Zac was awoken by the jarring sound of his telephone ringing.

"Hello?" He croaked sleepily.

"Wake the hell up, Reynolds! I need you at this office! NOW!" Captain Roark Williams shouted.

"Why? I'm asleep, sir."

"Because we have the autopsy report from Kansas City! And we need to make an arrest!"

"Trevor Packers and Bobby Woods…"

"Will you shut the hell up and get here already? Would I call to arrest the Packers boy? Don't be a fool, Reynolds. Be here in five minutes. NO JOKE!" Roark shouted at him and hung up.

Zac knew if Williams was pissed, then he better be there in five minutes. Williams was a good captain, but if he said it was serious, you better move your ass like it was on fire.

Zac jumped out of bed, hurriedly dressed and jumped in the car. The clock said 8:05. Thankfully there was no ice on the windshield to defrost. He made it to the station at 8:08, glad he only lived a short ten blocks away. Larned wasn't a very big town, really, and there was very little traffic. He was still rubbing his eyes, wishing he had gum for his morning breath, as he stepped into Williams' office.

"That was six minutes, Reynolds." Williams frowned.

"Car was cold, man. What's up?"

"Autopsy came in. Now, I'm the only one that looked at it so far. Called you the second I read it. It wasn't pretty, not at all."

"How do you mean? Internal bleeding?"

"You think I'd call you in FIVE HOURS early for internal bleeding?"

"Maybe…"

"Son, he was murdered." Williams stared at Zac waiting for a reaction.

"Murdered!? What?" Zac felt like he was still asleep.

"Did I stutter? M.U.R.D.E.R."

"But how?"

"Poisoned."

"What?" Zac swallowed hard. "How?"

"Same shit they use on death row. Some potassium chloride. Stops the heart dead."

"Shit… but he…" Zac stopped. He knew just what it all meant now. He understood why Williams woke him up.

"Ah, caught on, have you? That means the hospital did it. Only doctors have access to drugs, especially this shit."

"Who was the doctor?" Zac asked, afraid of the answer.

"Rumsfield, of course."

"Larry? Oh, shit. Did he do it?"

"Fucker had to! Why? No damned idea, but we're going to get his ass!" Williams grumbled.

"Yes, we are." Zac was furious. Larry was known to everyone in town. He had never been mean to anyone, so why would he kill Nick? It made no sense at all.

"I'm calling the judge for a search warrant of the hospital and his house. If he did it, he'll be in jail by tonight."

"Good. I don't want anyone to know until it's certain, especially Patty. This would kill her, man. " Zac sighed.

"Of course. But you ain't killing a cop on my fucking watch and getting away with it. Ooh, we're coming for you Larry." Williams snarled through his teeth. "You sick son of a bitch."

Chapter 19

November 25, 2014

BY TEN O'CLOCK IN THE morning, Williams, Reynolds, and a few other officers were at the Rumsfield house with a search warrant.

"Remember, leave nothing untouched. Larry is an extremely rich and well-connected man. If there's evidence we need every damn bit of it." Williams ordered as they walked to the front door. "Every damn bit!"

Larry was home and opened the door when they knocked.

"Oh hello, Captain Williams." Larry smiled.

"We are here with a warrant to search your premises."

"Excuse me? A warrant for what?" Larry exasperated, clutching a hand to his chest.

"Please, step aside Larry. We must search these premises." Williams waved the search warrant. "You're more than welcome to look at it, but we are coming in."

"I assure you, I'm innocent. Step in, search all that you wish. I have nothing to hide." Larry waved his arm to welcome them into his home. He knew that they would never find anything to incriminate him.

The team of police began to comb through Larry's large two-story house. It had two large bedrooms, two bathrooms, a study, a large kitchen, a small basement, and a living room. It would probably take most of the day to search it. And that didn't even cover the large two-car garage with all the vehicles in it. It was definitely a lot to search, and they'd be lucky to finish it in one day.

Another team was at the hospital checking records, files, and Larry's office. If they were lucky, they could find the evidence by the end of the day and get an arrest. But the sheer amount that they had to search, it was very unlikely to get an arrest in one day.

Zac had started searching upstairs in Larry's master bedroom. It was very large for a bedroom, about the size of a studio apartment, with a large walk in closet. He began rifling through the dresser first, pulling out socks and underwear, looking for hidden items. He then moved onto the bed, still finding nothing peculiar at all. Larry was a very clean man, so it made the search easy enough to go through the very organized room. It was almost too easy at times. Zac moved on to the large walk-in closet, seeing that half of it was empty. He knew that Larry had been through a divorce about two years ago. He either hadn't moved on from it, unable to fill the empty space, or maybe he simply didn't care enough to fill it. Zac had a feeling it was the latter.

While searching the closet, Zac found a black coat and a ski mask. It could have just been winter wear, as Kansas winters are very cold, but a gut feeling said to bag it for evidence. He grabbed an evidence bag from his belt pouch and stuffed them inside. Hopefully it would lead somewhere in this case.

As he was exiting the closet, he pulled out his cell phone and sent Zacchya a text message: "Sorry can't call today. Important work stuff. I can text you later though. Didn't want to be 'that guy'. LOL."

He didn't want it on his conscience, being the guy that promised to call, but never did. He was not that guy and hoped to never be. He decided to move on to the bookshelf that was built into one of the walls. He was in the middle of skimming a book when his pocket vibrated.

"It's okay, thanks for letting me know," she texted back.

His stomach flip-flopped at the sight of her name in print. He already had such a crush on her. She just had that spark that every man looked for in the right girl. Her blue eyes called to him. Maybe it was the way she twirled her long, blond hair around her fingers when she was nervous, or her soft giggle. Whatever it was, he liked her. And it scared him. He told himself to just go with it, but it had been over two years since he'd been in a relationship. The idea of jumping into another one caused him a bit of hesitation. She was a few years younger than him, still in high school, which kind of made him feel creepy. But she was eighteen, going to be nineteen in May, and he was twenty-two, so it wasn't that far off of an age gap. She was perfectly legal to date. Oh, to *date her*. Those words shook his core.

Romance was exciting, made you feel ridiculous and hopeful, but it also slowly broke down your protective walls. It made you feel so vulnerable. Was he ready for that? Was anyone ever ready for that? To slowly give your heart away was the scariest thing he could think of, and he faced danger as a cop, quite often. Knowing one day you could be shot and/or killed seemed way less scary, heroic even, than falling in love. He wasn't sure if he could do it. It was easier to hide behind the walls he'd built around himself to keep him protected. People couldn't always be trusted. He'd seen the scum of the earth with this job; people did awful horrible things to each other. How did he know that the next person he decided to care for, wouldn't do something awful to him? He didn't, no one did. That was the scariest thing he could think of. Take all the odds of the human race, which does nothing but turn on itself all the time, and believe that one person is different and beautiful, full of love and hope. Was he willing to take that chance on Zacchya? He'd done it once with Rachel, loved her so completely. But it wasn't enough then. She chose to end her life, focusing more on her pain than the hope of their future. But Zacchya seemed different than most girls, and maybe she was. It was a bit too soon to tell. He hoped that if Zacchya was the right girl for him, it would show itself in due time, so he wouldn't have to worry about it.

Or maybe you're being a girl, Zac. Focus on the job, dude, he thought to himself.

He went back to the search, checking every book, every page. There were at least a hundred books on the shelves to search through. Somewhere he would find the evidence he was looking for. He was too invested in this case, to not do everything he could. He would find what he was looking for. As he grabbed the book, *The Catcher in the Rye*, a note fell out and landed at his feet. He leaned down for it, hoping for a clue.

Dear Liz,

Oh how I think of you day and night. Your beauty has changed me more than any other experience I've had in this crazy life. I believe that all humans have the capability of light and dark. We all have seeds for evil planted in us, one way or another. Life throws us so many curve balls, and we must act accordingly. It's not always easy to pick the right path. I'm sure you remember all of our conversations on humanity and its choices. I love my long talks with you. But the day life threw you at me, I was near dumbfounded!

You know that I had a rough childhood, to say the least… but when I saw those eyes, those glorious hazel eyes, shimmering on that beautiful June day, I knew my life had changed forever. All the evil I faced as a child was over. A new leaflet in my story was to be written.

Oh the words you filled in my soul. You've touched my soul with your words, your heart, and your utterly complete beauty! No other event in this world could ever shape me the way you do. When I hold you, I know the meaning of love, of peace. You hold the sun in your eyes and it pushes out all of my darkness. Nothing will ever compare to you. Nothing, my love!

I wish I was there to kiss each one of the freckles that sprinkle your nose. I dream so much of those freckles. I dream of your lips, your touch, and the warmth of your body next to mine. I long to caress your cheek, brush your hair with my fingers; caress you in ways I can only imagine. You deserve only the best, my dear, Liz. If God exists, like you say, then he broke the mold when he made you! You make me want to believe in God. Because in you, I see all the goodness of this world. I see a life and a future and want to spend every moment with you.

I hope you love me as much as I love you! Oh, how I love you! You've torn down my walls, broken all my defenses. You give me strength. You give me hope. I need you, Liz. I've never needed anything as much as you.

Oh, hold this letter next to your heart and let it beat next to my words. Then, I will feel you, and you'll feel me beside you. We'll never be apart. I believe in forever. Forever, I will love you. Forever, I will need you. Take my hand, Liz, walk with me into that beautiful future. I don't know what it will hold for us. But I know that it's enough if I have you. I need you.

Don't write back. Don't call me. Run to me! Let me kiss you, hold you, take care of you! Please, Liz, let me stay with you always. Marry me.

Forever, Larry.

Zac stood dumbfounded, holding this very private love letter. Why would Larry keep it all of these years? There was no date on the letter, but the paper was yellowed and brittle with age. Whoever this Liz was, Larry had really loved her, a life changing love. But Larry never married a Liz; his ex-wife was Alberta. As he scratched his head, he was surprised to see Larry walking into the room.

"Sorry to interrupt you, I came for my coat." Larry said hastily, clearly not happy with the search of his belongings.

"Oh, go ahead. I'm done searching the closet there," Zac replied.

"Is that…" Larry's face went pale as he stared at the letter in Zac's hands. "Did you read it?"

"Yes, I had to… looking for clues and all," Zac replied.

"Oh… of course, yes. Well she never got the letter. It was meant to be a surprise. I had left town for a few weeks, and planned on being nearby when she read it. Then I would come out and propose." Larry's eyes glazed over with sadness. "But she broke it off with me after she met Edward. We stayed friends, of course. But she never knew I planned to propose. It's for the best, really."

"I'm sorry. I never… knew you were an item."

"Long time ago, a lifetime really. But love changes us, for the better or the worse. If you ever find a love that strong, that life-changing strong, you hold onto her. Never let her believe a better man exists than you. Be her prince, her white knight, whatever she wants. A woman's love will change your life. Don't ever lose it." Larry wiped one small tear from his left eye.

"If she comes, I hope I never lose her," Zac said quietly, feeling awkward talking to a man about love, whom he thought was a murderer.

"Good. Okay, I must be off. Work calls. I hope this silly search is over and done with by the time I return."

"No promises there."

"Of course, of course. Goodbye, then." Larry, with his gray pea coat draped over his arms, shuffled out the door.

Zac stood quietly, the note still in his hand, unsure of what to do or think. Larry confided in him something that was so private and deep. Why? He had no idea. But Larry's love for Liz Track had never died—he'd seen that. Zac wondered how anyone could hide a love that strong, convert it to friendship, and never crack. He would lose his mind hiding something so deep and powerful. Love was hard enough to feel, confusing and overwhelming, without it being returned. Zac felt a pang of sadness for Larry. That had to be a heavy burden to carry.

But he had to focus on the case. Larry was possibly a murderer, so Zac's sympathies would have to be put up far away. It wasn't the time or the place for it. As Larry walked to his black Jaguar, which they had already searched through, he kept a calm face. He wouldn't let anyone see a drop of guilt for anything. As he was almost positive they'd never find anything on him. He'd covered his tracks too well, made sure of it. Unless they found the entrance to his underground lab, which was very unlikely, he was safe. Maybe he'd been stupid to use such a traceable drug to kill Nick, but had only done that because he actually liked Nick. Nick's death was meant to be quick and painless, as it was. He didn't want Nick to suffer. It still came to him as such a shock that Patty had ordered an autopsy in the first place. Clearly Nick must have said something to her. She cared too much for him to let his "killers" go free. Larry wished he could just figure it out. It was ruining his plans for Trevor going to prison, and that was unacceptable. With the cops searching his place, he couldn't plant thoughts into Trevor with 33X. Otherwise he'd do just that and have Trevor confess to the murder. He would figure something out… he always did.

* * * *

November 25, 2014

Zacchya sat with the rest of The Misfits crew at lunch. Well not the entire Misfits crew, as Alicia was no longer hanging out with the group any more. Her break up with Trevor had caused too much awkward tension and she found herself spending time with her new boyfriend, Kevin. The last time they had all hung out together was Bobby's birthday party, then Alicia drifted away. She didn't answer their texts or anything. So The Misfits were one less person, but it was okay with them. If Alicia wanted out, she was free to walk away. Zacchya munched on a turkey sandwich as she talked to April.

"So I've only gotten a few texts so far. Maybe I read into it too much. You think?"

"It's hard to say. Guys are a weird breed of people!" April laughed.

"Too true!"

"If you bonded as much as you say, then maybe he really is just that busy!"

"Well he better be busy! Kiss me and then leave me hanging, ugh!"

"Gross! Gross!" Trevor said. "No boy, old or whatever, needs to be kissing my sister."

"Don't be a weirdo, Trevor," Zacchya said, rolling her eyes.

"How's it weird to imagine my sister Frenching some cop? That's just… sick!"

"Well I'm not a little girl, you know. Guys, cops or not, find me quite attractive." Zacchya smiled.

"She's right, bro. Zacchya's a dream woman… well not as good as my woman, that is." Bobby winked.

"Such a charmer." Trina rolled her eyes.

"Just tell me why he hasn't called, please! First guy I've liked since… you know… and he won't call!"

"Dude watches are different from girls, it's a completely different time table. Just give him a few days, he'll call," Bobby said.

"Definitely different! Those texts said he was sorry and he'd been busy. He doesn't seem to be the type to lie about it. Why would he text you at all, if that were the case?" April said.

"True. I just wish he'd tell me what's been so hectic. At least that!"

"Maybe he can't… confidentiality and all that jazz," Tim said.

"Wouldn't want my dirty laundry hanging all over the place." Bobby nodded.

"Definitely not, Bobby, your underwear is all streaky!" Trina winked at him.

"Ha. Ha. Ha. I can barely breathe from laughing," Bobby said as he rolled his eyes.

"Just give it another day or two. He will call." April smiled, avoiding the topic of underwear streaks.

They all laughed at the underwear joke that April avoided. The group continued laughing and talking. Zacchya smiled back at April. She was probably just over-thinking the whole situation, as girls do. It was difficult not to, when she liked him and wanted to get to know him better. She saw so many good qualities in Zac. She wanted to spend more time talking to him, kissing him, and just getting to know him. She didn't want to rush the future of the relationship, but he made her feel something she hadn't felt since Jacob. It was scary to feel that way again. In a way, she just wanted to know if it was real or just a phase. Her heart felt like it was cheating on Jacob, which was silly, of course. But sometimes love grabs a hold of you and not even death can rip it out of your heart. She had only been seventeen years old when they loved, but it didn't stop it from being real. Love doesn't know age, distance, life, or death. As hard as it would be, maybe it was time for her to move on finally. She'd held onto Jacob's memory for so long. She wasn't sure how to live a life where he wasn't constantly in her thoughts, in her heart. But all she could do was take one step at a time.

* * * *

Zac was tired. His normally coifed hair was a mess. There were puffy bags under his eyes. He wished deeply for more than three hours of sleep a night, but hadn't seen it in days. The search on Larry's house and office had been tedious and still ongoing. Captain Williams was not taking "no" for an answer. He knew Larry had killed Nick and would find the evidence to prove it, even if it killed him in the process. Zac had become obsessed with finding the truth as well. He had searched the house with a fine-toothed comb and found nothing. He was sitting at his desk at the station, combing over phone records for the past three months.

As he got to the records for the month of November, he noticed an odd pattern. One number had been called the night before Nick died. And then it was called the night of Nick's funeral over three times. It wasn't a local number and had an area code Zac had never seen before. There was only one thing to do about it, call it. He had to see who Larry would call before Nick died and then after the funeral. It was too fishy. Zac dialed the number, it rang.

"C&I Corp. How may I help you?" a cheerful female voice answered.

"Hello, This is Officer Zac Reynolds from the…"

Click. The line went dead.

Zac dialed again, thinking it was just a faulty signal dropping the call. The operator chimed in, "I'm sorry the number you dialed is no longer in service."

"No longer in service? But I just called two flipping seconds ago!" Zac muttered to himself in shock. He tried again and got the same message, no longer in service.

He decided to find another way to research the company. He Googled C&I Corp and found nothing on it. He Googled the phone number and found nothing, not even a link to a spam account. Something was definitely off. It only pushed him further in his quest for answers. He would go back to the house and look again. He was missing something; he knew that now. This mysterious call had proved that. Who had the power to make a number disappear in less than thirty seconds? Larry clearly knew people higher up than anyone realized. And he was clearly covering something up, dealing with this imaginary company, C&I Corp. He had to find the answer. If it killed him, he would find the evidence they needed to nail Larry to the floor.

He told Williams he was off again to search Larry's house one last time.

"Find something, Zac. We can't keep this warrant valid for much longer without evidence. The judge is already jumping my ass." Williams sighed, his mustache ruffling from his breath.

"I will. I can feel it, sir."

Zac drove across town to Larry's house. Larry was at the hospital, but they still had access to the house 24/7, but not for much longer. Zac stepped inside, shaking off the cold air and snow flurries. He had checked every room over the past two days. He wasn't sure where to start. Finally, he decided to start in the basement and work his way up. If he had to be there all night and day, that was fine. He was going to find the thing that was missing, the clue that was apparently well hidden.

The basement was surprisingly small for such a large house. It was furnished with an old couch, fridge, twenty-seven-inch TV, and another bookshelf. It was about twenty square feet total. He stared at the room, looking for any clue that he might have missed previously. He decided to start with the fridge, as the bookshelf would take the longest to re-search.

The fridge was mostly empty, except a few frozen dinners in the freezer, and a few beer bottles in the fridge. Zac let out a sigh and decided to check the bottles, in case one had something hidden inside. It seemed silly to check beer bottles, but when he grabbed the bottle nearest the back wall of the fridge, he heard a loud scraping sound nearby. Zac jumped, surprised by the sound, looked around the room to see where the sound came from. He noticed that there was now an opening in the wall to his left.

Zac was beyond surprised, flabbergasted really. He walked over to the wall and seen it was really a hidden doorway. He pushed it open, seeing a small hallway. His heart began to race. This is what he had been looking for. The answers he needed were there beyond that short five foot hallway. How did they miss that the first time? Who would have thought to even check inside a beer bottle, anyway?

He stepped through, grabbing the flashlight from his belt, to help navigate the dark concrete hallway. It was about five feet long, and then opened up into a much larger room, full of tables, medical equipment, and a lot more. Zac blinked, unsure of what to think. He let out a small chuckle. Only heroes and villains had secret lairs. Which one was Larry?

Zac walked a few feet, overwhelmed by the sheer amount of space he now had to search. Tables were full of medical equipment; it was like an entire laboratory! He noticed a metal door, a few feet from him that looked like the walk-in coolers he remembered from his high school days of working at McDonald's. He decided to start there. He pulled open the heavy, stainless steel door. A high pitched scream escaped from his throat.

Chapter 20

November 26, 2014

"Good evening, I'm Cindi Sims and this is your six o'clock news." Cindi smiled brightly at the camera, her white teeth sparkling against her red lipstick. Her blond hair was perfectly curled, not a single hair out of place. She was camera ready. "The small town of Larned, Kansas received a shock today as Dr. Larry Rumsfield was arrested on two counts of murder."

Trevor looked at the TV screen in shock. "WHAT?"

Zacchya and Hollie sat beside him on the couch, slack-jawed, saying nothing.

"After an intensive two-day search of Rumsfield's residence in Larned, on suspicion of murder, Officer Zac Reynolds found a body hidden in the basement."

"A body?" Hollie could barely even speak. How could her wonderful brother kill someone? And why on earth would he keep the body? Larry wouldn't do that. There was no way, not Larry!

"Larry's premises were being searched on suspicion of murder. Officer Nick Walker, who had been presumed to die from his injuries after a vicious beating last month, however, after an autopsy, it showed that Nick had in fact, been poisoned." Cindi looked sadly at the paper on her desk, shaking her head.

"This news has shocked an entire community. Larry Rumsfield was a well-known and respected doctor. He was also well known outside of Larned for his research with Alzheimer's and trying to find a cure.

"We have an official statement made today from Captain Roark Williams that I will play for you." Cindi nodded to the camera.

Roark Williams' speech began. He was standing in front of the police station in Larned.

"Today, we are saddened to announce that Larry Rumsfield has been arrested on two counts of murder. Larry was well known in this town for the good that he achieved. However, evidence has proved otherwise to his darker deeds. It comes as a shock to us all. The whole community will feel the effects of this news; I have no doubts. I hope that you respect the police force to do their jobs without interference. Also, please be respectful to his family members in this hard, trying time. Justice is not always easy, but it is always right. Thank you."

Cindi came back on the screen, her face somber. "There is no known identity of the body found in Rumsfield's basement. Any new information on this case will be heard here first, on KXBN."

"Turn it off, Mom," Zacchya spoke quietly. Hollie clicked off the television without a word.

"I don't believe it! I can't, man!" Trevor paced in front of the blackened screen. "I won't! There has to be some kind of explanation!"

"Trevor…"

"Zacchya! Seriously, there has to be! Larry wouldn't kill…"

"Stop, please," Zacchya begged.

"I just can't keep quiet. You heard her! Nick died and it wasn't my fault! What the hell does that mean? What does it mean?" Trevor's face was red with anger, confusion, happiness, sadness, and every other emotion he could think of.

"None of us know, Trevor. We're all in shock here. But please… he… he is my brother," Hollie said, tears leaking from her eyes.

"I'm sorry, Mom. I just…" Trevor walked over to her, putting his arms around her.

"I know me too," she cried into her son's shoulder.

"We've all had such a hard year. I just don't understand how this could happen. He wouldn't. I know he wouldn't." Trevor hugged his mom tighter.

Zacchya had run up to her bedroom upstairs. She threw herself on the bed. None of it made sense to her at all. She looked up to Larry so much. He had always been a good uncle to her, always there to talk to her. But some part of her was glad he was in jail. And that made no sense to her at all. She loved Larry, why would she want him in jail? Sadness and confusion overtook her. Would Larry really kill two people? Why would there be a dead body in his basement?

Something twitched in the back of her brain at the thought of his basement. She curled into the fetal position, holding herself tightly. She never wanted to even see pictures of that basement. She was petrified of it. But why? It made no sense to her at all. She was scared of a place she had never been. A bubble of fear erupted in her mind. Had she been there? She tried to calm herself down. She knew she was upset about Larry's arrest, but it didn't feel like sadness or anger. She was scared, truly scared.

Her phone vibrated next to her. She looked down at it, hoping for a distraction. It was from Zac.

"How are you? Did you hear about the arrest?"

She replied, "Yeah I did. I'm okay. Not sure how to feel about it."

"Captain gave me the night off. You want to talk about it?"

"I think I'd just like to be distracted from it."

"Can you leave?" he asked.

"Yeah."

"Be ready in ten."

Zacchya smiled, glad to have something to distract her from her overwhelming emotions. She ran to the bathroom, threw on some blush and mascara. She was one of the lucky few that was blessed with great skin and hair. She barely ever wore make up, and when she did it wasn't much. She ran downstairs, kissed her mom's head, saying, "Going out with Zac for a bit. I love you."

"Love you too, sweetie. Be careful. Don't stay out too late, you have school tomorrow," Hollie replied quiet and flat.

"I won't stay out too late. Are you sure it's okay I go? I don't want to leave you alone…" Zacchya asked, lightly touching her Mom's face. She felt bad leaving her mom at a time like that.

"It's fine. Sometimes the best thing is to distract yourself from the problem. Go out with Zac. He might help you cope." Hollie tried to force a smile, but it wasn't genuine.

"Okay, I love you. I'll be back later. If you need me, just call me." She kissed her mom's forehead and headed for the front door. She heard a soft car horn outside, so knew Zac was there. She grabbed her pink coat and headed outside. The air was bitterly cold when she stepped outside, and she wished she would have grabbed a scarf and hat. Her nose felt almost instantly frozen as she rushed to Zac's car.

"Wow! It's too cold out here!" she said, shivering as she buckled her seat belt.

"Yeah, the wind has a bite tonight. My goodness, you look so beautiful, even as a frozen popsicle." Zac's dark eyes gazed deeply into hers.

"Oh… thanks." She blushed.

"Any place you want to go?" he asked.

"Not really. I just don't want to think too much."

"I agree on that myself. I've had the worst few days myself," Zac replied quietly, "A distraction would be much welcome."

"Oh shit, Zac! I'm an asshole! You… oh my God… you found it… didn't you?" Zacchya shook her head, mad at herself. How could she forget Zac found the body?

"Oh, yeah I did. It was awful. That's why I have the night off. But let's not talk about it. Really, I don't want to. And you're not an asshole." He gave her a half smile. They drove around town listening to The Killers, which happened to be their favorite band.

"I love the Killers so much, so much!" she said with a smile.

"Me too! Who doesn't love 'Mr. Brightside'?" Zac smiled and turned it to that song. The two of them sang their hearts out. Zac was banging his fists on the steering wheel, making Zacchya laugh from how adorable he was. For a moment it was as if nothing bad had happened to either of them. The music overtook the moment and that was all there was.

Zac eventually pulled the car over at the park, but left the engine on to stay warm. He turned the music down, but still loud enough to hear but not be distracting.

"I know it sounds weird, but I missed you the past few days. I really did. Is that weird to say so soon?" He leaned toward her, holding her hands in his.

Zacchya swallowed hard. "No, not at all. I missed you too actually. I was afraid you didn't like me."

"No! How could I not like you? You're so beautiful, inside and out. I wanted to see you every day since that kiss. I couldn't get it out of my head."

"Kiss? I barely remember a kiss… how did it go, again?" She smirked and leaned into his soft lips. Her hands wrapped around him, memorizing his back, shoulders, and his amazing hair. Their lips stayed intertwined for quite some time. She never wanted the kiss to end.

*　*　*　*

Larry was in a cold six-by-six concrete cell. They thought he was too dangerous to share a cell with anyone else, so he was alone. There was nothing in the cell except an uncomfortable plastic mattress and a toilet. He was beyond furious with himself. He had let himself get caught. There was still so much work to be done! He never expected that young cop, Zac, would find anything at all, especially the entrance to his lab. It had been so well hidden. He longed to take that prick cop and smash his pretty face into a brick wall. If that asshole hadn't found his laboratory, there'd be no evidence at all. He'd be a free man, but oh no, he went and found Jennifer.

He remembered Jennifer very well. He had been on a business trip in Kansas City. After the boring meetings ended, he was feeling horny and went looking for an easy lay. He found a surprisingly sexy high-class hooker and took her back to his hotel room. Jennifer was a sexy blond, with perky enhanced breasts, and the most scrumptious ass he'd ever seen. He played her with for hours, getting all of his money's worth. Before he was ready to send her off, he realized she would be an excellent test subject for the drug he was working on.

He told her about an elaborate fantasy to fuck outside under a bridge where the homeless liked to hang out. He drove across town to the bad side of town, parked under a homeless infested bridge, and fucked her until she screamed. Their screams upset a homeless man who threw a beer bottle at them, which just made Larry laugh.

Once the homeless man had run off into the night, Larry knocked Jennifer unconscious. Her naked body slumped into his arms and he carried her light-framed body to the trunk of his car. He had a lot of fun with her, but still planned on killing her. He drove the five hours back to Larned, where he ended up playing with her for a few days. She was a great lay and fun to mess with. When he had his fill of her, he drowned her in a bathtub. He had plans for her, but the cops showed up the next day with the search warrant. He unfortunately never got to run any of the tests he wanted, so her death was a complete waste.

The memory of Jennifer was giving him an erection. He didn't want to be the guy that jacked off the first night in jail, though. He had a reputation in this town and was not ready to lose all of it in one day. He denied knowing how the body got into his refrigerated cooler, therefore refusing to identify her at all. Plus, he had no idea what her last name was, or if Jennifer was even her real name.

What he did know was that he'd been in this jail for over three hours and needed his phone call. His life's work depended on it. If the police found his files on 33X and the LZ Virus, he would never be able to perfect and finish them. He only recently had a successful trial of the LZ Virus. There were so many more tests to see how it worked, and if the effects would even last over time. Jail was the last place on earth he needed to be. He needed that phone call tremendously.

Larry saw an officer come toward his cell with his supper tray.

"Oh thank you, sir. I was wondering why I would be able to my phone call. I do believe I'm allowed one, correct?"

"Yeah you are. Even cop killers get a call. Eat your supper and I'll take you to the phone afterwards," the man snarled and slid the tray through the special flip down slot, the wicket they called it, that could open and then relock without having to open the door completely. It was a little bigger than the lunch tray he received.

"Thank you, sir." Larry smiled and took his tray. He quickly munched on the egg salad sandwich and potato chips. He wanted that phone call more than supper. Food wasn't on his list of important things at the moment, but he ate for appearances.

About fifteen minutes later, the officer returned to pick up his tray. "Okay, I'll be back to give you that call in a minute."

Larry smiled and began pacing his cell. He hoped it wasn't too late. The officer returned a few moments later, cuffed Larry using the wicket, and then unlocked the door. He was led down to a small empty room with a phone on the wall.

"You get ten minutes, make it fast," the officer said and then stepped outside the door, shutting it behind him. The door had a large window on it, so they could watch him but they couldn't hear his conversation.

Larry dialed the number, hoping again that he wasn't too late to fix the problem.

"C&I Corp, how may I help you?" a cheerful woman said.

"This is Larry Rumsfield, number 37834."

The line clicked once and a man with a deep voice answered. "Where are you Larry? I don't recognize this number."

"I don't have a lot of time, sir. I'm in jail. You have to get the data out of my lab."

"Do they know about the lab?" the man asked quickly.

"Yes, found it earlier this afternoon. It's all in one spot, separate from the 33X files. But those should be taken as well."

"Where are they?"

"Underneath the floor. There is a loose tile on the west side of the room. There's a hidden compartment with all the files."

"We will extract them tonight. Do you know if they continue to watch the house?"

"No, but I suspect they are, yes."

"It will be done. You have been a great service to us, Larry."

"I can do more for you, sir. I won't go to prison. Trust me, sir, I will finish the LZ Virus and perfect it. Don't give up on me just yet."

"I hope that is true as you've been a valuable asset. For now we must go further without you. Our analyst will read your data and go from there."

"Understood, sir," Larry replied.

"If anything changes in your status, please let us know immediately," the gruff-voiced man said.

"Of course, sir, thank you again. This isn't the end." Larry hung up the phone. He had done the only thing he could do at the time. The man, Larry didn't know his name, would fix it. The data and the files would be safe, and that was all that mattered.

When Larry returned to his cell, he lay down on his plastic twin mattress. His head was spinning. He had to get out of this jail and soon. The man wouldn't wait for him. He would just have to think of a plan to escape this jail. His only hope was to break out. It would have to be well thought out, something that no one could pin on him. There was too much against him, even without the files. Finding Jennifer's body was enough to send him to prison without a doubt.

Larry sat up quickly. He knew just what he had to do. Why hadn't he thought of it earlier? He had to fake his own death. It was the only thing that made sense. Fake his death, so he can finish his life's work and help the world. He thought he knew just the man that would help him achieve his goal, too.

Chapter 21

November 26, 2014

THREE MEN WERE SITTING INSIDE of a large moving van. They were sitting in the back, which was completely enclosed and full of surveillance equipment. The man in charge, a square-shouldered, muscular man, called "The Boss" was reading over his notes. It was near midnight and he hoped to be out of Kansas before 1:30 a.m. If everything worked accordingly, as it usually did, they would be on the plane in time.

"Like I said earlier, this is a cut and dry operation. We go in, get all the data on the LZ Virus and 33X, and we get out. Simple as that," the Boss growled at his team. He had a very commanding voice that sounded menacing, even if he wasn't trying for it to.

"Understandable, sir, but why the nicknames?" A]a slender dark haired man sitting beside him asked.

"We do not know if they are bugs. And that is not a chance I'm willing to take. So you are P3 and he is Q4," The Boss said pointing to an extremely large, dark skinned man.

"Such odd nicknames, sir…" P3 said.

"Two characters will make it hard for a pattern or code to be spotted. It's simple and to no point at all. It means nothing, so they will never suspect anything of it," The Boss said. He had been the leader to these men and quite a few others for many years.

"Q4, get to the front of the truck and take your shot," The Boss commanded.

"Yes, sir!" Q4 walked to the front of the moving truck ducking, as it was not tall enough for his six-foot-five frame. He reached the front, grabbing the large rifle lying on the seat. There was a cop car in front of Rumsfield's house, keeping watch for thieves or whatever else might appear. After someone was convicted or arrested for murder, people tended to vandalize or steal their belongings. People were not to be trusted.

Q4 set up the shot carefully, aiming at the officer's in the police car. The rifle was filled with special high-powered tranquilizer darts. The men would sleep for approximately twelve hours, depending on weight. Since it was such a powerful gun, the tranq-darts would break the car window on impact, so they would hit his target. The second man would be out before he could even pull out a gun. Q4 waited for the right moment and then pulled the trigger. The dart zoomed through the air, flying the twenty yards to the car. The glass of the window shattered, and hit the officer in the driver's seat. He was slumped over the steering wheel almost instantly. Q4 took the next shot before the passenger even realized his partner was unconscious. The men were fast asleep.

"It's done, sir," Q4 said, facing the back of the van.

"Great, let's move and quickly!" The Boss said. The three men pulled down their night vision goggles, and quietly exited the van. Larry lived on the west edge of Larned, and didn't have many neighbors; the furthest was a few blocks away. The men were quick and silent, heading to and entering the house. It wasn't their first break in and it wouldn't be the last. They walked quickly, in a straight line, to the basement. The entrance to the laboratory was open and they headed in.

"West side, look for the loose tile," The Boss ordered.

P3 headed to the west side. The floor was covered in large two-by-two square tiles. He checked each one that was by the west wall. P3 was never one to question a supervisor, but he wondered if the man's research was worth all the trouble. He knew what 33X did and it made him very nervous. In the wrong hands, too powerful of hands, it could bring more trouble to the world than it could help. If the wrong people had 33X, would anyone not be brainwashed? No person would be safe. It could be added to water supplies across the world. When he pictured it in his mind, he could only see destruction from it. Sure it could be used positively, but most people would rather control than help. He felt a shiver up his spine, wishing it would be destroyed instead of saved and protected. It belonged in the trashcan. He would never break an order, though. Plus, there was always a small chance that it wouldn't fall into the wrong hands. He trusted The Boss and who he worked for.

P3 finally found the loose tile, pried it open to find a metal box underneath the floor. He grabbed it, opened it and seen a large manila envelope on top labeled, "LZ Virus Data 2010-2014. CONFIDENTIAL." Inside the envelope were numerous papers and a few memory sticks. Still laying in the box was a small black case, about the size of an eyeglass case. P3 shuddered as he opened it. He had also heard rumors about the LZ Virus, and was glad it wasn't finished yet. He feared 33X and its possibilities, but that was nothing compared to the LZ Virus. He forced himself to focus on the job and not put his opinions into it. Inside the case were two small glass vials of a green liquid and another memory stick.

"I thought it wasn't finished?" P3 asked himself out loud.

"What?" The Boss asked, as he searched a nearby table.

"LZ Virus… I thought it wasn't finished." P3 held up the small green vials.

"It's not supposed to be!" The Boss huffed. "Be very careful with those! Clearly the analysts will have to read the data as soon as we get back!"

P3 gently put the vials back into the case and scooped the envelope out of the metal box. He pulled out a mesh bag from his pocket, placing all of the information inside.

"All done over here, sir," P3 said.

Q4 was in the cooler looking for evidence, but having no luck. He decided to go search in the small side room, which was apparently Larry's office. It had a computer, desk and video camera equipment. The video camera did not have the memory card inside, so that was a bust. He turned on the computer and did a quick search for any files that contained the characters "33X". He found one folder titled "Subject 2" and clicked on it. There were numerous folders inside of it: pictures, video files, and word documents. He pulled out a memory card from his jacket pocket and moved all of the files over. He was surprised the information on Subject 2 was so easily accessible. He searched more and found another folder "Subject 1" that he moved the contents over to the memory card as well. There were not near as many files on Subject 1. He had clearly put more time and effort into his second test subject. Q4 knew that Larry's niece was Subject 1, but he was unsure who the second subject was. He honestly didn't know much about the research, and he wanted to keep it that. It was easier to just do his job with the least amount of information.

He continued to search the computer for any more files, there were a few that he found and moved over to the memory card. He was glad that The Boss gave them 20GB memory cards, as there were a lot of video files that took up a lot of space. To be extra cautious, he searched for any files with "LZ Virus" as well. There were no files on the computer at all, except a video file address to an Elizabeth Track. He figured it was the search picking up the letters "L" and "Z" in her name, but moved it over to the memory card, just in case it was related.

"I think I'm good over here, sir. Plenty of files on 33X subjects," Q4 shouted out.

"Did you find any vials of it?" The Boss asked.

"No, I checked the cooler but with no luck. It must be hidden somewhere else."

"I'll check the cooler again, sir," P3 said as he walked toward it. "What's it supposed to look like?"

"Blue liquid. I've seen one of his test videos," The Boss replied.

"Blue, gotcha." P3 entered the walk-in cooler. It was full of random chemicals that apparently had to be refrigerated. P3 didn't know much about science. He gently moved items around, looking for anything hidden, being careful not to break any of the glass beakers.

After about ten minutes of searching, The Boss opened the walk-in cooler door. "Leave it. It's 0100 right now and we have to be back at the airport and in the air by 0130."

"The vials though…" P3 said.

"I'm sure there is a formula on the files that Q4 retrieved. We really must go." The Boss rushed. The men snuck out of the house as quietly as they entered. They were in the air and back to their home destination right on time.

Chapter 22

November 28, 2014

Captain Roark Williams and Zac Reynolds were in the car for the short drive to a nearby town, Rozel. Rozel had a population of only a few hundred people, but they only wanted to talk to one. To gather information on Larry's case, they needed to talk to his ex-wife, Alberta.

Alberta lived in a small two-bedroom white house. She had gotten plenty of money from the divorce, but she had used it wisely. She had never been much of a big spender anyway. She moved to Rozel after the divorce to be near her mother and aunt.

Zac and Roark reached the house, knocked, hoping that she would answer quickly. The December wind was biting cold.

"Hello? May I help you?" Alberta, a tall, slender brunette answered the door.

"We need to ask you a few questions about your ex-husband, Larry. May we come in, ma'am?" Roark asked politely.

"I figured as much. Yes, come in, that wind is terrible!" She hurried them in the doorway and found them a seat.

"Thank you, ma'am." Zac smiled as he was seated, glad to be out of the cold and in a warm house.

"No problem at all. I knew you'd be showing up soon enough. After I'd seen the news… well, of course you'd want to question the ex-wife." Alberta sighed and sat in a brown chair across from them.

"It's been a terrible circumstance all around. My name is Captain Roark Williams, and this is Zac Reynolds. We will be as quick and thorough as possible. We do not wish to intrude upon your privacy."

"Good I don't prefer to live down memory lane for too long." She spoke quietly, fidgeting with her fingernails.

"What kind of husband was Larry? Loving? Cold? Abusive?" Roark asked, his notepad in hand.

"Larry was charming and wonderful when we first got together. I met him after college, when he came back to Kansas from NYC. He was so smart and ruggedly handsome. He offered to buy me a drink one night and that was that. We were together all the time after that.

"Oh he was a romantic—always buying me flowers and presents. Made me feel like a princess, every girl's dream, really. It was great at first, so we got married about two years later. It was a big, beautiful wedding, a fairy tale." She paused, still fidgeting with her fingernails.

"Did it change after the wedding?" Zac asked.

"No, not right away. About a year after we were married, our… oh, heavens this is embarrassing!" Alberta blushed.

"If it's necessary, please tell us anything that could help. Don't feel embarrassed about it. We've heard some bad stuff…" Roark stated.

"Well, he started to get… violent in the bedroom. Asking to choke me or hit me. Things I didn't feel comfortable with at all. And the requests only got worse. He even asked if he could cut me. I obviously said no! I was repulsed!" Alberta stared at the ground, her cheeks still a shade of crimson. "And when I continually said no, he began to get abusive. Mostly yelling and belittling me at first. Then he'd hit me, always in places that could be covered up. Never hit my face, couldn't let anyone see what he did to me.

"I was just a small town girl that married a gorgeous man, what I had always dreamed of. I did everything I could to save that marriage, eventually caving to some of his perverse fantasies." Alberta's eyes misted with tears.

"I'm so sorry, ma'am," Zac said sincerely. He couldn't understand how a man could do that to a woman he loved.

"So he'd abuse me, often. And I'd hide it to save face. He'd threaten worse if I told anyone. I thought I was doing what I was supposed to, staying in my marriage. Divorce is a sin, right?"

"Not always, especially in that situation," Roark replied softly. Cases like that broke his heart. A woman should never have to stay with a man who abused her. A woman should be loved and supported, cared for gently, not abused. Yet so many women were ridiculed and abused, made to feel like nothing by a man. They would stay with that man who never loved them, never could love any woman, because it's their "womanly duty." It about made Roark sick to his stomach.

"Well about two years before the divorce, he changed. He worked constantly, always going out of town. And when he'd get back from work trips, he'd come later in the night. Then he'd spend all of his free time in the basement. He quit hitting me, quit talking to me. It was an empty loveless relationship. We became strangers, but I was okay with it. I didn't care what he did, just as long as he wasn't near me. By the time we divorced, we hadn't been intimate in over three years." Alberta sighed. It wasn't easy recalling her life with Larry, but it did feel necessary.

"Did he talk to you after the divorce? Or harass you at all?" Roark asked.

"No, not at all. He gave me a hefty chunk of his money and that was that. He had other plans, I guess. I was no longer his concern."

"Thank you, Alberta, you've been very helpful today." Roark smiled at her.

"Sure. Um… when he quit talking to me… was he… you know, hurting other women?" She asked, wanting and not wanting to know the answer.

"That I'm not sure on. But by the looks of the things we found in the basement, I would say yes. We only found one body. But I doubt it was his first, sadly. That's not fact; that's just my guess."

"Some people never know they married a monster. They go on blind-eyed and happy while their husbands kill women. But Larry was a monster to me, a villain for so long, that I'm nowhere near surprised by it. I'm just saddened that he hurt other people. I hoped I would be his last victim." Alberta wiped away a solitary tear from her cheek.

"In this job you hear about all the bad guys. Most of them are hiding in plain sight, blending in with the crowd. A lot of them are like Larry, well known and re-spected, even. But eventually, their deviancies come out. All dark eventually comes to light," Roark stated.

"Very true, sadly, very true." Alberta nodded. She smiled slightly at Roark. He seemed like a good, trusting man. She even found his balding head, bushy mustache, and large stature attractive. Maybe it was because he was nothing like Larry at all. She'd had enough of the typically handsome men; they weren't to be trusted.

"Well thank you for your cooperation. You've been so helpful." Zac stood and shook her hand.

"And we promise, Larry will never leave his jail cell… unless he's headed to prison." Roark nodded toward her, shaking her hand.

"Thank you, I'm glad you caught him and stopped him. You've probably saved a lot of lives." Alberta smiled as she led them to the front door.

Roark and Zac snapped their coats and headed toward the car. As they were letting the engine warm back up, Roark looked at Zac and sighed.

"It really sucks, doesn't it?" Zac said.

"Yeah. No one deserves that shit. We have to make sure that asshole rots in prison."

"Definitely." Zac nodded.

"Alberta seems like a great woman… we have to make sure there's no more victims at the hands of Larry," Roark grumbled. There was something so sweet and likeable about Alberta. He knew a lot of women that were abused like her and it bothered him so deeply. He didn't want another good woman to fall victim to a senseless asshole.

"Yes, definitely. Let him rot in pieces, the stupid bastard." Zac rolled his eyes and drove off.

* * * *

Larry was sitting in a small plain white room. There was nothing in the room at all except a wooden table and some chairs. There were no pictures on the walls, nothing to add personality at all. The only significant feature, besides the table and chairs, was the window on the door, so the officers could occasionally check in on him. He was waiting on a visit from his lawyer, and all lawyer visits were confidential, of course. Larry had a lot of money—millions in his bank account—and could have chosen any lawyer he wanted. But he only wanted one. There was only one man that would do the job correctly for him. He had no intentions of staying in jail, let alone going to prison. His work was too important for him to stay locked up like an animal.

The door finally opened and in stepped a handsome, dark haired man in an expensive suit.

"John! How lovely to see you!" Larry smiled.

"Yes, and you too. I was surprised that you called me." John Woods smiled politely and sat down in a chair across from Larry. He pulled out a leather briefcase and laid it on the table.

"Of course you're the one I'd call! You're the best defense lawyer in the area. And how long have we known each other? Ten to twenty years?"

"Eighteen actually, you helped birth Bobby." John nodded.

"Oh yes, Bobby… how is the boy?"

"Same. Moved out, thank God. I couldn't take much more of him to be honest. Always been a bit of a menace." John shrugged.

"Yes, my nephew Trevor is a bad seed as well. I think they are friends actually," Larry stated.

"Yes, they are." John rolled his eyes.

"But we didn't call this meeting for chit chat about troubled youth, now did we?" Larry smiled.

"No, your case, Larry…"

"Sshh… the case looks hopeless. Unless there is a technicality, I'm looking at severe prison time," Larry said matter-of-factly.

"Yes you definitely are. What WERE you thinking?" John sighed.

"Don't you worry about my thought processes… there is more than one reason I asked for you, John."

"Aaahh, I see…what more?" John's eyebrows raised.

"If you can't find that precious technicality, John…. you're going to help me escape," Larry said flatly.

"Excuse me?" John gasped.

"Oh, please let's not pretend you have grown morals, John! You're as ruthless and determined as I am! It's why we've always gotten along so well!"

John didn't reply, but glared intently at Larry.

"I'm an extremely rich man, John. I could get you anything you want. New job in NYC? Got it. House on an island? You got it. Whores every night, which I know you love? You got it. Ask for it and it's yours!" Larry smiled.

John sat quietly for a moment, pondering all of his options.

"Anything you want, John. Anything at all, you just have to ask!"

"There is a little something I've wanted… I think you could help me with. Plus the money and the new job sounds great, I won't lie." John scratched his chin, deep in thought.

"What else?" Larry licked his lips. He had John just where he wanted him, in the palm of his hand. Freedom was so close, it was breathing on his neck.

"I want… to kill someone," John whispered, leaning across the table. "It's the thing I miss the most about the military."

"Now that's more like it! Glad to have you on board!" Larry leaned over the table, looking into John's eyes. "You can definitely have that. Oh, yes, you can."

"But how?"

"We're going to blow this place the fuck up!" Larry smiled wide, his teeth gleaming in the fluorescent lights.

"And you're sneaking out while it burns, I take it?" John smiled.

"Of course! The correct placement of explosives, I live. I escape, this place burns crispy. You get to kill. I get to be free. You can get your job, money, whores, or whatever." Larry sneered.

"Yes, absolutely, yes. It will take some time to plan of course." John smiled wide.

"Of course, of course!"

"It will take some time to get in with the officers who can be bought. Well, most of them can be bought, actually… but it can be done. It will be done. Then just make sure I have the explosives at the right time."

"Good. Good. Nothing I love more than a good fire, you know?" Larry smiled. "Make some s'mores while the destruction falls all around you. Sounds fucking splendid!"

"Can't agree more." John winked. "Fucking splendid."

Chapter 23

November 30, 2014

Liz's eyes were glazed, staring at a word on the newspaper in front of her. She wasn't sure how long she'd been staring at the word "arrested," but she couldn't move. In a moment, her whole life had changed. Her best friend and ex-lover was arrested for murder. She had been so busy with Marcus the past few days, that this was the first she'd seen of Larry's arrest. She had no way to understand it or believe it.

Larry was one of the most kind and giving people she'd ever met. He was always helping the less fortunate, giving generously of his time and resources. He couldn't be capable of murder, could he? She just didn't believe it.

All she could remember were happier times. She saw a flash of when they dated in high school, and he serenaded her under the stars. He was there for the birth of Jacob and Marcus. He even helped Edward get the job at the bank. She remembered Larry taking Jacob to his first water park, laughing and smiling as they went down a large water slide. Jacob always loved his "Uncle" Larry.

She'd never forget all the laughter and good times they had shared over the years. Larry was there in pieces across her life, a jigsaw puzzle that wasn't complete without him. He had never once shown anger or violence toward her or her family. He was loved and respected. It didn't make sense.

Edward walked into the kitchen, seeing Liz's eyes locked on the newspaper, unmoving. He slipped her hand around her waist to comfort her.

"Oh, you scared me!" She jumped.

"Sorry. You just looked like a lost puppy. I wish I knew how to make it all better." Edward frowned.

"Tell me it isn't true, Ed."

Edward leaned down and softly kissed her forehead. "I wish I could do that. Larry's been a friend to us for years. It just plain sucks."

"Yes, it does. How did we become the people that never knew their friend was a … oh, God…" she cried.

"I don't know how that happened. It's not like we have some horrible scum detector. We know what's right and wrong. And Larry was good to us, all the time…"

"Yes one of the best guys I ever knew... well besides you, of course."

"Of course!" Edward winked, lightly flipping his blond hair.

"Should we go visit him? I just… want answers." She sighed.

"I don't know if it's a particularly good idea, sweetheart. If he confesses to you why he did… whatever he did, could you handle it? It would mean that everything he lived could be a lie. No friendship can last through that mistrust. I know you, Liz, you'd never forgive him, and you're the most forgiving woman I know," Edward said as his arm was wrapped comfortingly around her shoulders.

"I know… I just want answers. How could he kill Nick? He was here helping me with Marcus the day after Nick was beaten. He was very upset about it, like, genuinely upset. He was always so damn sincere!" Liz was so frustrated. She wanted to throw her fists into a wall, but she wouldn't. It wouldn't fix anything. It was just beyond her comprehension to understand how Larry could kill Nick, someone he considered a friend.

"We don't always get the answers we want. And then sometimes, we get the answers and wish we wouldn't have," Edward stated.

"True." She sighed.

"I know I never said it before, but I always wondered about him. Not like thinking he would kill someone… but he always seemed too perfect. Deep in my mind there was a red flag, but I chose to ignore it. Felt like giving him the benefit of the doubt. Chose to see him for his actions, not what I felt," Edward explained.

"Really?"

"Yeah, I never told you before because I know how close of friends you were. I didn't want to upset you."

"Hmm….I would have never believed you, anyway. He was too good to me for so long."

"Exactly." Edward went and grabbed a cup of coffee from the counter. He was so distraught to see his wife in pain. It was hard to trust someone for so long and find out that you were wrong. He wished he knew what Larry had done, but was truly afraid to ask. There unfortunately wasn't a book titled *How to Understand and Cope When Your Friend Turns into a Murderer.*

As he sat down beside her at the kitchen table, bringing her a coffee as well, he knew that they would find a way to make it through the ordeal. They always found a way to cope with troubles, even when it didn't seem like they could. But he hoped that they didn't have to go visit Larry in jail. He knew Liz couldn't handle the environment. She was tough, yes, but it would be too much for her. She was too trusting and loving to cope with her best friend admitting he murdered someone.

* * * *

December 4, 2014

John was happily soaking in his bubble bath. He had been so busy the past few weeks reading over Larry's case files and simultaneously trying to get everything he'd need to help Larry escape. He was almost positive there'd be no loopholes to get Larry out legally. The only real hope was the escape plan.

He had made numerous phone calls to his contacts and had a bit of luck. He knew a man in New York that could get him C4 blocks without raising any warning flags. John had contemplated using homemade bombs, but it was a bit risky. Most bombers had a signature style, using specific techniques to achieve their goals. Certain items could be traced and he couldn't have that. He did not plan on being in the U.S. much longer after the explosion. He would stay long enough to make sure there were no suspicions raised from his involvement. Then he planned on taking a long, quiet trip to an island he hadn't picked yet.

Oh, just thinking of the white sandy beaches, busty tan women, and overflowing alcoholic drinks gave him a bit of a boner. He began touching and caressing himself to relieve his sexual tensions. He couldn't wait to leach off of Larry's influences. All he had to do was sit back and demand whatever he wanted. And he wanted a lot. He daydreamed of busty, topless women until his tensions were relieved. The warm bubbly water calmed him immensely, and he was soon asleep.John was awoken suddenly by the fact that he couldn't breathe. His head was being pushed under water by strong hands around his throat. He kicked his legs, flailed his arms to try and break free. The hands however stayed firmly around his throat. He never expected to die in a bathtub. Honestly, he never saw himself dying at all, always thought of himself as invincible. He wasn't a weak man and didn't plan on going out like that. He quickly decided to not panic, but fight back. He brought his hands up to his attackers, using all the force he could muster to pry the fingers away from his throat. John was feeling very light headed as his oxygen decreased, but he continued to claw and pull at his attacker.

Without any warning, the attacker's hands released John's throat. He began coughing and gasping for air, as he broke the water's surface.

"Oh, we have a fighter here, boys." A deep-voiced man laughed.

"Who?" John asked between coughs, trying to see who his attacker was, but his vision was blurry and the room was quite dim.

"Help him out of the bath, please." The gruff-voiced man pointed to a slender, muscular man next to him. They pulled John out of the tub, plopping him carelessly on the tile floor. John sat naked and dripping wet, still trying to catch his breath.

"Do not get water on my boots, John," the man sneered, stepping away.

"Why… did you try to kill me?" John asked the man, his breath slowly returning to normal. His defenses were up, watching this large man with as much precision as he could. The man was dressed in dark colors, possibly black, but the room was dim and full of shadows. John guessed it was after sunset. It was hard to get a clear description of his face. The man was large, over six feet, broad shouldered, heavy but not from fat. The man was built well, definitely all muscle.

"Please get dressed and meet me in your sitting room. Hurry, we have much to discuss," the man said and then exited the bathroom with his companions.

John grabbed a nearby cotton towel, dried himself, and then grabbed the clothes he brought with him earlier. He changed quickly, still not sure what to think about the whole situation. He wished his handgun wasn't on the opposite side of the house. If he lived through the ordeal, he planned on putting a gun in every room.

John's pure curiosity and needing answers drove him to his own living room where the men awaited him.

"Please have a seat, John," the large man said. John was not happy about being offered a seat in his own house, but he sat in the chair opposite them.

"What's this all about?" John asked.

"I do apologize for the choking incident. It was a mere test to see if you are indeed the man we need. I think that you are."

"A test? What the hell kind of test is that?" John was furious, his face reddening with anger. He could still feel where the fingers were grasped around his throat. What a terrible test that was.

"The man we're looking for must be strong willed, determined, smart, and sure. We feel you live up to those qualifications. With your legal prowess, military experience, and your clear determination to live, we find you worthy." The man nodded.

"Worthy of what?" John asked, staring intently into the man's dark eyes.

"Perhaps you'd prefer a bit more information," the man said, gazing strongly back into John's eyes. "My name is Magnus Cain. Most everyone calls me The Boss, however. I am in charge of these fine fellows here. We supply Larry with certain equipment and items necessary for his… side work."

"The Boss? What is this, the mob?" John fought the urge to laugh. He would've laughed if the man hadn't just tried to drown him in a bathtub.

The muscular black man to Magnus' right stood up, looking extremely angry. "How dare you!" he spat.

"Sit down, Tyrell. It was just a dumb question." Magnus said calmly, lightly touching Tyrell's hand. "We are not the mob. The mob is a disgusting mess of hoodlums in shiny cars and fancy clothes. We are much, much more than that. But I prefer not to give all the details on what we are just yet. Just know that we have power on our side and we use it well."

"Alright… so why do you want me? What use am I?"

"It's quite simple, really. Larry, as you know, is in jail. After a correspondence with him early last week, we know that you plan on helping him escape."

John was flabbergasted. "Uh…" He couldn't imagine why Larry would tell anyone of their plans.

"There's no need to lie to us, we know it's true. Truth from you would be best."

"Yes, it's true." John swallowed hard.

"We have numerous connections that can help this endeavor. We would like to help. Larry is… not always the best choice morally, but his mind is far beyond most men. We need his help for certain… oh, let's just call them, resources. I'm afraid I can't divulge more than that. But we need him. He is very important to us and what we work for. Because of that, we are willing to look past his moral flaws for the time being."

"I see…"

"We are willing to help you in any way possible. If you need explosives, that can be arranged. If you need Larry's dental records changed with a random cadaver's, it can be done. We are full of resources. We'd prefer to do this with as few casualties as possible, though. But we are more than willing to help you, John," Magnus stated.

John sat quietly for a moment, thinking. He had no idea who these men were, or who they worked for. But he could imagine if they could do all they claimed to, that he wasn't safe. Powerful men were not safe men. Most would slit your throat if it would help them succeed. If they wanted Larry out of jail that bad, after all he'd done… it didn't sit comfortably with John. John wasn't always straight morally, but something was dark here, and he couldn't help but see it.

"So what do you want from me, then? It quite sounds like you could easily do it alone."

"Honestly, we could. But we prefer to fly under the radar. The operations we work are extremely confidential. Our involvement must not be known, ever. We need you to do the dirty work, so to speak. Ask of us what you will, but you are the one that will play it out."

"You want me to be the fall guy, then? The guy that gets caught and takes the blame?" John asked accusingly.

"I prefer you do not get caught, no. But it is a possibility, of course." Magnus shook his head. "But you will not decline, of that much I'm sure."

"Oh, you're sure, huh?"

"Yes, I am, John. Because know this, if it's not you that helps us… we will replace you… by any means necessary." Magnus' eyes darkened. John could see exactly what he meant. If he didn't help them, he'd end up dead. He was a pawn they wished to play with. But pawns are completely replaceable. But Magnus was right… John would never refuse. He longed for the payout, plus valued his life too much. He would play along with them to get what he needed. It was his only option, anyway.

"I have a few ideas… Do you mind if I share them with you?" John smiled.

"Of course…I knew you'd be the right man for the job," Magnus sneered, leaning in closer to hear John's plans.

Chapter 24

APRIL WAS SCARED; HER HEART was near beating out of her chest. Her hands and feet, tied to a chair, were rubbing raw. She wasn't focused on the pain, however. Her thoughts were focused on the fact that Tim had a knife held to his throat. It was all of her fault. Tim wouldn't die if she would just stop it. She screamed for it stop. She couldn't sit there and let Tim die. She'd do anything in the world to stop it. She could feel the arteries in her neck pumping, each beat telling her to save Tim. She had to stop it.

Darkness.

She was strapped down to a chair again. But this time she wasn't scared. She was feeling surprisingly clear headed and fearless. There was a soft, warm buzz in her head that comforted her. It was like being drunk, but without the desire to burst out laughing. She didn't even mind the ropes around her arms and legs. It would be okay. Everything would be okay. She felt like smiling, but didn't. He wouldn't be mad at her for feeling peaceful, quite the contrary, but she didn't like the man. She didn't like him at all. She didn't feel scared of him anymore, but she didn't want him happy, either.

She looked around the room for Tim, but he wasn't there. The man must not have woken him yet. She sighed. It was always better when Tim was there. She loved him so much it was nearly overwhelming.

The man finally pulled a chair to the side of her. He smiled, unmasked this time, trying his best to look charming. He always looked charming, not like the creep he really was. He had switched on a video camera in front of them. He liked to video tape her.

"What do you remember about Vegas, April?" the man asked, still smiling ear to ear. April woke up in a cold sweat. For a moment she thought she had gotten the flu and was trying to sleep off the fever. But that wasn't the case. She had gone about a perfectly ordinary day, and then fell asleep next to Tim, like she always did. But then the nightmares came. She'd had a few recently, always the same or similar. They were always of her and Tim kidnapped and tied to a chair. She had never in her life been kidnapped or tied to a chair, so they made no sense to her. The fear that came along with them was very real, however. She'd wake up sweating, heart pounding, head swirling in fear. She'd grasp for reality, anything to tell her that the dreams weren't real.

Tim lay sleeping quietly next to her. She longed to squeeze onto his warmth, his safety, and forget about her bad dreams. She didn't want to wake and bother him, though. The clock read 2:15 in the morning and they both had school in the morning. She didn't want to burden him because of a nightmare. It was stupid really; she was overreacting. Dreams were just some part of her subconscious giving supposed clues to what she thought, or needed in life. Maybe she secretly felt trapped. No, that wasn't it. She loved her life with Tim. Patty was supportive and grateful for them staying with her.

Maybe she felt like someone in her life wished her harm. But that was laughable as well. No one wanted to hurt her. She had good friends and family. She had had a little trouble forgiving Trevor and Bobby for injuring her father, though. But the truth about his death came to light, and she couldn't blame them anymore.

But she did miss her dad, a lot. She found it easier to pretend his death wasn't real. Denial was a stage of the grieving process, and she quite liked it there. To her, Nick, was out of town for a while. He'd be back eventually…

April tossed and turned, trying to get comfortable again, hoping to gently doze off. But she knew that sleep would probably not come. Tears slowly formed in her brown eyes. She was being stupid, having a dream scare her that much. She rolled over, wrapping her arms around Tim's chest. He was warm, actually sweating. But she didn't mind. She loved the smell of him, sweat and all. She cuddled closer to him, nuzzling her head into his neck. His presence calmed her immensely. She could feel her body getting lighter, almost ready to fall asleep.

"April?" Tim whispered next to her.

"You're awake?"

"Yeah... bad dream." He sighed.

"Me too actually." She faced him, seeing that even in the dim light, he looked just as scared and sad as she felt.

"I've had one like it before...last night, actually. It's so damn scary." Tim shuddered.

April hugged him close, kissing his neck. "Mine too. What's yours about? Do you want to talk about it?"

"It's stupid... I'm being stupid."

"Oh, tell me, please."

"Well... we were kidnapped, tied to a chair..."

"What?" April sat up suddenly.

"We were tied to a chair..."

"Are you making this up right now?" She frowned angrily at him.

"Why on earth would I make this up? Those dreams about scare me to death!" Tim looked at her, offended.

"I'm sorry. I'm sorry... I have the same dreams, Tim."

"You do? How?"

"No idea. But he's always threatening to kill you and I can't handle it. I just can't!" She tried to fight the tears welling in her eyes.

Tim hugged her close. "In mine I watch him kill you. It's... awful. The worst." Tim sobbed into her shoulder.

"Oh, God, I'm so sorry!" She squeezed him tighter, wishing to relieve all his pain.

"What do you think it means?"

"No idea, but I hate it!"

"It's weird that we're dreaming about the same stuff, though."

"Yeah but it never happened. Clearly I think we'd remember that!" She smirked.

"Clearly! Did you ever see his face in the dream? In mine he was wearing a black ski mask."

"He's not wearing anything in mine, but..." She scratched her head, trying to remember.

"What? You can't remember?"

April's mouth fell open. "No... I do. I do remember."

"Who?"

"It was Larry! What in the..."

"Well that makes perfect sense, though!" Tim replied, smiling.

"It does?"

"Yes! He's a monster right? Of course you'd see him as the bad guy! I bet the reason we're having these dreams in the first place is us trying to make sense of all the bad he's done. It's all come to light that he did some really bad things… our subconscious is just trying to give us answers." Tim nodded, happy with his hypothesis.

"That makes a lot of sense, actually." April smiled. It was nice to have some kind of answer instead of just the fear. Now maybe she could face the dreams head on for what they were.

"See, just dreams playing tricks on us. That's all it is."

"Thank God for that!" April smiled, leaning over to kiss her smart, wonderful husband.

* * * *

December 31, 2014

Zacchya and Zac had been seeing a lot of each other, when time allowed, of course. School was off for Christmas break, so she had plenty of free time. Zac would use any days off he had to spend with her as well. They had made their relationship official on December 12 and were growing closer all the time. She spent Christmas Eve at his parents' house. She found his parents to be loving and sweet. They welcomed her graciously, which was nice because of all the stories of her Uncle Larry floating around. Not to mention her own sketchy past as well. But they welcomed her flaws and all, told her to visit any time. She was quite fond of them already.

Zac ended up coming to Christmas at her house. Hollie and Trevor were both very pleasant, not holding it against Zac for being the one that put their brother/uncle in jail. Both understood that Larry had committed the crimes and had to pay for it. Plus, Hollie found Zac to be handsome and charming. He seemed to be very good for Zacchya. She couldn't help but be happy for her, when she saw the way Zacchya's face lit up in Zac's presence.

Zacchya and Trevor's relationship was healing as well. She no longer harbored deep feeling of anger or dislike toward him. They were back to being best buds and siblings. Trevor liked Zac, even though he thought he was a bit old for his sister, but he let it slide. He was just happy that she was happy again, that was all that mattered. He loved his sister and wanted the best for her.

He secretly wished that life hadn't taken the turns it had. He always thought that Zacchya and Jacob were perfect for each other. When they were together, the world seemed lighter, more beautiful. But life never seemed to work out the way anyone wanted or planned. Jacob was unfortunately murdered, and she had to find a new place. Trevor hoped that Zac would treat her as well as she deserved and needed.

Christmas was a good occasion for everyone. For at least one day, people forgot about their selfishness and focused on loving others. Trevor wished people would do that all the time, but it never did work out that way. At least they had one good day of the year. He tried to focus on his family and friends instead of his loneliness.

Before the break, school was getting difficult for him. Not from the schoolwork, but from Alicia. She hadn't hung out with The Misfits since Bobby's birthday party. She was constantly hand in hand or mouth to mouth, with her new boyfriend, Kevin. Trevor tried to play it cool, like it didn't bother him, but he was torn up about it. He had really fallen for Alicia, and then she dropped him like a bad habit. She refused to talk to him anymore, too. That made the sting of it all even worse. He had hoped to salvage a friendship, at least, but she chose otherwise. She had Kevin now, which was apparently enough for her. Trevor's heart just silently broke. He fought his loneliness in silence. He didn't want anyone to know that he missed having a girlfriend. He was supposed to be a strong man, a football player, not an emotional sap.

It didn't help the situation that high school students loved to focus everything on relationships. If you were single, you were usually pegged as a loser or a player, and he was neither. A few girls tried to get his attention, but nothing caught his eye. He was trying to not end up with a girl that only wanted him for his looks or the fact he was on the football team. He knew that most girls his age found him attractive with his shaggy blond hair, bright green eyes, and freckled nose. But he didn't want a girlfriend just to have one. He was trying to not be shallow and pick only a "hot" girl. He'd rather be alone than settling for something because he was lonely.

Some days his teenage hormones begged of him to find the first girl that smiled at him and jump her bones. But he always found a way to control himself, thankfully. He had lost his virginity to Alicia, and wasn't quite ready for another sexual experience with anyone else yet. It was New Year's Eve and he was feeling quite lonely. He went over to Bobby's place to hang with the crew for a bit. Trina, April, and Tim were there as well. They watched some movies, pigged out on food, and even had a few beers that Bobby used a fake ID to get. But none of them got drunk. Trevor still had to drive home after the party and wasn't one to be irresponsible enough to drive drunk. Plus if his mom smelled alcohol on him, he'd be dead by the morning. He was feeling a bit like the fifth wheel partying with nothing but couples, but he tried to not let it bother him. Bobby jokingly offered to kiss him at midnight.

"Just a little smooch, Trevor. I'll try my hardest not to slip you the tongue!" Bobby laughed.

"Oh, man I was hoping you WOULD slip me the tongue." Trevor winked.

"Trina, I'm afraid I'm going to be bisexual tonight…" Bobby pumped his fists in the air, laughing.

"Well Trevor can enjoy your sloppy kisses then. Thank God I'm off the hook tonight!" She winked, flipping her blond hair.

"Want me to kiss you too, Trevor?" Tim asked.

"It's been a lifelong goal to get kissed by a soulless ginger!"

"Isn't it everyone's life goal?" Tim chuckled.

They continued to laugh and joke, talking about their hopes for the rest of the school year. They were less than six months from graduation. It was a scary and exciting thought to know they were almost free to be responsible adults. Soon they'd be filling out college applications and thinking about what to do with the future.

As the clock counted down to midnight, Trevor hoped that 2015 would be better than 2014. He hoped for less drama, more hope, and that Jacob would find peace and eventually pass on. It was weird to him that no matter what they did, Jacob was there in the background. He was an unspoken past, a truth they didn't want to face. Trevor wanted nothing more than to have Jacob find peace and move on. He didn't deserve what he had become. It was hard for all of The Misfits to find their place, when their past leader was undead and at unrest. He knew Trina and Alicia both would never forget their injuries from their encounter with Jacob, even though the memories were still foggy and unclear.

The clock struck midnight and Bobby leaned over jokingly to kiss Trevor. Trevor laughed and pushed him away. So he was alone on New Years, so what. There was a brand new year ahead of him. New possibilities were just lying around the corner, waiting to be picked up. Maybe the perfect girl was hiding there for him in 2015... he could only wait and see.

* * * *

Zacchya was beyond happy. She hadn't felt depressed in weeks, but that wasn't the only reason. She was on a date with Zac. They went out for a romantic dinner in Wichita. She ordered crab legs and tiramisu, her favorites. Zac decided on steak and potatoes with tiramisu, as well, for dessert. He looked into her eyes, so sweet and lovingly, that she barely wanted to eat. After supper, they drove back to Larned. They talked about everything and nothing, sang songs along with the radio, dancing like fools. It was a wonderful night that she didn't want to end. She couldn't believe it was a page out of her own life. It felt more like a dream. They parked on an old, dirt road, kissing and touching each other, the car fogging up with their warm breath.

Zac finally pulled away, catching his breath. His short brown hair was messy from her hands, but she found it utterly adorable on him. She was sure he could never look bad. He was almost perfect.

"I can't hold it in any longer. I love you, Zacchya," he said softly, trembling with nerves.

"Oh, Zac, I love you too!" She smiled, reaching out to touch his face.

"It's hard to believe that I knew a life before you. I can only see you in it now… and the future with you."

"I feel exactly the same way. I love spending time with you. I hope it never ends." She leaned over to kiss him again. For a moment, the world stopped turning. All there was was her and her Zac. Nothing else existed but their love. Her mind was lost in the sound of his breathing. Nothing mattered at all, just her and Zac. Nothing could break them apart in that moment. 2015 would be an amazing year, to that she had no doubts. As the announcer on the radio said it was now January first, she hoped that in a year's time, she'd still be doing just that: kissing Zac.

Chapter 25

January 14, 2015

LARRY WAS PACING IN HIS cold cement cell. He had only about three feet of space that wasn't occupied and it was pissing him off. He'd had a call from The Boss the day before that set his soul on fire. Things were being delayed. His preliminary court date was set for February 16th, so they still had some time to plan things and get the escape situated.

He tried to compose himself, but really he just felt like punching or stabbing someone. He was surrounded by buffoons and it was near driving him mad. As he made another lap around the cell, he kicked the stainless steel toilet out of frustration. His toes throbbed, but he didn't care. He waited for the guard to take him to his visit with his lawyer, John. John would be lucky if Larry didn't claw out his eyes. He couldn't take another minute in that cell. He was at his wits end. He'd been too smart, too free to end up in this place. Maybe he'd taken it all for granted. Enjoyed the finer pleasures a bit too much, and now he paid the cost. Once he escaped, he could never legally be Larry Rumsfield again. That name would be tarred with disdain forever. He would get out to help The Boss perfect 33X and the LZ Virus. That was his main goal, and apparently The Boss' facilities were well hidden. But if a time came when he was no longer needed, and they didn't kill him, he'd have to get a new identity. He would possibly even need a new face to go along with a new name. He was still well known in a lot of circles.

Thankfully all of that was still a long way off. He still had plenty of research and testing to do on both drugs. 33X was almost perfect, but just needed a few more test subjects to check for side effects. The LZ Virus still had a bit of fixing to do, but it was coming along nicely. He had actually had a successful test before he was arrested, that he had not shared with The Boss yet. He figured The Boss would be extremely angry when he found out Larry hid those tests from him.

As he paced the cell waiting for John, he remembered the first time he met The Boss. He'd just given a speech for his college final in New York. Besides the physical tests and on the job training, it was one of the last parts of his grade. He was very close to graduating and becoming a doctor. He received a standing ovation from the speech, which was quite rare from a student, and was feeling proud. After class was over, he headed for the bus stop. A large man stopped him as he waited in line.

"Excuse me; you're Larry Rumsfield, right? May I have a quick word with you?"

"Oh my bus is… I suppose as long as it's quick," Larry replied, glancing at his watch.

"I happened to be sitting in on your speech today. I quite enjoy the topic of the hippocampus, don't you? It was a splendid lecture. I don't even think the teacher could have understood as much, or explained as well as you did."

"Thank you very much. It is quite an interesting subject. I believe a lot of our medical questions on memory loss could have answers with the proper testing. Hopefully that will happen within my lifetime." Larry nodded.

"I 100% agree with you. It's all very fascinating. Would you mind missing your bus and having supper with me? My treat, of course. I'd love to sit down and have a good long chat about you and your future." The man smiled sweetly, which was odd coming from such a strong burly faced man.

Larry contemplated for a moment. He sized up the man, trying to decide if he was a serial killer or actually interested in science. He decided on the latter and they were off in the man's car, an expensive black Lexus to a restaurant a college kid couldn't afford. The man bought Larry a drink, an expensive Irish whiskey.

"Oh thank you, this is quite good." Larry nodded with gratitude.

"It's quite my pleasure. I'm afraid that I haven't even told you my name yet. It seems quite silly, but I wish to not divulge that information yet. You can just call me Boss."

"Boss? Hmmm… well I do appreciate the dinner." Larry smirked. He was beyond curious as to why this man wouldn't give his real name and only a nickname. But the man did look like he would be in charge of a lot. He was tough, manly, with a face and a demeanor that was not to be messed with.

"It's no problem at all. I wish this was to be more of a social visit, but it's not, Larry. I would like to offer you a job."

"A job? But I haven't even graduated yet!"

"We both know the degree is merely a formality. Your IQ alone sets you above and beyond all other students, and some of the teachers, to be quite honest. No one else seems to see things the way that you see them. Your mind is an untapped resource we desperately need. I believe with your quest for knowledge, genius abilities in chemistry and brain functions, you're just what we need." The Boss leaned over the table, his dark eyes wild with excitement.

"You've piqued my interests… what kind of job?" Larry listened intently, leaning across the table as well.

"You're going to build us new drugs. Some to help cure diseases, some to… help the bigger causes." The Boss' eyes twinkled mischievously.

"Bigger causes?"

"Let me put it to you bluntly… You accept the job, I'll tell you everything. But you never heard a word of it. Understand?"

Larry's mind ran wild with imagination. Whatever the Boss did, it was beyond secretive. Was it CIA or FBI? He didn't know what, but he *HAD* to know. It scratched the darkest parts of his mind. He couldn't handle not knowing. Plus, he knew that he was destined for something more, something bigger, and something that most people only dream of. The Boss might be the one that could help him achieve those goals.

"Yes, I accept." Larry smiled widely.

"Glad to have you on board!" Boss shook his hand, smiling. "I work for a secret part of the government. They don't even give us a name, because we technically do not exist on paper. We need your help to make us new drugs to help create the perfect army. The U.S. Army is already one of the best in the world… why not make it perfect?"

"Are you saying…?" Larry's eyes widened with wonder and understanding.

"Yes, we need you to help us build the perfect soldiers," the Boss whispered, excitement glowing in his eyes.

Larry understood what he was implying. But was it possible? He leaned over the table, almost spilling his whiskey. "You want me to make a drug that deals with memory… like commands and such, I guess?"

"Yes. With a soldier that never disobeys, we'd be the perfect army. A soldier that never forgets the vow he took to protect our flag, our honor… that is more than we could ever hope for. Some soldiers along the way forget what they're fighting for. Why not remind them? Then they would go to battle in places most wouldn't wish on their worst enemies, but do it with a smile on their faces. They could eliminate our enemies, by any means necessary. There'd be nothing but a perfect soldier sent to do his job and get the job done."

"Yes, of course, that makes sense. A soldier's job isn't easy… I'm sure there is hesitation from time to time."

"Yes, there is. But that's not all. We hope you might be able to create more drugs for us. One that might… oh, reanimate the dead…" the Boss said nonchalantly.

"Reanimate the dead?" Larry would have shouted, but he remembered how secretive their conversation was. Even with the chatter of voices around him, clinks of plates and dishes wasn't loud enough to cover up if he shouted. "That's too dangerous! It's not possible!"

"Oh it's quite possible. If anyone could do it, it would be you. You're one of the smartest men I've ever met... and I know A LOT of smart scientists."

Larry shook his head in disbelief. They were asking him to bring back the dead! No one had been able to do that successfully! Oh, sure there was reviving someone after a few minutes... he thought that the record of reviving someone was over eighty minutes, but that was keeping the body refrigerated at the correct temperatures on ice. Most of the U.S. wars that he knew of seemed to be lacking on refrigeration or ice. It seemed near impossible to bring back the dead. He was unsure of how to respond.

"Ok, fine. We'll put that one on hold then. What about some kind of drug that helps the soldiers keep their nutrients longer? Something that would keep them from starvation or dehydration?"

"Hmmm... that seems more plausible at least. I could do research on that easily enough. It could be a very good starting point." Larry made mental notes about where he could start on the project.

"Good, good, glad to see you're on board." The Boss smiled again, reaching his hand over to pat Larry on the shoulder. "Take this card. Call this number when you need our help or have something for us. Follow the instructions exactly as they are written on the back."

Larry nodded, grabbing the card and flipping it over, which read: "ID Code: Larry Rumsfield # 37834."

"We can help you as much as you need and we want to. I hope our partnership is a long one."

"I surely hope so! I do love this country, sir. I'm glad to help out in any way that I can." Larry smiled, raised his glass for a toast. He would help the army create the perfect soldiers and save countless lives.Larry's memories were cut short by the clink of metal on metal. The guard was standing outside his cell, tapping his keys on the metal bars. "You ready for your visit?"

"Yes please." Larry stepped back away from the door, letting the guard come in to cuff him. They walked down to the visitation room where John was already waiting for him. Larry walked into the room, nodded to the guard as he shut the door behind him.

"So what's the word, John?" Larry asked as he found a seat.

"Well as you know, I've had no luck finding the loophole you need to get out of here legally."

"Yes, yes I do know."

"However, Magnus and I are working closely on a plan that will give you the perfect escape."

"He said there was a delay…" Larry drummed his fingers impatiently on the table.

"Oh just a slight delay, really."

"A slight delay? You realize that I've been in this shithole for over a fucking month?" Larry slammed his fists into the table. The cuffs around his wrists jammed into his wrist bones, making shallow cuts. He barely felt the pain though.

"Larry, I know! I know! We are trying everything we can!"

"Well hurry it up! I'm not paying you for NOTH-ING!" Larry snarled through his teeth.

"Well I'm sorry that it's not damned easy enough to plan an escape without causing suspicion! Do you even realize the amount of work that goes into a venture like this?" John shouted. He was glad that the room was sound proof and made specifically for lawyer visits, which were not allowed to be overhead or recorded.

"I'm sorry. I shouldn't have snapped. I'm just so fuck-ing sick of this place! I'm sure Magnus told you about my research…"

"No, he didn't actually. He just stated that it was very important and you're better on the outside."

"Well that is true… it's very important." Larry nodded, his anger slowly subsiding.

"We are trying to be as quick as possible. I promise that."

"When is your estimated date?"

"Soon… I'd say before February, I hope. Just a few loose ends left to tie up. You'll be out of here before the preliminary court hearing. We are just working on cutting back a few causalities."

"Causalities are not important to me," Larry said flippantly.

"Nor to me… but Magnus cares. He hopes to have as few as possible."

"Oh, well he would care about that. Whatever works the fastest and the best, is good by me."

"I will give you a heads up the day before the attack. There is a…" John leaned over the table. He knew that no one could hear them outside of the room, but he was just being extra careful. "There's a body we're sneaking in with your dental records. That's been a lot of the hold up, actually."

"Oh… I see! That is brilliant!" Larry smiled, slapping his hands on the table.

"Yes, it really is. I would say it shouldn't take more than another two weeks to work out the fine details." John smiled. He and Magnus' plan would work. He knew that it was planned out well. Once the final kinks were ironed out, the police station would be set ablaze and Larry would be a free man. No matter how wrong or right that was.

Chapter 26

January 24, 2015

ZACCHYA KISSED HER MOM ON the forehead. "I'm going to see Zac for a bit." She waved and walked out the front door. She hated lying to her mom, but she had to. Over the past month, her mind had become so clear and she needed answers.

Her depression was almost gone, which had been wonderful. She no longer faced each day with forced smiles and emotional ankle weights. All that sat upon her shoulders was breaking loose. She was happier and more at peace than she had been in over a year. But even with her newfound peace, there was still something bothering her. She couldn't shake the gnawing in the back of her mind. It was as though a dark fog covered a corner of her mind, and she couldn't see through it. It bothered her immensely. She knew that fog was related to Larry somehow.

When he was first arrested, she was overwhelmed with sadness and hurt, but more than that, fear. They had been so close her entire life, so it made no sense. She longed for the answers that hid from her sight. The fog was connected to Larry and she had to find out why. So she drove her car across town to the jail. She would visit him, sit face to face with him, and get the answers she needed. There was plenty of hesitation in facing him. There were consequences she might not be ready for, but she couldn't stop.

She parked on the street, looked in the mirror to prepare herself.

"Find the answers. Try not to run out of the visit. Don't slap him across the face," she said aloud to the confused girl in the mirror.

She opened the car door and the brisk January air hit her. She wrapped her arms tight around herself and headed for the door. As she entered the jail, a guard she knew as a friend of Zac's, Seth, came to greet her.

"Zacchya it's good to see you. How are you?"

"Doing well. I'm here to visit Larry, actually."

"Oh sure, of course. I forget you two are related. I will take you to the visiting room." Seth smiled as he led her to room. It was a large open room with numerous tables and chairs for visitors. She sat an empty round table, thanked him.

"I'll go get him for you." Seth nodded.

Zacchya fidgeted with her hair as she waited for them to return. Her heart was pounding. She was slowly regretting coming at all.

Finally Larry walked in, wearing an orange jumpsuit, handcuffs around his wrists. His eyes widened with surprise at the sight of her.

"Zacchya! I'm surprised. I didn't expect any visitors." Larry smiled as she sat in the seat across from her.

"Hello, Uncle." That was all she could manage to get out. Her anger and confusion were boiling inside her.

"I can't imagine how angry you are at me."

"Anger is definitely one emotion I'm feeling towards you," she said flatly.

"I know it looks awful, it really does! But I didn't do the things they say!" Larry exclaimed.

"Sure you didn't! You expect me to believe that! Everyone says they're innocent." She rolled her eyes.

Larry leaned across the table, trying to catch her gaze. She refused to look directly at him.

"What can I do for you then? Since you clearly came for a confession I guess."

"You can tell me why you killed April's dad! And why they found a body in your… basement," she spat.

"So you did come for a confession! Typical!" Larry rolled his eyes.

Zacchya glared at his smug smile. She longed to punch him, watch him suffer. A large part of her wished to see him in pain. She knew she had wasted her time. She went to stand up to leave.

"That's not the only reason you came, is it, Zacchya? Your mind has to be… oh, how do I word that…" he whispered, winked at her.

"What?"

"Feeling chipper and happy are we? Not a care in the world, I'd imagine." Larry's eyes twinkled. "Depression is gone. Your relationship with Trevor is back to normal."

"How do…" She stopped. Her hands were on the table, half standing, half sitting.

"I know more than you could ever know," Larry whispered again.

Zacchya sat back down, stared at him. "Then tell me."

"I don't have to tell you. Soon enough you'll remember. And then you'll really hate me." Larry quietly chuckled.

She knew at that moment he was evil. The man she'd known her whole life, respected even, was hidden behind pretty, happy layers. Her whole life had been a lie. She had faced his evil throughout her life and smiled at it, wished it well. Her stomach swirled with anger.

"I don't have time for your mind games, Larry. Tell me something important or I'm going." She glared at him.

"I thought you loved my mind games." Larry licked his lips.

Zacchya felt a wave of nausea hit her stomach. "You're disgusting."

Larry reached for her hand, barely grazing her fingertips before she moved.

"Hey! No touching!" Seth said from across the room.

Zacchya's eyes widened with disgust. She remembered his hands. Those disgusting hands touching her in ways no uncle should ever touch his niece.

"You!" She shouted as she jumped out of her chair. "You sick… sick bastard!" Tears poured down her cheeks as she bolted from the visiting room.

Larry smiled at the table, looking innocent. "What did I do?"

Seth wanted to follow her, but he had to stay next to Larry in case something happened, or he tried to escape. He watched her run past him and into the hallway.

Zacchya didn't hesitate until she was outside, the brisk air feeling harsh against her face. She jumped in car and sped off. She had to get out of there, away from Larry.

Her stomach churned and she knew that vomit was nearby. She made it to the highway, only a few blocks away, and turned west. She wanted out of town, then she'd pull over. She forced the bile and vomit to stay inside her stomach. She just had to escape.

The memories were slowly pouring back into her mind. She had seen herself strapped to a chair. Larry's hand was touching her body, unbuttoning her pants.

She pulled to the side of the road, unable to take any more of the memories. She bolted out of the car expelling her breakfast and lunch. She prayed the memories would be expelled too.

Never in her life had she felt so violated and manipulated. The worst part wasn't even the abuse, which was already unspeakably awful; it was the fact that he did something to her to make her forget it all. Somehow he had planted new thoughts and ideas into her head. All the worthlessness she felt was fueled and planted by him! All of her suicide attempts were his fault!

Did she ruin Jacob's funeral because Larry wanted her to? The idea was too awful to consider. Why would anyone want to purposely ruin a funeral? Weren't they bad enough on their own? Who would want to put poor Elizabeth and Edward through that, hadn't they been through enough?

She wiped the vomit from her mouth. Tears poured from her eyes, her nose leaked down her face. She didn't care what she looked like. Her soul was crushed, dirty as though she'd never get clean again. She reached into her pocket for her cell phone. There was only one person she needed.

"Hello?"

"April?

"What's wrong, hon? You sound awful!"

"Can you come get me?" Zacchya sobbed into the phone.

"Where are you?"

"I'm outside of town, on Highway 56, towards Garfield. I'm parked on the side of the road."

"I'm on my way," April said, hanging up the phone.

Zachya cried into her hands barely feeling the cold. She was glad that April was her best friend. April didn't even hesitate to help her. She asked; April said yes. That's what a best friend was supposed to do. She could have called Zac, but she didn't want him to know about the molestation. It was too awful and embarrassing. Plus, Zac already hated Larry; he didn't need another reason. April was the only person she could trust with the information.

Less than five minutes later, April's Buick was pulling up behind Zacchya's car.

April ran out of the car to Zacchya, hugging her tightly.

"Sweetie! Talk to me! What happened?" April asked as she caressed Zacchya's hair.

"Went… to… see Larry." She sobbed.

"Oh my… get in my car. It's too cold out here. We'll get you warmed up and you can tell me all about it." They walked to the car, April's arm around Zacchya, supporting her.

They got situated in the car. "So what happened?"

"He was being a douchebag. Wouldn't answer a damn thing straight. I went to leave… and he… said something stupid. Just enough to keep me there." Zacchya cried. April listened intently, her arm still around Zacchya's shoulder.

"He said something about remembering. And then I did. Oh, God, I did!" She bawled into April's shoulder.

"What did you remember?" April asked, worried of what the answer might be.

"He… he…" She was crying too hard, gasping for breaths.

"Just breathe, sweetie. He can't hurt you now."

"He brainwashed me," she said when she finally caught her breath.

"WHAT?!"

"Gave me a drug to do things. I don't know what it was. It's why I was so depressed." She sobbed.

"Oh my God! Are you serious?"

"Gets worse." Zacchya tried to compose herself, but it was just too awful. She broke down again, sobbing into her hands, snot leaking through her fingers.

"Take your time, sweetie," April said, rubbing her back. She found her a tissue to wipe her nose and eyes. April couldn't possibly imagine anything worse than being brainwashed. How was that even possible? Larry was clearly too smart for his own good if he was concocting drugs to control people's minds. Larry had probably made Zacchya kill Jacob! It made so much sense. She had never told Zacchya what she'd seen nor did she ever plan to. The girl had been through enough. The whole situation with Jacob's murder had never added up in April's mind. Now she knew why. She had chosen to see Zacchya as the hurt girl she was, not focusing on a mistake she made against her will. But why would Larry want Jacob dead in the first place?

Zacchya sat up again, trying to catch her breath. She just had to say it and get it off of her chest. Maybe then it wouldn't be so heavy to carry.

"He… molested me," she whispered between her sobs.

"NO! God, no! No! No!" April gasped. How could anyone do that to their own family? April squeezed Zacchya tight.

"I will never let him touch you again! I promise! Never again!" April cried with her friend. All of her nightmares made so much sense. Larry was a monster of the worst breed. He ruined so many lives without batting an eye. She had no dad. Zacchya was forced to murder someone, and not even remember it! Jacob was dead and for what? The extremes that people went to boggled her mind. She hoped that Larry would get his justice in the end. He didn't deserve to live. Only hell could ever welcome him with open arms.

"I hate him, April." Zacchya shook her sad fists.

"I hate him too. He'll get his in the end. I know it. He has to." April held onto her friend. Things that had never made sense over the past year were adding up. It all came back to Larry. She wished that she were violent for a moment. She'd kill him herself. He deserved to die. No, he deserved much worse than death. Death was an easy out for such a despicable monster like Larry Rumsfield.

Chapter 27

February 1, 2015

WANDA AND MARVIN DUNTZ, RESIDENTS of 823 Main Street, were awake watching the morning news. Wanda worked day shift, eight to five, at Sunnyvale Hospital. Marvin was retired, but liked to get up and spend the morning with his wife. They'd sip on coffee while talking about the world going to hell in a hand basket. It was a bonding moment for them. Relationships weren't always about sharing the things you loved, but also the things that pissed you off as well.

"Marvin, dear, will you let the dog out? I'll make us some eggs," Wanda asked, as she headed toward the kitchen.

"Sure. Come here, Pepper, you menace," Marvin growled at the small terrier mixed dog lying on the sofa. Pepper came running towards the front door, ready for the fresh air. Marvin and Pepper walked out to the front porch.

"Is someone barbecuing this early, Marvin? I smell smoke or something." Wanda shouted toward the front door.

There was no reply. Marvin could be a bit hard of hearing at times. She strolled lazily to the front door. The smell of acrid smoke filled her nostrils.

Marvin stood on the lawn, staring across the street at the local jail. Black smoke was pouring out of the second floor.

"Shall we call 9-1-1?" Wanda gasped, her hand on her chest, as she ran to his side.

"It's the damn jail! Wouldn't they know already?" Marvin asked, unable to peel his eyes from the smoking jail.

"They might not! I'm calling!" Wanda turned to head back into the house. She made it about three steps when she was thrown across the lawn. Her face crashed painfully into the cement steps of her own front porch. Blood immediately poured from her nose and mouth. She felt the pain before she heard the extremely loud BOOM. She tried to crawl up the stairs, but was blinded by the white lights in her eyes. Her body was unable to move, something pinned her to ground. She stretched her arm out, the nerves jerked it unnaturally. She was dead.

Marvin was thrown in another direction. He landed with a horrible crunch into the middle of the street. His spine snapped paralyzing him instantly. The moment he hit the pavement, a car came rolling towards him. Unable to stop in time, the car hit Marvin, his body bounced over the tires. He was dead.

"Oh God!" The driver from the car screamed as Marvin's lifeless body rolled under his car. He slammed on the brakes. He jumped out of the car unsure of what to do. The entire scene was overwhelming. A man flew in front of his car. He killed a man! The jail on the adjacent street now had a gaping hole on the first floor, black smoke pouring out. Orange and red flames licked the brick building. The ambulances were parked next to the jail, originally, he knew, but one lay across the street, upside down in a front lawn. He thought he saw an arm underneath a piece of jangled metal from one of the ambulance doors.

He suddenly remembered that the town's fire trucks were also parked with the ambulances. All of the first response vehicles were there. If they were damaged, which looked extremely likely if ambulances were flying across the street from the impact of the explosion, no one could stop the fire. Another town would have to come to the rescue. It would take too long.

The shock of the situation took over his mind. The screamed frantically, running madly through the street. "HELP! HELP!" he screamed into the open morning air.

People began to scatter from their houses to see what had caused the loud boom and shockwaves. The scene was utter chaos. People ran wildly through the street, trying to get closer to the jail, but too afraid. Some simply ran in large circles, wanting to help but unsure of what to do.

One man, Isaac Partridge, a large black man, had been one that had run inside to help. He kept low to the ground, half crawling over the piles of bricks and debris.

"Anyone in here? Hello?" Isaac shouted out. The acrid smoke burnt his nostrils, making it difficult to breathe. He coughed and hacked as the smoke slowly coated his lungs, but he continued on through the wreckage.

Ahead of him was a hallway, but it had numerous holes blown through it from the explosion. It was littered with bricks, broken glass, and pieces of metal and wood. He wondered if it was a terrorist attack. He couldn't imagine who on earth would want to attack a small farming town, unknown to the rest of the world, like Larned?

"Is anyone alive? Do you need help?" Isaac shouted again. There were large flames to toward the left of the hallway, so he took the right. Destruction was everywhere. Smoke still poured through the building as it tried to find any open space to free itself. Isaac coughed and coughed as he tried to stay low to the ground, trying to not get smoke inhalation poisoning. He found an office nearby. The front door was blown off and sticking out of the wall across from the hall. He ducked to avoid the large piece of broken door and entered the office.

A young woman was lying on the ground. She was on her side, looking as if she were sleeping, her back towards Isaac.

"Are you ok, ma'am?" Isaac asked, tapping her on the shoulder.

When he touched her, she rolled toward him. Her brown eyes were glazed. There was a large sharp piece of metal protruding from her abdomen. She was dead. He fought his panic and fear. He had to keep searching. Someone had to be still alive. Please, God, let him find someone alive. There was no time for him to breakdown, even though he wanted to. He had to be strong. He wished more help would come. Where were the EMT's and firefighters? He was only one man and could do so much. He hadn't seen anyone else yet. He felt alone, but he trudged on.

He searched anything and everything he could get to safely. Sweat poured from his body, the building was still so hot. Flames were still above him on the second floor. He could feel their heat radiating towards him. His lungs burned from the smoke, making him dream of fresh air. He doubted that he would ever take the cold air for granted again.

At the end of the hallway was a large pile of rubble. He tried to sort through it, in case someone was underneath.

"Is anyone there? Hello?" He shouted. Grey ash was flying through the air, coating his skin and face. He coughed, tried to brush the ash from his eyelashes.

"Help," a soft voice croaked.

"Where are you? I'm here to help!" Isaac shouted.

"Help," the voice croaked again. Isaac couldn't tell if it was male or female. But the voice did seem to be coming from under the rubble pile. He fought the dizziness that came from breathing in too much smoke, and the falling ash impeding his vision. He tore the bricks and debris as fast he could. Wood and glass cut his hands, but he didn't notice.

A hand finally broke through the debris. Isaac grabbed it and squeezed.

"I've got you! I've got you! You're going to be okay!" He fought back tears. He had found someone alive! He let go of the hand, pulling broken brick and debris from the pile with a fervor. He was going to save a person's life.

He unearthed the rest of the person's arms and torso. Only a bit to go. Sweat poured excessively from Isaac's pores but he wouldn't stop. He couldn't.

Finally a body was visible; a man's face broke free, coated in black ash, gasping for air.

"I've got you! I'm going to get you out of here!" Isaac used all of his strength to pull the man from the wreckage. His body and face were blackened from smoke and ash, his clothes torn, blood was oozing from his arms and torso.

"Can you walk?" Isaac asked as he pulled the man free, and into a sitting position.

"No. My leg." The man coughed. Isaac noticed the man's left leg was caked in blood and ash, it looked broken.

I'll carry you. We're getting out of here." Isaac picked the man up, trying to be careful of the injured leg. They stumbled through the rubble and debris back toward the opening the bomb blew.

"What's your name?" Isaac asked, as he kicked aside bricks and glass.

"Seth." The man moaned in pain.

"I'm Isaac. We're almost out now. Just a few more steps." Isaac groaned. His muscles were weak from carrying Seth and the lack of oxygen. The hole was visible now, people stood outside in the fresh air. Oh, how he longed for that air.

He stepped through the threshold. "Take him!" Isaac shouted at the crowd in front of him. One was dressed as an EMT. Seth would get the help he needed. He'd be okay. The EMT grabbed Seth, laying him gently on the grass.

Isaac's nostrils filled with clean air. He was out of the smoke and ash. He made it to a safer area away from the jail. He fell hard to the ground, unconscious.

"I need O2 stat! Anyone!" the EMT worker screamed. "Someone get me some O2!"

People scrambled around, scared and confused. The buildings upper floor burned ferociously. The sky above was no longer blue, but grey from the smoke and ash. The destruction was absolute.

The EMT worker scrambled for help as she searched for any kind of oxygen for the two unconscious men on the grass in front of her. How could she help them without proper equipment? The ambulances were blown apart, scattered in pieces around the block.

Finally her co-worker ran toward her, carrying an O2 tank and face masks. She sighed with relief. As she placed one of the masks on the man who pulled the boy from the building, she felt hopeful again. Her co-worker started CPR on the kid, administering life saving breaths. At least two lives would be saved throughout this horrible situation. She hoped there would be more saved, though.

A horrible rumble shook the ground. For a moment she thought it was an earthquake. Then realized the top floor of the jail was falling down upon itself.

"RUN!"

Bricks, wood, glass, pipes, bars, and everything else that made a building, came tumbling from the sky above her. She prayed they would be spared.

Chapter 28

February 2, 2015

JOHN WOODS LAZILY YAWNED AS he flipped through the channels, looking for the local news. He found KXBN, a Wichita station he preferred. Of course, they were covering the bombing in Larned from yesterday. He rubbed his eyes and leaned closer to hear.

"The tragedy that struck the small farming town of Larned, Kansas yesterday is still causing heartbreak today. Around 6:30 AM a bomb exploded in the local jail. The bomb was powerful enough to blow the building apart, sending debris and destruction all around. Unfortunately, the bombs were well placed enough to paralyze the first response vehicles parked next door. As you can see from this photograph, an ambulance was blasted across the street into an unsuspecting neighbor's front yard." Cindi Sims didn't even have to pretend to feel upset about the situation. She really was. If there were bombs going off in Larned, they could go off anywhere.

"A few civilians entered the tattered, broken jail to look for survivors. Unfortunately there were few to be found. The estimated causality rate right now is at eleven, which is beyond tragic.

"However, one local hero, Isaac Partridge, did manage to escape the building with one survivor, Seth Bell, twenty-five, whom he uncovered from the rubble. We now take you to Tom, who is on the scene live in Larned."

"Thank you, Cindi. I'm here with the local hero, Isaac Partridge. Isaac, you were one of the few brave souls that climbed through the destruction and fire to find survivors. What motivated you to jump into a burning building?"

"People were dying. Who knew if any was still alive just waiting for a helping hand," Isaac said, shrugging his shoulders.

"Very true, but most people wouldn't go into a building that was very much still on fire, and threatening to cave down upon them, though," Tom said.

"They would. It's the only human thing to do. If someone's in trouble, you help them. That's it. There's no alternative."

"Now, excuse me for saying so, but you're not exactly a young man."

"No, I'm fifty-five years old, but young at heart, I guess." Isaac shrugged.

"Bystanders told me that you carried Seth from deep inside the destruction, back to safety. That's an amazing feat for a man of fifty-five."

"Like I said, it's my humanly duty. The boy was buried under bricks, glass, wood, metal, and God knows what else. It was pure luck that I found him alive. The building was a mess inside, but we got out alive. That's all that matters." Isaac half-smiled, feeling uncomfortable with the cameras.

"This community owes you so much for your bravery and honor." Tom bowed his head.

"No, no. The people that helped us when we got out, they are the real heroes. Not me."

"Thank you again, Isaac. It's been an honor to meet you." Tom shook his hand. Isaac nodded and walked off camera.

"The community of Larned is already trying to repair and begin the daunting task of rebuilding. I think as long as there are citizens like Isaac Partridge here, they should be fine. Back to you, Cindi."

"Thank you, Tom. Somehow the city of Larned will pick up the shattered pieces of their lives and rebuild from this tragedy. There has been no word on who caused the bombing or why. We will keep you updated as the story develops. Hopefully the culprits behind this heinous act will be caught soon. Stay tuned to KXBN for all your local news."

John flipped the TV off. He still couldn't believe that he had been a part of that. Of course, he was safe and sound by the time the first bomb exploded. He was still awaiting confirmation that Larry was out, alive, and in the safe compound. It had been twenty-four hours and he had expected to hear back from Magnus much sooner. If Larry didn't escape, he knew he'd be in trouble. Magnus was a strong man with a whole military behind him. There's no doubt John's life wouldn't be spared if Larry was dead. They wouldn't need him anymore. The thought didn't settle well with him.

He tried to push the thoughts out of his head, focusing on the soft growling in his stomach. He headed toward the kitchen to make a sandwich. But he found out he wasn't alone. A figure came from the shadows, grabbing him, putting a cloth over his mouth. The world went black.

John stirred uncomfortably. His stomach churned, empty but very sour. His vision was blurry but slowly coming to focus. He was in his own living room, tied to one of his dining room chairs.

"Must you always try to kill me?" John huffed angrily.

"Good morning! I didn't even try to kill you this time, John. A little chloroform never hurt anyone." Magnus stepped in front of him, smiling widely.

"I'm really starting to get the feeling you don't trust me."

"That's neither here nor there." Magnus waved his hand carelessly.

"So what's with the ropes, then? I mean, it's better than near drowning, but still…"

"Formalities, really. So… the explosion…"

"It worked right? He is free?"

"Did you receive a confirmation?" Magnus paced in front of him.

"No… that's why…"

"Doesn't matter right now. What matters is you and me."

"Doesn't matter? How does it NOT matter? I don't understand."

"You didn't cut back on the causalities, John."

"Oh, yes I did! That's why the bomb went off so early. There was less staff there that early on in the morning. "

"An ambulance blew across the fucking street! It crushed a civilian!" Magnus growled, his face growing red.

"Oh no… I didn't mean…"

"Of course you didn't!" Magnus laughed.

"I just worked our plan, sir. We knew there'd be causalities," John replied.

"But you wanted death, didn't you? You missed the battlefield, huh? The smell of burning flesh. The destruction. You missed all of it." Magnus continued to pace the floor.

"No! No!" John shook his head.

"Yes, you did. I know men like you. I've been around them my entire military career. It's punks like you that only join up for the army so they can kill someone. You're no better than serial killers. Killing is not meant to be fun. It's not meant to be enjoyed! In wars, people die, yes but it's for a cause." Magnus had quit pacing; he was staring at John full of hate. "It's people like you that make me want Larry's research finished! It's the only way to fix the broken ones! The only damn way!" Magnus' eyes were aflame.

"Larry's worse than I'd ever think of being! You know what he's done! Who he's killed!" John spat angrily.

"Larry has something I need. There are things in this world worth killing for. Our freedom and this country... I love this country! And if saving one psychopath can save it from becoming a shithole... then I will do that. America deserves the best! And Larry can help with that. Throughout his flaws, he does see a bigger picture.

Even though he stumbles occasionally, he sees the bigger picture. You do not."

"I love America…"

"No! You don't! You DO NOT!" Magnus' nostrils flared. He pulled out a gun from his belt. He held it at John's temple.

"Don't be rash, Magnus. I can still be of use! There's no need to kill me!" John pleaded.

"Yes, yes you can be of use to me. But first learn some damn manners. I told you to call me Boss."

"Boss, I'm sorry! I'm sorry! Just let me help you in any way I can! I'm still quite useful!" John begged.

"There's just one thing left I need you to do for me," Magnus sneered.

"What's that? I'll do anything! ANYTHING!"

"Fucking die, you broken piece of shit." Magnus pulled the trigger. "It's all that you're good for."

Chapter 29

February 14, 2015

Zac was nervous—the heart racing, palms sweating, feeling nauseated kind of nervous. She was across the table from him, looking more beautiful than ever before. Her long blond hair fell into beautiful waves that kissed her shoulders and beyond. The sight of her alone was enough for him. Her pout red lips and large blue eyes called to him every moment. It took all he had to not reach across the table and kiss her. He longed to kiss her every day. No, he must play it cool. She was talking about something, but he couldn't hear her words. He was too distracted by her beauty. She was the most beautiful girl he'd ever known. He loved everything about her. He couldn't believe that she loved him back. He felt like the luckiest guy alive. Hopefully this night would go just right.

"So I told Trevor to zip his lips! That brother of mine is so ridiculous! If he wasn't my brother I'd shake him to pieces!" She giggled, her eyes sparkling.

Zac blinked at her. Was he supposed to laugh? He hadn't been listening at all. He forced out a chuckle. "Oh, that Trevor!"

"Right?!" She smiled back at him. She had perfect white teeth underneath her plump lips. He tried to not stare at her lips. He was daydreaming of kissing her again.

"Zacchya, you're so damn beautiful," Zac blurted out.

"Oh! Thank you! You're not too bad yourself! Every girl in this place is staring at you!" She blushed. No matter how many times he told her, she still blushed. And she was right, numerous girls were checking out Zac. He was so handsome.

"It's true! I can barely focus! I don't think I could make it without you. I love you so much!"

"I love you too, Zac. Baby, are you okay? You seem…. Oh, I don't know, different."

"I'm better than okay! I have you, don't I?"

"Yes, of course you do." She smiled at him, getting lost in his dark eyes.

Without warning, Zac jumped out of his chair, rushed to her side, kneeled at her legs. He rested his arms on her knees, staring up at her.

"Oh, Zacchya! I love you! I need you with me all the time! Do you love me as much as I love you?" He gazed into her eyes, waiting for the perfect answer.

"Yes, I do. Please get off the floor, baby. I love you, you know that!" she pleaded.

"Marry me? Make me the happiest man alive!" Zac pulled out a ring from his pants pocket. Inside was a beautiful one-carat round cut diamond on a gold band.

Zacchya's mouth flew open in surprise. Tears formed in her blue eyes.

"Zac… I…"

"Just say yes!" His eyes stared up at her, lost in the beauty and the nerves of the moment. His heart was pounding so loud, he was sure she'd hear it.

Tears leaked from her eyes, but not from joy. "I… can't, Zac. I love you so much, I do! But not yet. Oh, God! I'm so sorry!" she cried. How could she do this to the man she loved?

"Why?" Zac frowned up at her, confused as he fought back tears. How could she say no? He was sure she'd say yes.

"I feel like such an asshole!" she whispered, as the people in the restaurant were now staring at them. "It's the worst time in the world for me. I'm… no good. I'm not a good person. And I have to make it right. Please, Zac, ask me again later! I'll say yes. I just can't say it now!" she cried, her mascara running down her flushed cheeks. She reached down to hug him, but he didn't return the hug.

"Please don't hate me! I love you! Ask me again, but wait. I'll say yes. I promise. I just can't say it now." Her tears fell harder and faster as she grabbed her purse and ran from the restaurant. She felt like the most horrible person alive. The man she loved had just proposed, and she left him alone, embarrassed. She couldn't forgive herself. But she knew the truth about herself. And until she dealt with the truth about who she was, she couldn't marry Zac. He was perfect, beautiful, and more wonderful than any other man. She was dirty and tainted. She'd make herself better, good enough to be with him.

The cold wind whipped her hair across her face as she ran through the streets. She hated winter, snow, all of it. But she had to get out of there. Since she found out, well actually remembered, that her uncle molested her, everything had changed. Years of hidden worthlessness flooded her. A man that she had loved and respected had made her a victim. Even though Zac would understand, she couldn't tell him. What did it matter anyway? Larry was dead from the horrible explosion two weeks ago. A part of her was glad her monster was dead, but it didn't help her cope any better.

But it was more than the molestation that had caused her to say no. Something bigger, worse actually, was bothering her. Something she'd forgotten so long, it didn't feel real. But it was real. And she had to make it right, even if it killed her.

* * * *

The sun was bright and warm for February. No snow or ice hung on the branches of the trees. The roads were clear. It was actually a beautiful winter morning that felt more like spring. If he didn't know better, he'd say the flowers were going to bloom soon.

Even as he stepped out of his worn out cottage, he glanced at the brown grass expecting to see flower buds. He hadn't thought about flowers in such a long time. There wasn't time for flowers when you were obsessed with revenge. There for a moment, even revenge plans were put aside. It was honestly that beautiful of a morning.

Jacob walked toward the bridge, stretching his arms. He always found it odd that even with being dead, he needed sleep, felt pain, felt hot and cold, all the things that alive people felt. But he didn't question it too much, at least not until today. Everything felt different, even the wind.

He'd had his first dream since he was revived so long ago. He couldn't remember what it was about, but maybe it was a sign that his plans would soon come to pass. Oh, maybe this would be the day he'd pass on! The mere thought of it put a spring in his step. He was near skipping as he reached the bridge. For whatever reason, it was a different day. Everything felt brand new. He wondered what he'd do if he could leave the bridge and live a real life.

Most likely he would run straight to his parents to hug them. Even in death, he missed them so much. Not even death could break that bond he shared with them. He wished to explain his afterlife quest, so they could understand him. Somehow he'd find a way to help them understand.

As he paced the bridge, like he did every single day, he remembered pieces of his life. A smile spread across his lips, remembering his friends. He missed them so much as well. Trevor, Bobby, Trina, April, Tim, Alicia, and Zacchya. The Misfits, Bobby had picked the name, was his band of friends. They had grown up together, been through good and bad times. Nothing could ever break them up… that was, until he died. One of the girls had murdered him, he knew that. He could almost see her face, but it slipped through his fingers. He'd never been able to understand how one of them could betray the bonds of friendship and kill him. It was unspeakable. He tried to focus on the better times, not the betrayal. He was taken back to the summer before he died. He was camping in his backyard with Trevor, Bobby, and Tim. They shared a four-person tent; sleeping bags were sprawled about between bags of chips, sandwiches, and other munchies. Bobby had snuck a *Playboy* magazine in his backpack.

"Just look at it, Tim! Boobs are good for you! Make you grow big and strong!" Bobby laughed as he pushed the magazine closer to Tim's blushing face.

"Oh yeah, Tim! You'll get hair on your balls, man!" Trevor laughed.

"It's not right, guys! Stop! It's just disrespectful to the ladies!" Tim pushed Bobby and the magazine away. "Sex is supposed to be private!"

"Guys, give him a break. He'll see tits when he's darn good and ready!" Jacob smiled.

"Oh, King Jacob! How dare we offend your clansmen!" Bobby smirked.

"I should behead you. But I might be the coolest king ever… so I won't. But keep it in mind, peasant!" Jacob flipped his shaggy blond hair, winking.

"You guys are really stupid assholes." Tim frowned, pushing his glasses back up his nose.

"Sure, sure! Coming from the ginger! Call me when you grow a soul!" Trevor laughed as he pushed a marshmallow in his mouth.

"One day you're going to be sick of that joke…" Tim rolled his eyes.

"The soulless ginger joke? Oh, God, I hope not!" Bobby smiled.

Jacob sat next to Trevor, eating marshmallows, as he flipped through the *Playboy*.

"Oh, shit, Trev! This centerfold looks like Zacchya!" Jacob laughed as he forced the magazine in front of Trevor.

"Please tell me you're kidding!" Trevor's face went pale. He looked away from the centerfold.

"He wishes he knew what Zacchya looked like naked." Bobby snickered.

"The hands are the eyes of the… um… body!" Jacob winked.

"Gross dude! Just gross!" Trevor mimed gagging.

"Your sister's hot, dude. Can't blame the man!" Bobby smiled.

"She is quite pretty, Trevor, sorry." Tim smiled.

"See, even the nerd agrees!"

"I'm a lucky man, Trevor. But one day soon we'll be brothers for real! That's what is important here." Jacob smiled, patting Trevor on the back.

"That part would be okay, being your bro. But not the banging my sister part!" Trevor smiled.

"I sure hope that after high school we're still friends," Tim said back in the corner.

"You had to take it there, Tim? Don't get all sentimental and cry on us! I'm fresh out of tampons!" Bobby joked.

"Ha. Ha. I do though! I'm sorry you have no feelings except for boners, dude," Tim replied.

"Oh, snap!" Jacob laughed.

"Tim fights back, kids! Tim, one; Bobby, zero!" Trevor chuckled.

Jacob was surprised by how much he remembered from that night. They had numerous campouts that summer and the summers before it. But that memory was so vivid and clear. There was something special about boys being boys, bonding over food, laughs, and porn. They were all secretly embarrassed by the magazine like Tim, but they covered it up and acted tough. It's just what guys did to impress their friends.

He missed it all so much. He hated waiting in this limbo, or whatever it was, waiting to seek revenge. He wanted to move onto heaven, preferably not hell, or just be alive again. This middle part was awful. He was the first person that he knew of that came back from the dead. There were no books for him to read to cope with his need for revenge. Nothing to help him understand what he was supposed to do. He had never been a revengeful person before he died. He guessed it had something to do with the horrible way he'd been murdered. He was now without his friend that came to visit him periodically too. He was alone and stuck.

He continued to pace the bridge, trying to not think about his future, or lack thereof. He heard a soft rustling in the trees. He hadn't had a visitor in so long, that he couldn't remember. Everyone was too scared to visit him.

Out of the overgrown tracks ran a wild-eyed girl with wavy blond hair. She ran towards him, full of emotions he couldn't understand.

He stepped closer to her, ready to play his part in finding out who she was, or if she was the one he searched for.

"Jacob!" she screamed as she ran toward the bridge. Her hair was tangled from the wind. Leaves were scattered in her long tangles. She looked very distraught.

Jacob stopped in his tracks, frozen. "You…"

Her face was wet from crying, chunks of blond hair were sticking to it. She tried to brush it away so she could see him clearly. "Oh, God! Jacob!" she cried, tears pouring down her red cheeks.

"Why are you here?" he asked. Confusion and anger swelled in his chest. He swore he could feel his heart pounding ferociously in his chest.

"I had to see you one last time. I heard the rumors, the stories. But I had to see you!"

"Why are you here?" he asked again more forcefully. But still he was frozen from fear, anger, happiness, and everything else.

"I remembered what I did! I did… to you!" She was sobbing hard in her hands, barely able to speak.

If he wanted to kill her, it'd be too easy… but he stayed put.

"It's all my fault! All of my fault!" She bawled. He felt sorry for her for a moment, but stopped himself.

"I know it was you. I remember now," Jacob said.

Jacob could see it all now. He had seen her face that night. She had lost her mind, obsessed, and then she stabbed him. So much betrayal. Zacchya, the girl he loved, killed him. There she was, finally, she had come back to him. He meant to kill her, dreamed of it for so long. But he couldn't do it.

"Why did you kill me, Zacchya?" Jacob asked as a solitary tear fell from his blue eyes.

"I don't know! I loved you! You were the first man… I wasn't myself. Oh, God, I wasn't myself! He…"

"YOU KILLED ME! And all you can say is 'I wasn't myself'! How dare you!"

"He planted it in my mind, Jacob! I didn't know! I only just remembered it! I thought you committed suicide! I never…"

"Suicide? I would never!" Jacob gasped.

"I ruined your funeral, Jacob! I went crazy and tried to kill myself. I missed you so much. God, I missed you more than anything! Not a day went by that I didn't think of you! Not a day!" She inched closer to him, still about ten feet away, sobbing.

Jacob stood quietly. Nothing made sense to him anymore. Someone made her do it? It was made to look like a suicide? How was that even possible? How could you kill someone and not even remember it? He had planned so long to see her, kill her and be free again. But this wasn't playing out correctly. It was going all wrong!

Zacchya inched toward him. "I never stopped loving you, Jacob. Never. Even now, there's a man that wants to marry me. I can't do it. I don't deserve that. I love him… but not as much as you. Never as much as you." She tried to dry her tears on her jacket. He stared at her, unmoving. She had to do something. Her heart was overwhelming her. She still felt so much love for him, like not even a day had passed since she last seen his smile. She wished he would smile now. She needed that. Obviously she didn't deserve to see him smile after what she had done, but she needed it.

"Can I… can I touch your face? I just need to feel you're real. One last time, please. Then you can kill me. I know that's what you want." She forced herself to stop crying. She inched closer to him, just barely out of his reach. She stretched out her arm, desperate to feel him. Maybe she could forgive herself if he was real.

Jacob stood still, staring at her. He didn't know how to react. This girl, he had once loved, had murdered him. Now she asked him for favors. Some part of him still loved her, still wanted her to touch him. But he couldn't figure anything out. He stood still, feeling completely overwhelmed.

She moved closer to him, slowly, barely a foot between them. She raised her hand slowly to his face.

"Please, Jacob. Just one last time. I know what I deserve. But let me say goodbye before you kill me." Her blue eyes, desperate and sad, looked into his. "I never stopped loving you. Not for a minute." Her hand reached his cheek, touching it lightly.

Jacob's world exploded. Every inch of him was covered in goose bumps. His heart pounded in his chest. Her hand gently caressed his face. Her sad, blue eyes peered into his soul. Oh, how he missed her fingers, those eyes. The second her skin brushed against his, he knew his mission had been wrong. He was made to love her, always to love her. He never knew how much he had missed it, been waiting for it. He stretched out his hand to reach the hand at her side. Thunder rolled in his veins. She brought him back to life with that touch. He was alive again. She had brought him back to life.

THE END

ABOUT THE AUTHOR

Natasha has been writing since elementary school, but this is her first published novel. She enjoys photography, music, and traveling in her spare time. Natasha lives alone in Larned, Kansas